THE DEAD DON'T PAY

A James Wolf Murder Mystery

By James Arthur Donzella

Three Ravens Publishing
Chickamauga, GA USA

James A Donzella has managed to reinvent the noir detective novel with The Dead Don't Pay. Aside from the refreshing paranormal twist, Donzella has impressive comedy writing chops and he's not afraid to use them. All the things you love about the hardboiled noir poetry of Raymond Chandler can be found on every page.
~Robert Morgan Fisher - Winner of the Chester Himes and Montana Humor Prize.

James A Donzella puts the don in a flat foot's donut in this noir murder mystery. Stylistic, crafty, surprising and fun. He puts the Zella in thrilla? Ok, I'm trying too hard. But Donzella makes it look easy because I couldn't put it down."
~ Gary Kroeger - Former child actor, adult movie star and SNL Alum.

As a fan of 40s and 50s private eye fiction, I appreciate what James Donzella has accomplished with his novel The Dead Don't Pay. He has pretty much provided the reader a time machine for stepping back into a well-realized late 1940's San Francisco and into the shoes of one James Wolf, a hard-drinking, chain-smoking private dick who gets involved in the usual convoluted tale of smuggling and murder after being hired by a classic femme fatale who is not what she claims to be. Told with the witty, sarcastic verve of a Raymond Chandler, coupled with the spare, masculine style of Ernest Hemmingway by way of Dragnet, The Dead Don't Pay pulls you along through all the twists and turns to a didn't-see-it-coming ending that should satisfy mystery fans everywhere.
~Thomas A. Swyden -TV Writer, Buffy the Vampire Slayer, Xena: Warrior Princess.

Table of Contents

To Kennetha,
My love and my muse.

Chapter 1

It was late in the morning. Sports page headline:

Cleveland Wins '48 World Series

Another sawbuck down the drain. I pushed aside the past-due phone bill notice and picked up a racing form. If I could find just one winner, going off at three-to-one odds, I could cover the bill for another month. I don't remember who said it, but the phrase—*It's always darkest before the dawn*—echoed in my head. That axiom is as true as anything. My office door creaked on its hinges. I had a visitor.

"Mr. Wolf?" she asked in a whiskey-soaked purr.

"Twenty-five dollars a day, plus expenses."

The scent of lavender hit me. I peered over the top of the racing form. Roughly thirty, blond hair, an angular face, high pink cheeks. Tight blue business jacket and skirt. An Indy 500 race car driver couldn't handle those curves even in low gear. So beautiful it hurt. The kind of woman I'd like to get to know better, but something told me that once you rode with her, you'd better fasten your seatbelt tight.

"James Wolf?"

"Guilty as charged. What can I do ya fer?"

"May I sit?"

I raised myself up an inch or two from the chair. An old chunk of lead lodged in my hip kept me from standing fully erect.

"Forgive my lack of manners. Please, take a seat."

Looking about as nervous as a Hula Dancer standing in the middle of a grassfire, she removed her white cotton gloves and perched herself on the edge of the chair. Placing her small leather handbag on the corner of my desk, gloves over the bag. I winced as I plopped back down into my seat.

"Are you alright, Mr. Wolf?"

"Yeah, sure. Just a souvenir I got back in '39. San Francisco Police in those days. I cornered Hap Larkin in the Union Bank shootout."

If she was impressed, she didn't show it.

"I would, on behalf of my employer, wish to engage you to perform a service for us."

"If I agree, as I said, I get twenty-five dollars—"

"It's very simple really. My employer is a collector of rare objects. This afternoon there is an estate sale at Brooklyn's on Geary. My employer wishes to purchase a ceramic statue, it's actually a pair of statues, but if he shows any interest in this particular item, he's concerned that, how shall I put this. . ."

"He doesn't wanna show his hand so he can cop the thing on the cheap."

"I guess you could say that."

I brushed away a generous amount of dust that had collected on my desk, and leaned back in my chair.

"So, you want me to go buy the thing?" I said. "Why not do it yourself?"

"The staff and many people who attend these sales would recognize me. It wouldn't take much to ascertain what I was up to."

Ascertain! No client had ever used that word in front of me before. I considered doubling my rate—call it a 'refinement tax.' She opened her handbag, and fished around in it.

"My employer is interested in someone who can be discreet and is bonded," she said, producing a white envelope, placing it on the edge of the desk. "The envelope contains five hundred dollars in cash. Two hundred is yours. If you're able to purchase the item for less than three hundred, you can keep the difference."

I clearly needed to learn how to read people better. Yeah, remind her again about your penny ante twenty-five smackers a day. Idiot.

"What if I can't get it for three hundred?"

"When you deliver the item, you will be reimbursed the difference according to the receipt. Are we in agreement?"

"Sure thing. Let me get you a contract, Miss . . . I'm sorry. I didn't get your name."

"Elizabeth Westrom."

"Okay, Liz. You've got yourself an errand boy."

"It's Elizabeth," she said as she removed a slip of paper from her purse and placed it on the envelope. "Once you've made the purchase, come directly to this address. We will expect you by six o'clock."

I picked up the paper.

"607 Paloma Street, Burlingame," I said reading from the slip of paper.

"You'll find the items in the ceramic section. Lot eleven-thirty-five. Chinese water carriers."

I opened the left drawer of my desk. Retrieved a standard contract form.

"I'll just need you to fill this out," I said as I slid the document across the desk positioning it in front of her.

I watched her closely as she filled out the form. My job is to fix people's problems. The money's good when you get it, but there's no retirement plan. There was something interesting about her. I knew for sure she wasn't all that she appeared to be. It's an instinct you get being in the business. Many people will come around in some kind of trouble, looking for help, but they never come out and tell you exactly what the trouble is. They all hold something back. Westrom was no exception. She'd avoided looking me directly in the eye from the moment she'd breezed into the office on a lavender cloud. It appeared as though she wanted to hide herself from my gaze. When she finished the contract, she handed it back. I looked it over.

I said, "Is this the best phone number to reach you?"

"Yes. That is my home phone number. I don't see that it is necessary for you to call my employer regarding this service."

"Understood."

I gave her my card, and said our goodbyes. Lavender hung in the air, reminding me that this wasn't some kind of daydream. The cash in the envelope was real enough, ten fifty-dollar bills. The customer is always right—especially when her fist is holding enough cash to make it right. When it's cash up front, I keep an open mind and do whatever is asked short of murder. And if one day it actually turns out to be murder? I'll at least consider all the slants before declining. Or not.

This proved to be my lucky day. Giacomo Lupo was back in business. I changed my name to James Wolf when I became a cop. It was my pop's idea. As I was the only son of an Italian immigrant fisherman, he thought it made our little family more American. With $3.75 in my bank account and owing my landlady last month's rent, I left the office with a spring in my step. I headed directly to my apartment on Clay Street to change into something more presentable.

I joined the police back in '37. The Monday morning after Pearl Harbor I tried to enlist in the Marines. The aforementioned ounce of lead in my hip kept me out of the service. In '45 my policing career went sour. I got myself kicked off the force for brutally beating a kidnapping suspect. I rescued the victim—but the beating left the suspect blind. D.A. Mahoney was bent on getting an indictment for police brutality—wasn't a fan of Italians. Spaghetti benders, he called us. I had a reputation as a good cop, but Chief Delp had to play politics since the D.A. and Mayor were old buddies. My old boss, Lieutenant Mike Rickman, went to bat for me. I would've done the same. According to Rickman the ends always justified the means.

Unceremoniously dismissed, private dick became my only option. Rickman made sure I was able to get my P.I. license. He regretted that decision immediately. I quickly became the biggest thorn in his side. The job prospects this past year disappeared as quickly as a sand castle at high tide, but this job would get my creditors off my back and maybe more work.

It was just before noon when I tapped on Mrs. Vondernon's door. Grey-haired, and in her early sixties, she had style. You could tell she used to be a looker.

"Yes, what can—Oh, Mr. Wolf!" she said with a wide smile.

Vondermon was now a round woman. Her face, almost a perfect oval, sporting rosy cheeks. Her hips also equally round. Full-breasted, she wore her customary flower print house dress, loose-fitting, just above the knee showing off her still shapely gams. Apron tied at the waist accented what remained of her hourglass figure. The old dame liked me. She also liked having a former cop living in the building.

"Good morning Mrs. Vee," I said cheerfully. "First things first. Here's last month's rent." I gave her a fifty.

"Thank you. I'll get my purse."

"No, no. You keep the ten bucks. I'll get you the rest for this month soon. Could you do me a favor?"

"What kind of favor?"

I couldn't decide if her tone was suspicious or flirty.

"Would you mind giving these a quick pressing?" I produced a pair of slacks and a shirt from behind my back. "I have an important meeting later this afternoon."

"Sure thing, Mr. Wolf. Getting more work, I see."

She winked. Yeah. Definitely some fight left in this fish.

When I answered the knock on my door a short time later, Mrs. Vee had my shirt and pants pressed and ready. Thought I detected a hint of gardenia perfume. I thanked her. Still, with a couple of hours to kill, I got dressed and popped into Nick's Barber Shop for a trim and a shave.

Looking sharp, I was back in my car, envelope with cash tucked inside my jacket pocket, it was just after four o'clock and I found a parking spot on Clement and 4th. By four thirty I'd hoofed the two blocks to the entrance of Brooklyn's Auctioneers and went in.

Brooklyn's didn't look like much from the outside. Cinder block exterior along the boulevard. No windows. Inside the building it was large and wide. The set-up was much like a warehouse showroom: open area with steel support beams spaced out across the floor; signs in sections indicating the type of items available for bid. The upper level was half the size of the lower level. It was also open, with stairs leading to it on either side of the interior and windows along the back and sides.

In the middle of the entrance to the showroom sat a desk marked RECEPTION. There were several people ahead of me, men and women dressed in expensive finery, given programs as they entered the showroom. This event was a pre-auction sale. All attending had paid a fee to have the privilege over the next forty-eight hours, to make offers on items before they opened to a general public auction. From where I was standing, I could see works of art, ceramics, silver trays, tea sets, desks, tables, and chairs from the 17th century, I would've guessed, not being an expert. Wide-eyed I must've looked like a teenager who'd snuck into a burlesque show.

"Can I help you with something?" the woman at the desk asked.

"Wolf. I'm on the list."

She gave me a look. I heard throats clear behind me and the couple ahead of me turned and gave me the stink-eye. The room suddenly became very warm. I felt like a ham sandwich at a Bar Mitzvah. Could feel my face flush red.

"Woool…f," she said. "Oh yes, you're right here."

She looked up at me again. Shrugged and gave me a card with a number and a brochure.

"All items have an inventory number on them. Any that you're interested in bidding on, write down the number and your bid. When you're finished with your selections, a floorwalker will assist you."

"Thanks."

"Do you have a pencil?" she remarked with a degree of disdain that couldn't be mistaken.

"Yes. Actually, I have a pen."

I removed the pen from my jacket pocket and spun it between my fingers. She looked past me, signaled to the person behind me to approach the desk.

I wandered around for a few minutes, looking like I knew what I was doing, before approaching the ceramic section. I was looking for a pair of statues—an old Chinese man and woman carrying water buckets suspended from yokes across their shoulders. The statue of the old man was around 22 inches tall, the old woman nearly 18 inches. According to what Miss Westrom told me, the statues were carved out of alabaster stone and painted with pastel watercolors, giving them the appearance of being fired but not glazed ceramic. The difference in value between alabaster and ceramic would be in the hundreds of dollars. If these two pieces were correctly valued, they'd fetch fifteen hundred to two thousand. Among the ceramic displays, I noticed a large table with a sign hanging over it that read: Asian Art. I casually approached the table and could clearly see the carved head of an old Chinese man peering from behind a ceramic urn. This was what I was looking for. The two statues were in line with each other on the table. Item number 1135. Ceramic Statues, $300. Looking around, I discovered a curly-headed young man standing in the area. He had on a white shirt, black bowtie, and a red vest.

"Excuse me," I said. "I'm interested in item 1135, in the ceramic section."

"Yessir," he said as he approached me.

"Do I see you regarding this purchase?"

"I'm sorry, no sir. I'll find a floorwalker for you," he said. "Wait right here."

I turned back to the table and moved the urn to get a better look at the statues.

"May I assist you, sir?" a deep baritone voice inquired.

I turned to see a tall thin man dressed in a black suit, white shirt, and bowtie. His skin was pasty white, almost translucent. His long nose came to a point; high cheekbones gave his face a distinctly gaunt appearance. I imagined when not working here he'd be at Playland, scaring little kids in the chamber of horrors.

"Yeah, I'm interested in the water carriers. Will you take two hundred?"

"We estimate the value at three hundred dollars, based on—"

"I know," I interrupted. "But who knows if you'll get that much when it's up for auction. I'm ready, here and now, to take it off your hands. I'll tell you what. Two-fifty."

I waited. He gave a shrug.

"I'll have to check –"

"I may not be here when you get back," I said. "Do we have a deal?"

I pulled cash from my jacket.

He observed the bank notes in my hand, pinched his bottom lip between thumb and forefinger.

"Deal," he said with a shrug.

In one swift move, a sales book appeared, a receipt written, and a bony finger signaled the curly-headed young man a sale consummated. The lad carefully boxed up the statues. I gave Count Dracula the money. The young man gave me the box and I was on my way, fifty dollars richer.

Locking the box in my car, I popped across the street to the coffee shop. As I gulped two cups of java while devouring a ham and cheese sandwich, I prioritized my list of creditors. It was 5:00 p.m. when I started for the meeting point on Paloma in Burlingame. The trip would only take me forty-five minutes—plenty of time to make the six o'clock appointment. I cruised west on Geary towards 19th. As I crossed Funston, my '36 Ford Coupe started to lose power, chugging and smoking all the way to 19th. I cut across the boulevard and limped my way to Hillside. Found my way to Zeke's Service. I'd known Zeke from back when I was on the force, but I hadn't been in touch with him for over two years. The old jalopy made it halfway into the service station driveway when she abruptly gave out, her derriere sticking out in traffic.

Zeke Sampson, a muscular thirty-three-year-old, jet-black hair, with a tinge of gray at the sideburns from years of stress, jogged out of the service bay, wiping his hands on a grease rag.

"Jimmy! Why, you old sonofa—" he exclaimed as I exited the vehicle.

"Zeke! I gotta problem."

"Your problem is this twelve-year old-junker. Get behind the wheel."

He waved to a mechanic working in the bay and the two men pushed my Ford up to the service bay. Zeke went to the front of the car and opened the hood.

"You're leaking everywhere. Looks like the water pump."

"I've got an appointment in—" I checked my watch "—fifteen minutes, can I leave my car?"

"Sure. Where ya headed?"

"Burlingame. Need to call a cab."

"Phone in the office. My brother should be back with my car in a few minutes. You can borrow that if you want."

"That'd be great my friend," I said, relieved.

"What say we get a cup of coffee?"

We went into the office and Zeke poured a cup of his famous brown sludge.

"Why don't you call and tell 'em you'll be a little late?"

"No phone number. Just the address. I'm sure they can wait a few minutes."

I plopped myself down in a chair and we chatted about old times as we drank our coffee. Zeke worked as a mechanic for the San Francisco P.D. while I was on the force. We became good friends over the years because of the abuse I inflicted on service vehicles.

"You need to take better care of that clunker if you want it to be reliable."

"I wish I could, my friend," I said. "You know me, I can't tell a wrench from a screwdriver. Cash's been hard to come by this past year."

"How are things?"

"Picking up. I'm on a job right now."

"Good to hear."

The day after Pearl Harbor, Zeke went to the recruitment center and enlisted in the Army. His expertise as a mechanic landed him in a motor pool where he moved up quickly in the ranks to Staff Sergeant. It was a pretty cushy deal in the beginning, stationed at Fort Hood training new recruits until he was sent to North Africa. Sand wreaked havoc on the vehicles. If that wasn't a problem in itself, Rommel and his Afrika Korps nearly sent Zeke to his eternal resting place twice.

The war experience changed Zeke. He didn't return to the police department when he got home. He and his wife took the money they'd saved and Zeke started his own business. He wasn't at all inclined to spend the next stage of his life working for someone else. A year and a half later, the business was showing a decent profit and he and his wife welcomed a baby girl into the family. Whenever Zeke and I talked, it seemed like no time had passed since our last meeting. Each time we did meet, I always felt a twinge of jealousy. Zeke had it all as far as I was concerned.

"How's the family?"

"Kelly's gettin' big. Startin' to help her mom around the house," Zeke said beaming. "Smart too. Gets that from her mom."

It was nearly fifteen minutes later when Steve, Zeke's younger brother and partner, showed. I gave Steve a five-dollar bill and he filled up Zeke's car. I called Liz's number but didn't get an answer. Zeke told me he would replace the water pump right away. I agreed to meet him back at the garage once I made my delivery. With the package next to me on the front seat, I headed for Burlingame, throwing caution to the wind, breaking all the speed limits.

When I pulled up to the address on Paloma, it was 7:23 p.m. The house was dark. I slid out of the car and walked up to the front door, holding the box firmly with both hands. I had a feeling no one was home but rang the bell to convince myself my hunch was correct. I couldn't hear a bell or buzzer so I pressed the button several more times. Windows covered—place sealed up tighter than a snare drum. My gut told me something wasn't right. I returned to the car and started back to Zeke's garage. I stopped at the first filling station I came to and gave him a call.

"Hello?"

"Yeah, it's me. I'm on my way back."

"Everything go okay?"

"Nah. Nobody home."

"Your car's ready."

"Should be there in thirty minutes."

"Tell you what. Let's meet at your digs and we'll grab some drinks. I'll call Lorna and let her know I'm meeting you."

"Sounds good. I could use a belt. I'll hit 'em again tomorrow."

As I drove back to my apartment, I rehearsed my future conversation with Liz—Elizabeth in my head: Cars breakdown. Sometimes it just can't be helped. I tried to call. Didn't get an answer. I'll offer to give her the fifty I saved making the deal. That should smooth things over. I turned on the radio and listened to some music as I drove back to San Fran.

As I pulled up the street to my apartment, there were a couple of police cars blocking the middle of the road. At least two dozen bystanders milling around forced me to park a half block away. I approached the crowd. A man in a brown suit turned and started to walk across the street directly in front of me.

"What's happened here? An accident?"

"Looks like some guy got mugged," he said.

"Mugged?"

I heard a siren approaching.

"Yeah. Got beaten up pretty bad."

I pushed my way through the crowd as an ambulance arrived. I couldn't see past the police vehicles but the officer directing the ambulance attendants where to go was Pat Tunney. As the attendants unloaded a stretcher, I approached Pat.

"Hey, Pat. What happened?'

He turned. His face registered surprise. He acted like a prepubescent high schooler asking the prettiest cheerleader to the prom.

"Jimmy! What are you . . . ahh . . ."

I shot a thumb toward the apartment building. "Yeah, I live here. What's going on?"

"It's Zeke. He's been—"

"*Zeke!*" I yelled as Pat's words kicked my guts for a forty-yard field goal.

In an instant, the past all came flooding back to my brain. Brad "Sully" Sullivan, my best friend and partner. The man who helped me get through the loss of my mother and stood next to me as a brother when Pops died.

The man I killed six years ago.

Chapter 2

I rushed past Pat and around the police vehicles. My Ford sat at the curb; Zeke lay in the street, half under the running board. His face looked like a couple of pounds of fresh ground sirloin. Ambulance attendants carefully moved Zeke's body from under the car.

"Is he. . ."

"Alive, but badly beaten," the sandy-haired attendant responded as he positioned his stethoscope on Zeke's chest.

A fragile feeling of relief came over me as I watched the attendants lift the unconscious Zeke onto a stretcher and load him into the ambulance. Why would anyone want to work over Zeke? It didn't make sense I thought as the ambulance drove away. It just didn't figure. I noticed Pat talking to a short bald man in shirt sleeves across the street. I walked over to them.

". . .so I look out my window, right there, second floor, when I heard this noise," said cue-ball head. "Car door slamming and a man's voice. I couldn't make out what he was saying. Heard only grunts."

"Whatcha got, Pat?" I asked.

"This is Mr. Stanley. He heard the altercation. Jimmy here is a friend of the man beaten."

"By the time I opened the curtains and looked out, two guys were crossing the street and getting into a black sedan. I didn't know what was going on until some woman walking up the street saw your friend lying in the road."

"Did you recognize the make or model of the car?"

"Coulda been a Packard. Newer car for sure. License had an H and L, or I, as the first two letters."

"Thanks," I said.

I moved over to my Ford. Key was in the ignition. I reached under the dash and felt for my .38. It was there. I exhaled a breath of pure relief. That's all I'd need, somebody roaming around town with my gun. I retrieved the box from Zeke's car. Something was sure nagging at me as I walked to my apartment building. Mrs. Vee was standing at the entrance when I got there.

"Oh dear!" she exclaimed. "Mr. Wolf, you're okay?"

"Yeah, I'm fine."

"When I came out to see what the sirens were all about and saw your car parked in front, well I thought—"

"That's it, Mrs. Vee!"

"What's it?"

"My car!" I responded.

I headed into the building with Mrs. Vee right behind me chattering away on how the neighborhood used to be so quiet when her husband was the property owner. She wondered what the world was coming to. When we got to her apartment, I assured her there was nothing for her to worry about and maybe if she had some coffee on the stove, I'd appreciate a cup to calm my nerves. We went into her apartment. She waddled off to the kitchen. When I heard the water filling the coffee pot, I stashed my box in the hall coat-closet behind some shopping bags. I yelled to her that I was gonna pop up to my apartment and I'd be right back.

I entered and flipped on the light. Small but cozy, my flop came with a Murphy Bed in the wall to the right as you entered. To the far left were two windows that overlooked the alley. Living area had room enough for a couch, desk and an oak chest-of-drawers that fit nicely in the far corner. To the left of the entrance as you entered the apartment, the closet. A recessed kitchenette and connecting bath were located across from the entrance and framed out the room. I opened the closet and retrieved the small, well-worn satchel from the shelf. I placed it on the couch, opened the top drawer of the bureau and scooped out socks and underclothes. I went to the closet, selected a few shirts, slacks, jackets and tossed them on the couch. Under the bathroom sink, I found my leather toiletry carrier. I filled it with a razor, shaving cream, toothpaste, toothbrush and closed the mirrored cabinet. I gazed at my reflection for a moment. This whole job was too easy from the get go. I'd been paid more than was required and at first that made it okay—but now things had changed.

"What a sap I am," I said, bending over the sink, turning the cold tap on and splashing water on my face.

You let money cloud your judgment.

"What?" I said, looking up into the mirror.

Sully Sullivan, with his signature gray fedora, pulled down over his forehead, leaned against the bathroom door jam.

You let the money cloud your judgment, he reiterated.

I picked up the wash towel and dried my face and hands. Inspector Bradley "Sully" Sullivan was my first partner when I became an Inspector. He'd been on the force for six years and was a very experienced detective. He treated me like a brother. We'd go fishing on my father's boat when we had time off. A day never passed without me thinking of Sully.

The day he was killed, we were working the night watch out of robbery. It was hot that day in September and the night didn't provide any relief. We were following up on a case when a call of a silent alarm break-in at Watson's Jewelers on Battery just off Sacramento came over the radio. We were two minutes away.

When we arrived at the location, we discovered the rear door jimmied open which led into a storeroom. Shelves were stacked with boxes of merchandise. Display cases lined the walls, covered with woolen blankets, boxes of office supplies on top. Sully told me to cover the rear. I was to wait for backup while he inspected the rest of the store. It was hot and stifling in that storeroom and each minute seemed like ten as I waited tensely for Sully to return.

I became jittery as the minutes passed. The waiting made me sweat more profusely than the temperature would justify. My hands were slick with sweat as I changed my .38 from right to left hand to wipe the perspiration from my palms on the leg of my pants. During one of these exchanges, I heard a crash followed by a quick report of a gun. As I moved to the door leading into the store several more shots rang out. I moved into the dark showroom and ducked down behind a counter. When I peered over the top, I saw a figure heave a chair through the glass window. I saw the muzzle flashes just to the right of the door as two shots fired in rapid succession followed by a thin man darting through the opening. A man to the left of the door made a move for the exit.

Sully, crouched behind a desk to my right, took a shot in his direction. When the man moved for the door again, Sully's gun misfired as the man moved toward the door. I fired three quick shots and he collapsed to the floor. Sully darted for the door in pursuit of the escaping burglar. At the same moment, two uniformed officers entered the showroom from the rear. I told the officers to check on the suspect as I sprinted to the entrance, turning north on Battery, tracking Sully.

I ran up to Commercial and found no trace of Sully or the suspect. Clay Street didn't provide any clues as to the direction taken by my partner. I returned to Watson's and one of the uniformed officers met me at the door.

"Any luck?" he asked.

"No!" I replied, still trying to catch my breath. "Sully must be hot on his tail."

"Sullivan's inside. He's dead! Shot three times."

Dead!

"Dead?" my voice repeated and echoed far off in the distance. "Sully's. . . dead?"

The room began to contract and spin very slowly. I looked down at my revolver as the spinning accelerated. Three rounds discharged. Three rounds hit Sully. The room began to tilt and I felt myself drifting to the left. It was as if the interior of the jewelry store had mystically transported itself to the deck of a ship caught in a storm.

"Inspector?" another distant voice. "You okay, Inspector? Hey—Inspector Wolf! You okay?"

There was a full investigation and it was determined that I'd accidentally shot Sully in the confusion. Not one night passed that I didn't dream of Sully and that jewelry store. The outcome always the same. Sully was dead and I killed him.

I returned to duty but there wasn't a detective left in the department who wanted me for a partner. From then on, I worked cases alone—took chances. Very dangerous chances because I didn't care anymore. My life wasn't worth a plug nickel to me. Nearly a year to the day later two young punks were holding up a liquor store on

Mission Street around midnight. I just happened to drive by. Glanced at the window. The night clerk had his hands raised over his head. I stopped, approached the building from the east. Familiar with the establishment I knew the rear entrance would be open on a warm night. I cautiously edged down the alley to the rear. I had my gun out and was ready to burst into the building.

Looking to heaven, I muttered: "Sure could use your help tonight, Sully."

I wouldn't go in there, guns blazing my friend, a voice said from behind me in the alley.

I turned with a start. There leaning against the wall of the building across the alley was a man in a trench coat, hat pulled down over his eyes. He reached up and with his thumb pushed his hat up from his forehead.

You're putting the clerk in danger if you bust in like that.

"Sully? Is that really you?! You. . . you're supposed to be dead!"

I am dead. You went to my funeral, for chrissake.

"What are you, a ghost?"

Definitely not that.

"What is this—a Wonderful Life remake?! You tryin' to earn your wings?"

No wings, pal. That's a load of bunk. There are times when people need help and the only way for them to accept that help is seeing something they can relate to.

"Are you gonna follow me around from now on?"

No, but I'll be around. I'm here to tell you something. You can't keep blaming yourself for what happened. Sometimes things just happen. You're a cop Jimmy. Think like one. You act like you wanna kill yourself. You need to snap out of it and straighten up. Go back around to the front and walk in as if you're a customer. Ignore the clerk and those two punks. Get the drop on 'em.

I holstered my gun and made my way to the front of the store. Whistling a tune, I casually entered the store and immediately turned to the right and behind a large shelf that stored varieties of wines, whistling the whole time. Once safely behind the shelf, I moved a few bottles and could see the clerk, arms at his side, nervously watching the two punks. The punks had their hands in their pockets concealing weapons. The taller of the two, a red-headed man looked to be in his late twenties. The younger one had curly brown hair. He was twitching and scratching like a nudist with poison oak.

"Where do you keep the Petri Burgundy?" I called to the clerk.

"In the corner, left side of the cooler," he said.

I whistled my way to the back corner, picked up two bottles of burgundy and sauntered toward the cash register. As I approached the two hold-up men, I reached my right hand around to my backside as if I was going for my wallet. I'd stashed my .38 behind my back, wedged between my belt and spine. I was six feet from the counter when I let the bottles slip from my hand. They crashed to the floor startling the three men at the counter. In an instant, I had my revolver trained on the two robbers.

"POLICE!" I yelled. "Don't move!"

The younger of the two bolted for the door while the redhead tried to extricate his gun from his pants pocket. I fired a shot into his thigh and he collapsed in agony.

The headline in the morning papers read *Hero Cop Captures Hold-Up Men*. The story included the recounting of Sully's killing. That night was the first time I saw Sully. Deep down inside I knew it wouldn't be the last.

Chapter 3

ot a theory yet?

Sully's voice brought me back.

"What?"

Theories! Have any ideas?! Police work—remember?

"I figure when I didn't show up to the meeting, Miss Wistrom must've thought I double-crossed her. She sent a couple of her boys to wait for me here. When they saw my car—"

Your gut told you there was something fishy going on with this deal, Sully said. *You need to trust your instincts pal.*

"You're right. You were always right."

Not always, he countered with a laugh. *Remember that dame from the East Bay? All she wanted was a gold necklace outta me. Never saw her again after that.*

"I figure I'll get a hotel room just in case those goons come by again."

Good. You got used and if there's one thing I know, Jimmy Wolf doesn't like? It's being used. Trust your gut. This Westrom dame been feedin' you a load of bunk.

Ten minutes later, I was back in Mrs. Vee's kitchen sipping a cuppa joe.

"I packed some things, gonna be stayin' at a hotel while I work on this case."

"It must be important."

"Very. Listen if anyone comes around looking for me, you haven't seen me."

"Okay."

"Anyone wants me can call my service."

I said my goodbyes and grabbed my bag. I booked myself a cheap room in the Mission District, had some dinner then settled in for the night.

Next morning, I was up early, had some breakfast and stopped by the Hall to see Rickman. I waved to the Desk Sergeant and he signaled me he was in. His door was ajar so I just walked in and plopped myself in the open chair as he did his best impression of a hardworking cop.

"To what do I owe this pleasure? You got nothin' better to do?" he intoned as he kept his attention on the reports.

Mike was a get things done guy. His loyalty to me got him passed over twice for a promotion to Captain. Police politics left a bad taste in his mouth but with a new Chief of Police, Captain's bars were just around the corner.

"You heard about Zeke?"

"I saw the report. Too bad. How is he?"

"I'm goin' over to the hospital this afternoon. I called and they said he'd recover. Got a nice concussion and a cracked rib to boot. Gotta question for ya. Anything on a Packard with the first two letters, HL or HI?"

"Nothing. You know something as vague as that could take a while," he said looking up from the paperwork. "Does this have to do with something you're working on?"

I shrugged. "Let me know if you find anything."

He went back to his reports. I got up.

"You'll be the first person I call," I heard Rickman say as I headed down the hall.

I drove back to Burlingame to check the address where I'd been instructed to drop off the package. The place was still closed up tight but at a window on the side of the house, the shade was raised just enough to get a good look inside. The place was as empty as a politician's promise. Not even a scrap of paper on the floor.

A quick canvass of the neighborhood only garnered me one piece of information. The man who rented the house just moved out a week ago. He was medium height and build. Kept to himself, didn't get many visitors. I got into my car and started back for the city. Sully sat in the back seat, scowling like he'd poured sour milk into a fresh cup of coffee.

Gonna track down this Elizabeth. Give ya odds that ain't her real name, Sully said.

"Smells like a set up," I said.

Sully opened his mouth to say something.

"And don't talk to me about the money again."

I wasn't. Just gonna say ya might wanna find the address the phone number is attached too.

I stopped at a service station dropped a coin into the slot and called an old girlfriend of mine who worked at the phone company to get the address to Elizabeth Westrom's phone number.

"Pacific Bell, can I help you?"

"Operator 23," I said.

The line clicked then buzzed in my ear.

"Operator?"

"Barb! It's James."

"Well, hello there," she purred.

"I need a little favor. Can you give me the address of Monroe-3-2486?"

"You only call when you need something these days."

"Just get me the address, please."

"You know we're not supposed to do that," she teased.

"You say that every time I ask."

"Hold on, please," she said in her operator's voice.

After a couple of minutes of waiting, I lit a smoke and started to flip through the classified section of the phone book. I opened to Private Investigations and found my number. There's a certain feeling you get seeing your name and number in the book, a kind of validation. It was a full five minutes before Barb came back on the line.

"You still there?" she asked.

"I'm here. What did ya find?"

"That number is a phone booth on highway one south of Pacifica."

"Phone booth. Huh." I sighed. "Thanks Barb, I appreciate it."

"So when you gonna call me?"

"I just did, baby," I said, then added. "Soon. Promise."

I hung up.

I'd been involved in some strange cases before but this one was one for the books. Nothing about this thing made any sense. Someone worked Zeke over because he'd been mistaken for me.

I stopped by San Francisco General to check on Zeke and maybe see if he could be of any help. Ward nurse Miss Bitters, a woman in her fifties, reminded me of my fifth-grade teacher, Sister Ursula Marie: Five-foot-six, round wire-rimmed glasses. Sister Ursula Marie's face registered a permanent scowl as if she'd just chugged a cup of vinegar.

"The desk nurse told me to see you. I'm James Wolf. Here to see Zeke Sampson."

"Yes. Mr. Sampson left word that he wanted to see you."

"Thank you."

"Mr. Sampson needs his rest. He suffered severe trauma."

"I understand, Miss Bitters."

"You can have five minutes and that's all. I'm responsible for my patient's recovery and I'll not have them disturbed."

"I understand."

"If you will follow me."

"Thank you."

She led me into his room held up her hand, fingers splayed.

"Five minutes," she said.

I moved to the bed.

"Jimmy!" Zeke's voice was barely above a whisper.

"How you doin', my friend?"

"Fair. Got some information for ya," he grumbled as he tried to sit up a bit.

"Easy buddy."

"Two guys were waiting when I got to your place."

"They thought you were me because you were driving my car."

"The short weaselly lookin' guy asked me for the package. A big guy. I mean big! He just yanked me from the car like I was a ragdoll. I told the little guy I didn't know what he was talkin' about. Then the big guy slugged me."

"Did you get a good look at this guy?"

"Hat pulled down over his eyes. Only thing I got a good look at was his chest."

"Anything else you can remember?"

"No. He slugged me a couple of more times with a sap and the next thing I remember I'm in this hospital room."

I could see Zeke was struggling to stay conscious.

"Listen boy. You rest up. I'm keeping your car for the time being. As long as whoever these mugs are who attacked you think you're me and in hospital, I've got some time to look around."

Zeke flashed me the OK sign and I left him to the tender ministrations of Nurse Bitters.

Chapter 4

I called Rickman's office from a payphone in the waiting area. Gave him a brief rundown. He tried to pump me for information but I wasn't about to give out any.

I said, "If I had anything concrete, I'd tell ya. I'm concerned that these goons might come after Zeke again."

"I'll put a man outside Zeke's room for the next coupla' days."

"Good."

"If I knew what you were workin' on I could be more help," Rickman said.

"I need to work a few angles. You and your guys flashing your buzzers around town will only make things harder. I'll let you know when I get somethin' solid."

"You'd better—"

I hung up the phone before he could finish.

It was 2:14 p.m. when I parked across the street from Brooklyn's. Front entrance was open and I followed an older couple into the building. I slipped past them as a gray-haired man greeted them. I moved to the reception area. A man, I'd say he was about 30, dressed in a brown three-piece suit was leafing through a folder of papers at the reception desk.

I cleared my throat.

"Can I help you sir?" he said, looking up, then back to the papers.

"I'm lookin' for a girl."

"This is an auction house, not a lonely hearts club," he said dryly.

"You must be a burlesque comic. What time does the main attraction start?"

He put the folder down with a slap. "Is there something you want?"

"I was in here yesterday and bought two figurines—"

"All sales are final. There are no refunds or exchanges."

"You're really fluent in English. I wish you were more fluent in listening."

"Excuse me?"

"I'm looking for the girl who was working the reception desk yesterday. Is she here?"

He thought for a moment. "You must mean Claire Regis. She's not here today. Is there anything else?"

"No. Maybe we can word wrestle again some other time."

One round with Kid Interrupter left me with a growing headache. I left and walked the half block down the street to a cigar store and called information.

"Operator, number please."

"I'd like the number for a Claire Regis. R-E-G-I-S."

"Hold please."

"Thank you, operator."

"That number is unlisted."

As I walked back to my car, I saw Count Dracula coming out of the alley next to Brooklyn's. I hustled up to him as he started across the street.

"Hey, buddy!" I called to him.

He turned and said as politely as you can in that baritone voice, "You called me, sir?"

"Yeah! Wanted to ask you somethin'. I was in Brooklyn's yesterday and bought a couple of figurines—"

"I'm sorry but at Brooklyn's all sales are final, no refunds or exchanges."

"I already heard that tune, number one on the Hit Parade in this neighborhood."

"I beg your pardon?"

"Listen. I didn't catch yer name. I'm James Wolf."

I extended my hand, offered my business card. He paused for a moment then took the card.

"Private Investigator indeed," he said.

He was legitimately impressed. I liked this guy.

"Your name?"

"Pitts is the name. Lester Pitts."

"May I call you Les?" I asked.

He nodded and put my card in his vest pocket.

"Is there somewhere we could talk? I'm looking for some information."

He pointed to a tavern across the street. Jake's Place. It wasn't fancy by any means. Your typical saloon: wood floors that smelled of stale beer, stools, bowls of salted peanuts at the bar, row of booths along the wall.

We stepped up to the bar. Bartender, broad-shouldered and potbellied, chewing on a toothpick.

"Whatcha havin'?"

"What's your pleasure, Les?'

"Vodka martini, please."

"And for you, Mac?"

"Bourbon with a splash of soda," I said, throwing a five-spot on the bar and pointing a thumb toward the booths. Barkeep nodded.

Lester and I slid into the booth.

"So what kind of information are you looking for Mr. Wolf?"

"I'm tryin' to get a fix on a dame."

He gave me a look.

"Young woman," I said sheepishly. "From what I understand, she's been to Brooklyn's a number of times. She told me that the people who worked there would know her by sight."

Bartender arrived with drinks, placed them on the table.

"Her name was Elizabeth Westrom. Ring a bell?"

Lester took a healthy sip of his martini. When he set the glass down it was half-empty.

"I'm sure I don't recall that name," he put the glass to his lips again and the cocktail was gone. "You see, I'm not employed by Brooklyn's on a full-time basis. I am considered somewhat of an expert on certain antiques. This Elizabeth person, could have been there many times when I wasn't working."

"I see. So, you're an expert?" I signaled the bartender. Pointed to Lester's empty martini glass.

"Yes. I specialize in crystal and pottery."

"Do you remember the Water Carriers I bought yesterday?"

"Yes indeed. You didn't haggle. That's rare."

"So I got a good deal?"

"Not too bad."

"So two hundred fifty clams for alabaster statues—not bad?"

The bartender returned with another martini.

Les chuckled and said, "Clams or dollars, it really does not matter in the least. Those statues are not alabaster. They're ceramic. Good quality ceramic I will admit, but not alabaster."

"What?"

"Mr. Wolf, believe me. I can spot real alabaster from across the street. Who told you they were alabaster?" he said with a laugh.

"Miss Westrom. She said they were carved alabaster that someone had painted to look like ceramic."

Lester shook his head. "I'm afraid not, Mr. Wolf. Not that you were taken, not by any means. You could still find a buyer for those pieces for at least three to four hundred dollars or more."

"You wouldn't happen to have an address or phone number for Claire Regis?"

Lester shook his head. This whole case was nuttier than a squirrel's bowel movement. I thanked Lester for his help, bought him an extra martini, and drove downtown to the phone company. I needed Barb's help again. I parked two blocks away on Montgomery Street and walked in. Barb Howell worked the day shift. She would be ready to clock out in about fifteen minutes, so this would be a delicate operation. Barb was nice-looking and had a great personality, but just wasn't the kind of girl I was interested in. She just wouldn't take no for an answer. Therefore, I stopped saying no and started saying maybe. We'd hit a couple of nightclubs in the past, but she tended to get on my nerves. She'd chomp down on a stick of Wrigley's and make the damn thing snap like the jaws of a junkyard dog. I don't know how she did it and she didn't know either because when I asked her to stop doing it, she told me she couldn't. "It just does it on its own," she said.

Get the picture.

I made my way to her area and caught her attention. She held up one finger and exactly thirty seconds later, she had her headphones off and was waving good bye to the other ladies at the switchboard.

As she walked toward me, I fought the urge to turn tail and run as fast I could out of there—but I needed her help so I just stood there with a silly grin plastered onto my face. I could see that hungry look in her eyes. I felt like a lion tamer wearing a meat suit.

"Jimmy Wolf, you better be coming here to ask me for a date," she said as her arms surrounded my neck.

Before I could respond she kissed me square on the lips. Have to admit, it felt good.

"Barb, listen. I need you to do me a favor," I said as I pried her paws off my neck.

"Another favor? It's gonna' cost you, Jimmy boy."

"I'm sure it will."

"Dinner. Tonight. And I'm hungry."

"I'm working a case."

"You're always working on one of your silly ole cases. You need to take some time and work on me," she said her arms back around my neck.

"I'll put that on my calendar," I said pulling her arm away. "I need to find the address of a person. The phone number is unlisted. It's important that I find this person."

"Important enough to buy me dinner and dancing?" Barb said.

"You win."

"Give me about twenty minutes and meet me at Café du Nord."

I took out a business card and wrote Claire Regis on it.

"This is the girl I'm looking for," I said handing her the card. "Unlisted number."

"Claire Regis, huh! What's she got I don't?"

"Information. See what you can do."

I was on my second bourbon and soda at the bar when Barb sauntered into Café du Nord. She slid onto the stool next to me and nodded to the bartender.

"My usual, Ted," she said.

He gave her a wave and began to assemble a Manhattan.

I'd been avoiding Barb for some months because of her expensive tastes. She never had a date take her to a place that was cheap. I couldn't afford a hot dog stand for nearly a year. I was about to enjoy this dinner date as much as Barb. I flagged a waiter as he came by.

"Can we have a table?"

"Right this way, sir."

Barb snapped her gum a couple of times, extracted the wad from her lips, and deposited the aforementioned annoyance into an ashtray. We picked up our drinks and followed the waiter to a table.

We spent the next hour and a half discussing the state of the world, my neglect of her, as well as the excellent quality of the meal.

Barb, as always, however, came through.

"So this Claire you're looking for lives on Steiner," Barb said.

"Nice work."

"It was work," she said waving a square of paper in my face.

I reached for it, but Barb pulled it back.

"It'll cost you another dinner and dancing," she said.

"You drive a hard bargain."

"You know how to make a girl blush."

We went out dancing. Around 11 pm, I decided I had enough exercise for one evening. Claire's apartment stakeout would start bright and early Sunday morning.

"How about a nightcap," Barb said as I pulled up to her place.

"Gonna have to pass. Stakeout tomorrow."

"Got a bottle of Bushmills just sittin' there, hasn't even been tapped yet."

"One drink won't hurt."

Famous last words I thought as I followed her into the apartment. She breezed through the living room, pointed to a whiskey set up on an oak sideboard.

"Fix me one, on the rocks, I'll be right back."

Barb had a bowl of ice in the freezer. With a couple of cubes in each glass, I poured two generous fingers of whiskey each. I sipped one. It went down as smooth as polished marble. I returned to the living room, about to set Barb's drink down, when she said:

"This is much more comfortable."

I turned. She was leaning against the bedroom door jam, dressed in a lacy nightgown. So thin you could see all the way to Sausalito. She moved toward me, took the drink from my hand, and sipped.

"Mmmmmm. Makes me feel all wet and warm inside."

Taking my hand, she backed into the bedroom. Guess I hadn't had enough exercise for one evening. The stakeout would start a little later than planned.

Up early. My body felt like it spent the night in a cement mixer. I successfully slipped out undetected after a quick shower. Had a cuppa mud and donut in the all-night coffee shop just down the street from Barb's place, then drove over to the Steiner Street address and parked where I could see anyone entering or leaving the building. Claire Regis lived in an apartment house. 1722 Steiner. Phone number Madison 3-5748. I was there nearly two hours when a late model blue coupe pulled up in front of the building and a woman behind the wheel honked the horn.

At 9:15 a.m. exactly, Claire Regis exited the front door and bounded down the steps to the street. First time I'd gotten a look at Claire Regis from head to toe. I could tell from a distance she was a mover. Kinda sweet and compact, but definitely built for speed. She got into the coupe and they pulled away from the curb. I ducked down in my seat as they passed by heading north. I gave them a comfortable lead then swung around and tailed them to Union Street where they turned right and parked across the street from a little café. I pulled to the curb on the corner of Steiner and Union and watched the two women as they crossed the street. It was a warm Sunday morning and I could see Claire pointing to a table on the sidewalk. The two sat down as a waitress approached.

They talked and ate breakfast for an hour and a half. Claire's friend looked at her watch and I could tell from her reaction that she had somewhere she needed to be. They both paid the check and Claire's friend rose from her seat. The two hugged. The friend crossed the street, got into her car, and drove away. Claire sat at the table finishing her coffee. This was a perfect opportunity for me to make my move. I crossed the street just a half of a block from the café and casually walked in Claire's direction. When I reached her table, she looked up at me and I stopped.

"Pardon me," I said. "But aren't you from Brooklyn's Auction House?"

She assumed a puzzled look. "Yes, I am."

"I was in Friday and purchased a pair of figurines. I was wondering if you had a moment. I have a couple of questions?"

"Well we don't have a refund—"

"What—you guys work off a script?!" Off her shock, I added: "Relax, this isn't about a refund. May I sit?"

"I guess that would be—."

Before she could finish I dropped down into the chair opposite her.

"I'm James Wolf," I said and extended my hand.

"Claire Regis."

"I was. . . let me put it this way, engaged to perform a service. I was to purchase that figurine set for someone."

"I thought there was something odd about you. You didn't look like. . . someone who was an antique hunter."

She flashed a bright smile. Even a blind man could see she was beautiful. I lost my train of thought for a moment.

"There was a mix-up and I was unable to make the delivery and I can't seem to locate the person who hired me. I phoned, but no answer. The person I'm looking for is Elizabeth Westrom. Does it ring any bells?"

Shaking her head, she said. "I don't recognize the name."

"She told me that she'd be recognized if she came into Brooklyn's since she'd been there any number of times."

I went on to describe Westrom in detail. When I mentioned her matter of fact and precise demeanor, Claire perked up.

"I do remember a woman like that. Her name wasn't Westrom, though."

"Any way you can find out what her real name is?"

"She'd have had to sign a receipt, the same way you did when you bought the water carriers."

She did remember me. I could feel my face warming as she continued to speak.

"I'd have to look through purchase receipts. If I remember correctly, she was with a man and they purchased a couple of brass statues of bulls. Attached to polished rectangular wood boxes. A matching pair I seem to recall."

"Very detailed," I said.

"I remember cataloging those. Had to write an accurate description. I'm working tomorrow so I can take a look at the receipt."

"That would be great. Here's my card. You can call me anytime day or night. My service will get a hold of me."

"Private Investigator," she read aloud. Then nodded with approval. Seemed impressed—but she might've been just humoring me.

"I have my car here, I'd be happy to drop you somewhere."

"Yes, thank you."

There was a bit of small talk as I drove her home from the café. The conversation was typical fare about the life of a private investigator. I provided stock answers not unlike her kneejerk "no refunds" gambit.

"What's the most interesting case you've been on?"

"This one. Mostly I'm workin' divorce cases or for lawyers settling accident claims."

"Not like the books, huh?"

"Not like the books."

After dropping Claire at her place, I headed over to my office. I wanted to pick up the contract Elizabeth, or whatever her name was, had signed. I parked on Leavenworth and slipped into the rear entrance of my building just in case someone was watching the joint. I was in and out of my office in less than two minutes. With nothing more I could do, for the time being, I swung by my apartment to grab a few things. I hoped to be able to relax and put this case on a back burner for the rest of the day.

As I walked up to my apartment, I mentally reviewed a list of things I'd want to take back to the hotel with me: couple of clean shirts, few extra pairs of socks. I put my key in the lock and opened the door. I remember that I was thinking of a couple of nice neckties Claire might approve of as I stepped inside.

I immediately froze. The apartment was different. A breeze ruffled the curtains covering a slightly open window. I caught a whiff of stale cigar odor. I heard a swoosh kind of noise. Like the sound of a large bird's wing against the air. The hair on the right side of my head fluttered. I heard a dull thump. At the same time, I felt something touch me behind my right ear. There was a flash of light and then the floor of my apartment opened up to reveal a deep black hole. My body tipped forward and I fell head-first into the abyss. I tumbled deeper into a swirling vortex, heard a distant sound of breaking glass.

I tried to pick myself up off the floor. My legs wouldn't work. My face pressed deep into the carpet and I took a little nap. The whine of a fire truck's siren brought me back to consciousness. Dazed and nauseated I drag myself to the couch. About to vomit, Sully's voice commanded my attention.

Better get to the bathroom before you mess up the carpet.

I staggered to my feet. "I'll be fine," I said.

Don't think so. You look about as bad as your first day as a plainclothes officer.

I made it just in time before what was left of my lunch was deposited in the sink. I rinsed out my mouth and splashed cold water on my face. Sully was right. I felt as sick as my first case as a detective. The Margaret Cabot kidnapping.

You remember what I taught you working the Cabot case?

"I remember you not havin' any sympathy for the way I was feelin'," I said as I made my way to the kitchen. I wrapped ice in a towel and held it over the lump growing on the back of my head.

Chapter 5

I was the last one in the squad room that morning after a night of celebrating my promotion.

"You look like hell!" Sully said as I dropped into the empty seat next to him.

"It was a rough night."

"Get any sleep?"

"A little."

"You'll learn," Sully said with a grin.

"All right, listen up," Captain Backstran said as he looked out over the squad. "One Margaret Scranton Cabot, twenty years of age, lives at 3559 Washington Street, Nob Hill, student at Berkeley—last seen leaving her home at 7 p.m. Monday. Margaret is the daughter of Johnathon P. Cabot, owner of Cabot Shipping Line. She didn't return home that evening. At 7 a.m., the following morning Cabot received a phone call. Kidnappers were holding Margaret for ransom. They demanded fifty-thousand dollars be brought to Golden Gate Park. Once the kidnappers received the money, Margaret would return home. It's been…" Backstran checked his watch. "Thirteen hours now since the ransom was delivered. Cabot contacted us this morning. Lieutenant Poland has the information.

Stan Poland opened a folder.

"I have recent copies of Margaret Cabot's photo for all of you," Poland said as he handed a stack of photos to Inspector Tucker.

As Tucker passed the photos around the room Poland moved to the podium.

"Cabot's instructions were to go to Shakespeare's Garden and leave cash in the bottom of a flower pot. Put it under Shakespeare's bust at exactly 5 p.m. Ransom note said his daughter would return home within two hours."

"That's it. Hit the streets. Find this girl!" Backstran said. "Hopefully alive."

"Doesn't fit," Sully said.

"How's that?"

Sully started the car and pulled away from the curb.

"Girl leaves the house at seven. Next morning ransom's delivered. Pretty quick for my liking."

"How do ya mean?"

"Would-be kidnappers got their money right away. No fuss. Let's have a little chat with old man Cabot."

We waited in the vestibule of the Cabot mansion on Washington Street. If the San Francisco Dons needed a practice facility, this would suit the purpose fine. The main entrance opened up to an area wider than a basketball court. The ceilings were at least twenty feet high. Crystal chandelier hung about 10 feet above a mahogany table holding a single stoneware vase. Fresh flowers, meticulously arranged, filled the room with a sweet aroma. Foot falls echoed off the walls of the virtually empty room as the butler returned from somewhere deep into the home's interior.

"Mr. Cabot will see you now," he said. "This way gentlemen."

The butler led us into an oak wood paneled study the size of a tennis court.

"Have you found anything?" Cabot asked, nervously pacing in front of his desk. "I've been frantic."

"We're following up a lead," Sully said. "When your daughter left the house the other night, was she to meet a friend?"

"Yes! I've told the other policemen this."

"Was this normal for her on a school night?"

"Well . . . no. She said she'd be back rather quickly . . . picking up something or other. I suggested she should let Martin, he's our chauffeur, drive her. But she said she'd only be gone a short while."

"Then what?" Sully asked.

"I had arrangements to meet some of my business associates at my club. I returned two hours later and Margaret hadn't returned from her errand. But I told you all this."

"When you got the call for the ransom you said you spoke to Margaret?"

"Yes, I did."

"How did she sound?" Sully said.

"Sound? What do you mean?" Cabot said.

"Did she sound like she'd been cryin'? Was her voice steady?"

"She sounded nervous. Told me she wasn't hurt. She was okay."

"What about the ransom money?" I said.

"I had plenty of cash on hand."

"You keep that much cash in the house?" Sully said.

"I needed it for securing a deal. I picked up the cash and stored it in my safe. I've done it many times."

"I see," Sully said. "We're gonna need a little help Mr. Cabot. Notify the newspapers. Get her picture out there. Someone's sure to have seen her."

"Is that wise?" Cabot said.

"Trust us, Mr. Cabot. We'll get your daughter back," I said. "One more question, sir. Did Margaret have anyone she's seein' lately? Boyfriend, possibly?"

"No, absolutely not!"

"Thank you for your time, Mr. Cabot," Sully said. "We'll be in touch."

We went back to our car.

"Had all that cash on hand. Pretty interestin'?" I said as Sully pointed the car west on Washington.

"We gotta work fast," Sully said.

"Where to?"

"Golden Gate Park."

A petite secretary ushered us into the office of a Mr. Hooper, Park Superintendent.

"Thanks for seein' us Mr. Hooper," Sully said, flashing his shield.

Hooper, mid-forties, stood about five-seven and carried a pronounced paunch over his belt buckle.

"Police?" a puzzled Hooper said.

"I'm Inspector Sullivan, this is Inspector Wolf."

"What's the trouble officers?"

"Last night around 5 p.m. a ransom package was dropped at the Shakespeare bust. We'd like to speak with any park employees that worked in that area yesterday."

"Yes, absolutely. I'll have Miss Clark draw up a list of names."

"We appreciate it, Mr. Hooper," Sully said.

There were only four employees that worked Shakespeare's Garden that day, our third interview hit pay dirt. Mr. Sam Saito, 25-year-old Japanese-American.

"You're a park gardener Mr. Saito?" Sully asked.

"Yes, that is correct."

"Yesterday, sometime after five, did you happen to see anything unusual at the Shakespeare bust?"

"I don't think so."

"Did anyone leave anything behind, for example?" I asked.

"Oh! Yes, I do remember someone had left flowers."

"You didn't think it was unusual?" Sully said.

"For a moment yes, but people do leave flowers, usually on the anniversary of the man's death," Saito said. "They were gone a short time later."

"Did you happen to see who took 'em?" Sully said.

"No."

"Was there anyone around about that time?" I said.

"Man and woman were sitting on the bench. They watched me weed the roses."

"Were they still on the bench when you finished?"

"Oh, yes. The man had his arm around her. Lovers, you know."

I handed Mr. Saito the photo of Margaret Cabot.

"Do you recognize the woman in the photo?" I said.

Saito studied it carefully and shook his head.

"Looks similar to the young woman. Cannot be sure."

"But it was a young woman?" I said.

"Yes. Young. Very nice clothes also," he said handing me the photo.

"You've been a great help, Mr. Saito," Sully said.

"You think that guy and girl were lookouts?" I said as we headed back to the car.

"Stands to reason. Gimmie the rundown on Margaret."

"Turned twenty this year—lives at home. Sophomore year at Berkeley—humanities—"

"I bet Margaret's in a sorority. One of the girls may know something," Sully said as we piled into the car.

Our next stop, the Berkeley campus.

I fired up a smoke as we crossed the Bay Bridge. "You gotta strong hunch?"

"Yeah. Rich girl wants to get off daddy's leash. I'm guessin' there's a boyfriend involved," Sully said shrewdly. "Betcha Cabot didn't want to mention a row they had. Keeping up appearances, if you know what I mean."

"I get it. Daughter forced to live at home with a domineering father. No mother to run interference . . ."

"Meets a young man. He starts to put ideas in her head . . ."

"Beginning to sound like a phony setup," I said.

"Never forget. Trust your hunches. Don't assume."

After a brief visit at the Administration building, we proceeded to Margaret's Social Studies classroom. With five minutes left in the class, we entered. Professor Fineman was wrapping up his lecture.

"Pardon us, Professor. We're from the San Francisco Police Department. I'm Inspector Sullivan, this is Inspector Wolf. We'd like to ask if anyone in this class has seen Margaret Cabot."

"She didn't come to class today, officers, is there a problem?" Fineman said.

"Just routine. We have a few questions for her," Sully said.

Professor Fineman turned to the class. "Anyone have any information for the officers?"

The students exchanged looks and indicated in the negative with shakes of their heads.

"Anyone know if Margaret is a member of a sorority?" Sully said.

"I do," a dark-haired female student in the rear of the classroom said.

"You are?"

"Linda Engle. Margaret is a Delta Gamma."

"Where is the Delta house?" Sully asked.

"On the other side of campus. I can show you if you like."

"That would be helpful."

"You know Margaret well, Miss Engle?" Sully asked as we walked across campus.

"Not really. I have another class with her."

"Have you noticed anything strange about her lately?" I asked.

"She has been kind of moody. Missed a couple classes last week."

Interviews with several of the other sorority sisters revealed much of the same. Margaret was distracted with school. She missed entire days of classes. Stopped coming around the sorority house, telling girlfriends she would be going home after school. Most of her friends confirmed her demanding father kept a close check on Margaret.

We got a list of her friends from one of the sorority members.

"Yeah, I saw her at a joint on Union Street—Cow Hallow," Brad Greenmore told us. "Hadn't seen her in English Lit for a while."

"Which joint?" I asked.

"I don't remember. Me and a bunch of the guys were hittin' the bars Friday night."

"Was she with anyone?" said Sully.

"Nope. Alone at a table. Could've been waitin' for somebody, I don't know. We didn't stay long. Kinda surprised seein' her there."

"How so?" Sully said.

"Never thought she was the kinda girl who'd go to a place like that. Strait-laced. All proper."

We checked in with headquarters then started back for San Francisco. It was late in the afternoon when we exited the Bay Bridge, swung by Red's Joint to formulate our next move and get a bite to eat.

"We'll split up on Union, you take the west side," Sully said. "One block at a time. Wait on the corner so we can compare notes before we move on. We'll swing by HQ. Pick up copies of her picture."

"Right."

We came up empty on the first three blocks of Union. No one recognized Margaret's picture. We left photos behind. On the next block, I hit pay dirt.

"Yeah, I seen her," the bartender said. "Sat in the corner, over there."

"She had some friends stop by? College boys?" I said.

"Yeah, I remember those guys," the bartender said. "They kept lookin' at her. Knew her from school or somethin'. She gave 'em the brushoff."

"Was—"

"I tell ya. She was an eyeful. A real looker, ya know?"

"Yeah, I get it!" I said.

"From what I could figure, she came from some money. Rich college kid, slumin' ya know?"

"Yeah. Was she—"

"We get a lot of 'em comin' in. Ya know. Gettin' a cheap thrill. She in trouble?"

"Gone missing. Was she *alone* the whole time?"

"Jeez, I can't really say. Kinda busy. She kept lookin' at the door. Like she was expectin' someone, ya know. Kept lookin' at her watch."

"You didn't see who she was waitin' for?"

"Nah! Them college boys left after a while. Joint got too crowded for me to eyeball her table. Hold on a sec."

Bartender waved to one of the waiters.

"Ralph was workin' that night. *Hey, Ralph!*" he called. "Come over for a minute."

Ralph was short, thin in build, looked to be in his forties.

"Remember the other night, when those two sailors got into a scrap?" the bartender asked Ralph. "Coupla gobs got into it," he said to me.

"Bet I do. My right hand still hurts," Ralph said.

"This guy's a police officer," the bartender said.

"Better not've put in a complaint!"

"Nah, nothin' like that Ralphie. You remember that dame? Rich lookin'? Sat at the corner table?"

"Bet I do! Nursed a drink for over an hour. Kept wavin' me off. What's she done?"

"Missin'," the bartender said. "Cops lookin' for her. When she was here, did she meet anybody?"

Ralph thought for a moment.

"Yeah, she did meet this guy. Young. Mid-twenties, maybe. All dressed up in a monkey suit. Starch collar and everythin'."

"Black hair slicked back. Movie star-like," the bartender said.

"Yeah, that's him," Ralph said.

"Seen him around. Musician, I think," the bartender said.

"You've been helpful. Thanks," I said tossing a fiver on the bar. "If you think of anything else, here's my card."

"Sure thing officer. Always glad to help the police," the bartender said with a wave.

I flagged Sully at the next corner.

"Got a positive ID," I said. "Margaret was waiting for a man. Could be a boyfriend. Bartender remembers seein' him before. Probably a working musician. Dressed like one anyway."

"It's a lead at least. Let's start checking the clubs."

We hit nearly a dozen joints that featured music to no avail. When the clubs started to close, we hit the all-night diners. It was three o'clock in the morning when we stopped in the Cable Car on Howard. Several men, dressed in tuxedos occupied a table. We approached the table.

"Police officers, gentlemen," Sully said, displaying his badge. "We're lookin' for a musician—"

"Need a band for the Policeman's Ball?" a dark-haired man said.

Table got a good laugh.

"Not exactly," Sully said. "We have some questions, routine. This guy's mid-twenties. Good looking. Hair black. Sports it slicked back."

The men at the table threw out a few names.

"Hold on fellas," the dark-haired man said. "This guy you're lookin' for. Trumpet player—sax—piano player?"

"We don't know," Sully said.

"Can't be Eddie Marrs," the redhead said. "He's in his forties. If it's trumpet, you're lookin' for—Chuck Barns. Piano—Billy Tramaine."

An African American man in dark glasses leaned in, said, "Tenor sax cat. Slick black hair. Dusty Lang."

"That's right," the redhead said.

"You know where we can find them?" I said.

"Chuck's in Outer Richmond. Clement, I think," said a dark-haired man.

"Yeah!" red hair said. "Tramaine's Sunset, on Noriega. Lang's in Mission District."

"Thanks for your help," Sully said.

"If you need a band for the ball, you know where to find us," dark hair said.

The table erupted in laughter.

"Let's get addresses for these three," Sully said.

We checked the phone directory. Neither of the men listed. We'd have to cool our heels for a few hours. Contact the Musicians Union later in the morning. We went home to grab some rest.

It was 8:05 in the morning when I arrived in the squad room. Sully was on the phone.

". . . thanks for your help," Sully said.

Pleased with himself, he dropped the receiver back on its cradle.

"Good. You're here," Sully said. "I got addresses for Barns and Tramaine. They both worked last night. Lang is out of town."

Lieutenant Rickman walked in looking like he had a hard night.

"You guys are chasin' your tails," Rickman said. "Cabot should've called us as soon as he got the ransom note. Little rich girl's dead by now."

Rickman had just got his promotion to Lieutenant. He liked to throw his weight around. With that bar on his collar, he quickly became insufferable.

"My gut tells me that's not the case," Sully said, holding up a slip of paper. "Let's go, Jimmy. We'll see what Mr. Barns has to say for himself."

"What's goin' on with Rickman, Sully?" I said as we drove across town.

"He's lettin' his brain override his gut. Gotta trust those instincts, Jimmy."

Fifteen minutes later we banged on Barns's apartment door.

"Who is it?" Barns said through the closed door.

"Police," Sully replied. "We want to talk to you, Mr. Barns.

Barns opened the door. Hair disheveled, wrapped in a striped robe he looked like a soaked rat that just crawled out of a sewer.

"You know what time it is?"

"Just eight thirty," I said, checking my watch.

"I know the time! What's this all about?"

"We're lookin' into the disappearance of Margaret Cabot," Sully said.

"Never heard of her," Barns said, trying to shut the door. Sully pushed his way in.

"She's been seen around town with a musician," I said.

"Listen pal. There's lots of musicians in this town. I never heard of this dame."

"You didn't see last night's paper?" Sully said.

"I don't read the papers."

Sully showed Barns a picture of Margaret.

"Never seen her before. Can I get back to bed now?"

"Sorry to bother you," Sully said.

We raced to the Sunset District, turned right on Noriega heading toward the ocean.

"I got a feelin' the boyfriends about to bolt," Sully said. "Margaret's picture in the papers. He knows the police are involved. Probably thought he had more time."

We pulled up to Tramaine's twelve minutes later. He lived in a small studio apartment in the back of a house. We knocked but there was no answer. As we walked back to the car, an elderly woman met us in the driveway.

"You boys lookin' for William?" she said.

"Yes ma'am. Is he around?" Sully said.

"He left in a cab. Not more than five minutes ago."

"Any idea where he's goin'?" I asked.

"Takin' a trip he said. Gone about a week."

"He left alone, did he?" I said.

"Only one stayin' in the cottage."

"Thank you, ma'am," I said.

I radioed dispatch to have Inspectors Hallis and Vincent stakeout the airport, looking for Margaret. Inspectors Billett and Maloney would cover the bus station. Rickman would meet us at the railroad terminal. We arrived at the Southern Pacific Terminal on Third and Townsend ten minutes later. Sully and I headed to the ticket windows. Rickman covered the entrance.

We showed the men in the ticket windows Margaret's picture and gave a description of William Tremaine. Neither individual had purchased tickets.

"Whada we gonna do?" I asked Sully.

"We wait."

"Maybe they're not takin' the train."

"Gut tells me, train. Tremaine went back to his place to pack. Margaret must've been stayin' at a hotel."

"We'll give it a few more minutes, but I think we're at a dead end," Rickman said.

Sully and I kept an eye on ticket windows. Rickman covered the main entrance. Less than ten minutes passed when a cab pulled up. A tall man, wearing a navy-blue suit and a dark grey fedora exited the rear of the vehicle. The cabby removed luggage from the trunk. Rickman gave us a nod. The man fit Tremaine's description. He entered the terminal, a valise in each hand, a small bag under his left arm. He approached a ticket window. We moved in. Rickman on one side of Tremaine, Sully on the other. I kept an eye on the entrance.

"Where to?" the man behind the ticket window said.

"Never mind," Rickman said. "Police, Mr. Tremaine. You're under arrest."

Rickman twisted Tremaine's arms behind him. Shoved him hard against the wall of the ticketing station.

"What's this all about?!" Tremaine said.

"Margaret Cabot's kidnapping, maggot!" Rickman barked.

"Take it easy, Lieutenant!" Sully said.

I glanced back at the terminal entrance. A woman entered. It was Margaret Cabot. She wore, a tasteful beige suit, black hat, and a worried look. She pulled a dark mesh vale over her face. Looped over her shoulder was a black long-strapped leather handbag, in her hand a small brown leather make-up case. I signaled Sully. He gave me a nod.

Margaret started toward the ticket windows. She passed the newsstand. Margaret's photograph made the front page of The *Call's* morning edition. She kept her head down as she passed the newsstand. She approached a ticket window. I moved in close behind her. She looked up. Saw the commotion. As Rickman led Tremaine away, Margaret dropped her bag and rushed to him.

"Oh my god. *Bill!*" she cried.

Chapter 6

Margaret threw her arms around Tremaine's neck. Tears flowed from her soft eyes.

"Back off, sister!" Rickman demanded yanking her hands away from Tremaine. "There'll be none of that."

Margaret took a step back. Wiped away tears. Took a breath and threw her shoulders back, regaining her composure.

"Don't say anything, Bill," she said. "I want to call my lawyer!"

"You'll get your phone call, once we're at the Hall," Rickman said. "Cuff her."

"I don't think that'll be necessary," Sully said.

"Cuff her!" Rickman demanded.

"I'm sorry, miss," Sully said.

We rode in silence for the twenty-minute trip to the Hall. Margaret made her phone call. We brought her to the interrogation room, where Rickman was questioning Tremaine.

"You live at twenty-one hundred Noriega?" Rickman said.

Tremaine looked at Margaret.

"We're not talking until I see my lawyer," Margaret said.

It went on like that for nearly a half hour. We asked questions, Margaret requested her lawyer.

Officer Banks opened the interrogation room door, poked his head in and said, "Cabot's attorney wants to see his client."

Attorney at Law, Efrem Waterman pushed his way into the room.

"I'd like to see my clients alone *please*," he said.

"Clients?" I repeated.

"That's what I said. Clients!"

Banks positioned himself at the interrogation room door. Sully, Rickman and I retired to the Squad Room. I poured two cups of coffee.

"This should prove to be interestin'," I said, handing Sully a cup.

"There's a lot more to this than meets the eye. My hunch tells me Mr. Cabot lied."

"Everything's not quite right in Denmark?" I said.

"Leave me alone with that mug for five minutes and I'll get to the bottom of it," Rickman said.

"The kid has rights, Lieutenant," Sully said.

"Always by the book Sullivan. That's why your arrest rate isn't up to par," Rickman said as he stormed out of the Squad Room.

We stood there, looking at each other for a long moment. Then Sully spoke.

"Way I figure it, Margaret got pretty fed up with pops hovering over her. Tellin' her what to do. He wasn't about to let some piano player marry his daughter," Sully said.

"Then you think she was in on the ransom?"

"I think it was her idea."

Fifteen minutes passed when Banks stuck his head into the Squad Room.

"Lawyer wants to talk to ya," he said.

We found Waterman standing at the interrogation room door.

"My clients would like to explain the circumstances of this incident."

"Okay," Sully said. "We'd like to hear it."

Sully and I sat on one side of the table. Margaret, Tremaine, and Waterman sat opposite.

"You wanna start from the beginning?" Sully said.

Margaret wore a stern look on her face. She patted Tremaine on the back of his hand, took a deep breath and said, "This was all my idea."

Sully and I exchanged looks.

"Father was being completely unreasonable. It was bad after my mother died but it continued to get worse. I thought that I would have some sort of freedom once I enrolled in college, but that was not the case. He became more domineering. Our chauffeur dropped me off in the morning and picked me up after classes in the afternoon. I had no time on my own," she said, clenching her fist and banging it on the table.

"You discuss this with your father?" I asked.

"More times than I can remember. No matter what! Football games . . . school functions—it . . . it didn't matter. I would arrive with a chauffeur and bodyguard by my side," she said, staring at her hands. "I started to lie about what I was doing."

Margaret's face turned red from embarrassment.

"I'd tell father that some of the sorority girls were having a meeting about a dance or something, just so I could get to see William," she said, gripping his hand. "Father found out I was seeing William. He was furious. He instructed the staff that I was to only attend classes. I was no longer allowed to attend school functions. It was like I was in prison. I begged him, but he wouldn't listen,"

Margaret dabbed her eyes with a handkerchief.

"I wanted to know why he was doing this. He said because I was the daughter of an important man. I could be kidnapped. I pretended to conform to my father's wishes. Told him that William had broken up with me."

"That's when you got the ransom idea?"

"Yes. I talked it over with William. He was against it. He wanted to run away. Go east," she said, lovingly looking into William's eyes . "He told me we could make it on what he earned playing piano."

"But you didn't want to do that, right?" I said.

"Father would disinherit me I thought. So why not take a part of what is mine so we could start fresh."

"It's still kidnapping," Sully said. "Once you sent a ransom note—"

"I know. I just wanted you to know William had nothing to do with it."

Banks poked his head into the room.

"There's a Mr. Cabot here. Wants to talk to you— pronto."

"Thanks George. We'll be right there," Sully said.

Cabot paced the Squad Room floor like a caged tiger who hadn't been fed in days. Teeth chomped down on a fat black Cuban, puffing plumes of smoke out of the side of his mouth. One look and it was obvious Cabot wanted a fight.

"Mr. Cabot," Sully said with a smile. "Thanks for comin' down."

"Thanks for comin' *down*!" he barked. "My attorney calls me and tells me you have my daughter in custody!"

"Relax, Mr. Cabot," Sully said.

"RELAX!" he shouted. "You better tell me what the HELL IS GOIN' ON, Inspector?! I'll have your badge for this."

"Can I get you a coffee or something," Sully said calmly.

"Coffee? You think I want coffee!"

"Nothing is going to happen until you sit down and control yourself."

Cabot angrily puffed on his cigar. Sully indicated with a hand, the empty chair by a nearby desk.

Cabot yanked the chair away from the desk and abruptly dropped his heavy frame onto it.

"I'm sitting, and I'm calm. Tell me what the—"

Sully frowned—Cabot cleared his throat.

"Would you please tell me *why* my daughter is in custody?" Cabot said in an even voice.

"According to your daughter, she has been frustrated with how she has been treated."

"Frustrated!"

Sully held up his palm.

"Sorry," Cabot said. "Continue."

"Margaret's twenty years old and feels that she should be allowed some freedom. Apparently, after that row you had when you discovered she was seeing this Tremaine fellow, she got the idea of faking a kidnapping."

"Faking?"

"Her plan, according to her statement, was to run away with Tremaine. I think these two are in love. If Tremaine was just after the money he'd be gone by now."

Cabot hung his head.

"Unfortunately, Margaret made a statement. We're gonna have to book her I'm afraid."

"Jesus! What have I done? Can I see my daughter?"

"Your attorney is with them right now. Follow me," Sully said.

The D.A. worked out a deal with Mr. Cabot. Tremaine and Margaret were placed on probation. Two years later they married.

Chapter 7

*D*etails, *details, details.* Sully said as I returned to the living room and flopped onto the couch.

"What?"

You were off in the clouds somewhere. You were hit with a sap.

"Or a gun wrapped in a cloth or something. I must have hit the end table by the sofa when I fell sending the lamp crashing to the floor. The breaking glass sound I heard."

I surveyed the room.

"Looked at this place. Did the 49ers run a few scrimmages while I was in dreamland?"

I stood and checked myself. I had my gun. Wallet still in my pants pocket.

"The only thing missing is my good sense."

If you weren't so preoccupied with a pretty face youd've been aware of someone in the apartment before you opened the door.

I went to the apartment door and opened it. There it was, right there for me to see. The

fresh scratches, lock picked. Picked by someone who knew what they were doing. How stupid am I?

Should've noticed those.

"You're right."

I closed the door and looked around the room again. I felt sick and my head was pounding. I knew I shouldn't take a nap after getting whacked in the head as hard as I had, but the thought of cleaning up the place made my head hurt more.

"I think I'll just rest on the couch for a bit until I feel better," I said.

I started to move toward the sofa. The floor began to open up again and I just dove into the warm blackness.

I came around about fifteen minutes later, made my way to the kitchen and got some more ice for my head. A couple of aspirin and twenty minutes later I was feeling better, at least good enough to add two and two and get five.

Feelin' better, Sully said, leaning against the closet door.

"You again," I chirped.

You gonna just sit around all day feelin' sorry for yourself? Or you gonna work on solvin' this case?

"Someone was either lying or there's something concerning the statues I hadn't figured yet. One thing's for sure, the mug who slugged me was looking for that package," I said. "Guy or guys—must've figured I hid it."

Look. You're still operating with an advantage, but that advantage won't last much longer. Whoever these people are, they are either very determined or beginnin' to get desperate.

"Tell me somethin' I don't know."

You need to keep your mind on the case and not on a dame.

"She's not a dame!" I said.

One-step at a time, my friend. You're movin' too fast. Jumpin' to conclusions. It'll only get you into trouble.

"I can handle a reasonable amount of trouble."

Don't go chasin' your tail, Jimmy. Remember Lyle Zangger.

"I was young. Thought that detectives could solve cases in one radio episode."

Young and impatient.

After dropping off some fresh shirts and socks in my hotel room I had some dinner at John's Grill. Sully was right. I'd thought the Zangger case was a lead pipe cinch.

It was a Tuesday night from what I remember. One of those nights where the fog hangs about fifty feet in the air, severing the tops of the downtown buildings. We were working the robbery detail. Eleven-fifteen we got a call. Gunman held up an all-night diner on Howard Street. Shots fired.

Ambulance had pulled away, siren blasting, as we entered Hank's Café. Two uniformed officers were already at the scene.

"Sullivan, robbery," Sully said to one of the uniformed officers.

"Officer Ross," he replied. "Officer Edwards and I were first on the scene. Found the owner . . ."

Referring to his notebook he said, "Hank Mooney, layin' behind the counter, shot twice—shoulder and left leg. He was conscious at the time. Edwards called for an ambulance."

"Mooney say anything?" I said.

"Yeah, said the man had a wild look. Somethin' about his eyes. Crazy like."

"Hopped up on drugs, maybe?" Sully said.

"Could be," Ross said.

"Old guy in the back there, he saw everything."

"You put in a call for prints?" Sully said.

"Just got off the phone when you showed up."

"Good work," Sully said.

Officer Edwards jotted in his notebook as he spoke to the old grizzly-looking man sitting at a table, bloody cloth held to his forehead.

"Whadaya got so far?" Sully said.

"This is Mr. Henshaw. He's a regular customer of Hank's. Witnessed the robbery."

"You saw the whole thing, Mr. Henshaw?" Sully said.

He looked to be 60 plus years in age, dressed in ill-fitting secondhand clothes. Face registered a hard life.

"Sure nuf, Officer. I comes in here most every night. Hank sometime 'ill stake me to a fried egg sandwich . . . you know if I'm a little short."

"Tell us what happened," Sully said.

I took out my notebook.

"Like I said, Hank would stake me to a sandwich now and then. He's about to drop an egg on the griddle when this man comes in."

"Can you describe him?"

"Maybe five foot nine. Brown hair, I think. He was wearin' a blue knit watch cap. Like we yousta wear back in the Navy."

"Any distinguishing marks?"

"Nah, didn't see any marks. Face, kinda rough, you know, like some kinda skin disease."

"Pockmarks?" I said.

"Yeah, pockmarks," he said with a laugh. "All on the sides, ya know."

"What happened next?" Sully asked.

"He comes up to the counter. Tells Hank he wants a cupa joe. Hank gets 'im a mug and when he turns around, guy's gotta gun on 'im. Just like that!" he said, pointing an index finger at Officer Edwardes. "Tells Hank to open the cash box. I sees this and I'm headin' for the door. Guy whips around—slugs me on the noggin with the pistol."

"What kinda gun? Could you tell?" I asked.

"Revolver. .38, I think. Long barrel. I goes to the floor. I seen Hank grab a cleaver. About to take a swipe at the guy. Guy starts shootin'. Two shots—maybe three. Really loud. Thought Hank was dead fer sure."

"Then what?" Sully said.

"Guy goes behind the counter and opens the cash box. Grabs the dough. Only paper money from what I could see. Then he runs out."

"You notice anything else?" Sully asked.

"This guy was kinda jumpy. Twichin' like."

"Was he alone?" I said.

"I guess," Henshaw said with a shrug. "He ran out the door. I hears a car drive off. Screechin' the tires like."

"You've been very helpful, Mr. Henshaw."

"Never did get my egg sammich."

"Make sure Mr. Henshaw gets a ride home. Swing by General and make sure a Doc takes a look at that cut."

"Sure thing," Edwards replied.

Sully peeled off a five-dollar bill.

"You go with Officer Edwards, Mr. Henshaw. He's gonna run you by the hospital real quick. Make sure you're okay." Sully slipped the bill in Henshaw's hand. "Get yourself somethin' to eat while you're at it. See to that Edwards."

Edwards smiled and said, "Sure thing, Inspector."

"Thanks," Henshaw said. "Much obliged."

That was one of the things I admired about Sully. His compassion. He never let a day go by without reminding me that we worked for *these* people.

"We'll send a car for you tomorrow morning. Want you to look at some mugshots."

We canvassed the neighborhood. Drug store manager, across the street from the diner, heard the gunshots. Saw a man drive away in a dark, late model coupe—Chevy or Dodge, he wasn't sure. We packed it in for the evening.

Six-forty the next morning, I arrived at room 324, Robbery Detail. Sully was stirring a cup of coffee as I stepped in.

"Coffee, Jimmy? Fresh."

"Thanks," I said, holding up a small paper bag. "I brought donuts."

We had our coffee and reviewed the details of the robbery. Then spoke with Lieutenant Rickman, head of Robbery Detail.

"Fill me in," Rickman said.

"Kind of in a holding pattern right now Lieutenant. Sendin' a car to pick up Mr. Henshaw. Have him take a look at mugshots," Sully said.

"What about the victim?"

"I got a call into the hospital. Doctor will let us know when we can talk to Mooney," I said.

"Okay! Let's get crackin' on this. I wanna see some results. Pronto!"

A few minutes after eight, Henshaw arrived. Next two and a half hours he went through the mug books.

"This is the guy!" said Henshaw emphatically. "See! He's got marks on his face. Whatchacallit?"

"Acne?" I said.

"Yeah. Acne."

"Albert Gehern," Sully read from the mug book. "Two-time loser—released from San Quentin last year. Served four years for armed robbery.

"Looks like Al's fallen off the wagon," I said.

We got a call from S.F. General. Mooney was conscious. Doctor would allow us to talk to him for five minutes.

"I've got some pictures here Mr. Mooney. I want you to take a look. Tell me if you see the man who shot you," Sully said.

I held one photo at a time in front of Mooney.

"That's him," Mooney said weakly as I held the fourth photo.

"Gehern," I said to Sully.

"Thanks, Mr. Mooney, you've been a great help."

I contacted Gehern's parole officer from a phone booth in the hospital lobby. Got a home address in the Tenderloin District, Gehern worked at a warehouse on 3rd Street.

"Wish all our cases were this easy," I said as I turned the car down 3rd Street. "Wrap this up by the end of the day. Put the bastard behind bars for good this time."

"Just take it one step at a time my friend," Sully said with a grin.

We arrived at Bay Area Wearhouse & Company ten minutes later. Worker supervising the unloading of a forty-foot trailer directed us to the office. We climbed up a metal flight of stairs inside the building, to a room suspended on steel pillars overlooking the warehouse floor. A bespectacled woman, about fifty, gray streaks in her hair, sifted through a pile of papers when we entered the office.

"What can I do for you?" she said without looking up from her work.

Sully gave me a curious look and said, "Police officers, miss."

She abruptly dropped the papers on her desk.

"I don't know how you people manage your paperwork, but I sent a check for trailer registration to the Motor Vehicle—"

"We're not here about registrations, miss . . .?"

"Miss Klann. Opal Klann," she said as she fussed with her hair.

"We'd like to speak with Albert Gehern. I understand he works here."

"Yes. He's on the south loading dock I believe. Look for a tall man in a green frock. He's the foreman, Mr. Peake."

"Thank you very much, Miss Klann."

Foreman Peake directed us to the loading area where Gehern was moving crates with a hand truck.

"Albert Gehern," Sully said as we approached.

"Yeah. Who wants to know?"

Albert Gehern stood about five-foot-nine, brown hair, ruddy complexion. He wore a blue knit watch cap.

"Police officers," Sully said.

"What's this all about?"

"Can you tell us where you were Monday night after you finished work?"

"Monday? Let's see. I got off work at five. Hit one of the bars on the wharf. Had a coupla drinks. Somethin' to eat. Went back to my place, listened to the radio."

"What about Tuesday?" I asked.

"Why ya wanna know?"

"Just answer the question," Sully said.

"Tuesday. I had dinner with some friends."

"Where was this?" I said.

"Over on Post Street."

"Who were these friends?" I said.

"Robbie Doran. His wife Ruth and a friend of theirs, Ed. Ed Parish, I think his name was."

"How long were you at this friend's house?"

"We played some pinochle. Had some drinks. Musta left around eleven—eleven thirty."

"Then what?" Sully said.

"Took the bus home. What is this?"

"You own a gun, Albert?" I asked.

"You *nuts*! You know I'm on parole. Ex-cons can't own guns. You guys check with Robbie Doran. He'll tell ya I was with them Tuesday night. I gotta get back to work. You guys gonna get me fired."

"What's this Robbie's address?" I asked.

"It's on Post. I don't remember the number. Apartment B. He's in the book for chrissake!"

We left the warehouse and radioed into headquarters. Dispatch got us an address for Robert Doran. Apartment house on the corner of Post and Steiner. No one was home. We checked the other apartments. One of the residents knew that Mrs. Doran worked at a bank but didn't know which. They didn't know where Mr. Doran worked.

We returned to the Hall, reviewed our notes then met with Lieutenant Rickman.

"Gehern claims he was at a friend's house at the time of the robbery," Sully said. "We'll check out the alibi this afternoon. Mrs. Doran works in a bank. Should be home sometime after three o'clock."

"In the meantime, I think we should get a search warrant for Gehern's place. We can pick him up for questioning. Give us a chance to find the gun," I said.

"I'll get a warrant. You check out the alibi. Anything hinkey . . . pick up Gehern," Rickman said.

Sully and I staked out the Doran apartment house. Three-thirty in the afternoon a woman about 30, walked up the steps to the apartments. Sully opened the car door.

"Mrs. Doran?" Sully called.

She turned, startled for a moment and said, "Yes?"

"We're police officers," Sully said flashing his badge. "We'd like to speak with you for a moment."

"Is everything alright? Something happen to Robert?"

"No ma'am. It's concerning Albert Gehern."

"What about 'im?"

"He had dinner with you and your husband Tuesday night?"

"Yes, that's right."

"Albert said he left your place around eleven o'clock. Can you confirm that?"

"I couldn't say. I decided to go to bed a little early. The men continued to play cards. I'm not sure what time Al left. You'd have to ask my husband. He's still at work."

"Where does he work?" I asked.

"Universal Printing and Binding on 26th Street."

"Thank you, Mrs. Doran," Sully said, tipping his hat.

"What's this all about?"

"Just routine ma'am," I replied.

Unable to confirm Gehern's alibi, we headed to Universal Printing. Office Manager told us Doran was in the back, loading orders for delivery in a company panel truck.

"Robert Doran?" Sully said as we approached the truck.

"Yeah, I'm Doran."

"Police officers. We'd like to ask you a few questions," Sully said.

Doran stopped loading boxes. "Police?" he said.

"You had dinner with Albert Gehern Tuesday night?"

"Yeah."

"What time did he leave your house?" Sully said.

"Little after ten."

"You sure about that?" I asked.

"Yeah. I was kinda tired."

"Sure, it wasn't closer to eleven?" I said.

Nah. Ten or a little after. We had a lot to drink but I remember the time Al left. Ed, my friend, left a few minutes later."

"Thanks for your help, Mr. Doran," Sully said.

Chapter 8

Sully tapped on Rickman's office door.

"Yeah!" Rickman called.

"You got that Search Warrant Lieutenant. Gehern's alibi doesn't add up," I said as we entered the office.

Rickman held up a signed warrant.

"Looks like Gehern's our guy. Left the friend's house around ten. Gives him plenty of time to hit the diner," I said. "We'll have this wrapped up tonight."

"Bring 'im in for questioning," Rickman said.

Sully plucked the warrant from Rickman's hand.

Sully and I met two detectives at Gehern's Tenderloin apartment. He was in his undershirt when he answered the door.

"What? You guys again?" Gehern said as he swung the door wide.

"Wanna put on a shirt? We'd like you to come downtown to answer some questions," Sully said.

"Yeah, yeah. Like I've got nothin' better to do."

Nearly three hours—half pack of Lucky's later, we weren't gaining any ground with Gehern. We took a break for dinner then met with Rickman.

"Why haven't you guys gotten anything out of this chump yet?" Rickman said.

"He's stickin' to his story, Lieutenant," I said.

"Well, unstick 'im," Rickman said. "I want this joker booked by the end of the day. You've got witnesses that identified 'im."

"Yessir!" I said.

"Get back in there and break him. You read me?" Rickman said.

"Yessir!" Sully said.

Sully and I headed back to the Interrogation Room.

"Without the gun, we're on shaky ground," Sully said. "Somethin's not quite kosher."

"We've got two positive IDs, like the Lieutenant said."

Gehern was visibly agitated when we sat down with him again.

"Doran distinctly remembers you leaving around ten o'clock," Sully said.

"I toldya! Had a lot to drink. I looked at the clock on the wall, thought it was eleven!" Gehern pleaded.

"You know we're gonna find the gun you used, Albert," Sully said.

"For the hundredth time. I don't have a gun."

It went like that for another four hours. Gehern kept denying he owned a gun. Insisted the witnesses had made a mistake. We took a break.

"He's stickin' to his story, Lieutenant," Sully said. "I think he may be—"

"Keep at it. *Understand!?*" Rickman said angrily.

Inspector Garcia, the detective who conducted the search of Gehern's apartment, poked his head into the room.

"Gotta' minute, Lieutenant," Garcia said.

"What's up?" Rickman said.

"No gun," Garcia said. "We checked every room in that guy's dump a dozen times. Nothin'!"

"Okay thanks," Rickman said. "*You two!* Get back at it."

"I'm not sayin' another word," Gehern said when we returned to questioning him.

"Just come clean, Albert," Sully said.

"You guys are tryin' to railroad me. But it ain't gonna work. Either book me or let me outta here!"

Sully sat there for a long moment, then let out a long breath.

"Once more from the beginning," Sully said.

"I don't have a gun. I didn't hold up that coffee shop. Your witnesses didn't see me doin' nothin'!"

Sully turned to me.

"Book 'im."

"*For what?!*" Gehern snapped.

"Armed robbery," Sully said.

"Let's go, Albert.

After fingerprints and mugshots, Gehern was locked up in a holding cell until he could be arraigned. Sully and I met in Rickman's office.

"We've got Gehern downstairs," Sully said. "Booked him for Armed Robbery."

"Good," Rickman said.

"I still don't feel good about this one, Mike," Sully said. "My hunch tells me he's tellin' the truth."

"*Witnesses*, Sullivan! We don't go by hunches," Rickman said.

There was a knock at the door.

"Come," Rickman said.

Sergeant Pope stuck his head in.

"There's been another robbery. Gas station. Same MO. Perp fits Gehern's description. Down to the blue-knit watch cap."

"*Shit!*" Rickman said.

"I'll see about gettin' Gehern's release," Sully said.

Ambulance Medical staff tended to the service station owner Dean Jovanski's head wound as we approached the victim.

"Back to the starting gate," I said.

"Okay if we ask Mr. Jovanski a few questions?" Sully asked the Medical Attendant.

"Yeah, sure. He's got a nice bump—won't need stitches though."

"Tell us the best you can, sir, what happened," I said.

"Guy hits me for no reason."

"Start from the beginin'," Sully said.

"Guy pulls into the station. Parks over by the tires— around the side there. Asks me if he can get change for the phone."

"Then what?" Sully said.

"He gives me a fiver. I open the register to make change and he pulls a gun."

"What kind of gun? Revolver? Automatic?" I asked.

"Revolver. I put my hands up and he takes all the cash. About sixty bucks. Stuffs the cash in his jacket pocket. I was just standin' there—lookin' at 'im. He halls off and hits me with the gun. I went down in a heap. I see lights turn into the station, and he charges outta here. I thought he was gonna kill me."

"Did you get a good look at the car? Get a license number?" I asked.

"It was a Dodge Coupe. Dark color. Maybe blue. Didn't see the license."

"What about the man?" Sully said.

"Wore a dark blue-knit cap. Five-foot-nine I'd guess. Crazy look in his eyes."

"Any distinguishing marks?" I said.

"His face. Pockmarked. I think there was a scar, right here," he said pointing to the bottom of his chin.

"You've been a great help, Mr. Jovanski," Sully said.

We approached the uniformed officer interviewing the customer who pulled into the station during the robbery. He looked to be in his mid-twenties.

"Sullivan. Robbery. This is Inspector Wolf."

"Kalligan," he said. "This is Mr. Brugess. He witnessed the perp driving off."

"Yeah, I come in, need gas, ya know. I sees this guy run out of the door there," Brugess said.

"Then what?" I asked.

"He jumps into his car and tears outta here tires squealin'. I honk my horn, but nobody comes out, so's I goes in, see. I find the station guy on the floor. Head split open. I kinda helped him up. Got 'im into a chair. Called the cops."

"Get a look at the car?" Sully said.

"Dark blue Dodge coupe."

"Sure about that?" Sully said.

"Yeah. Had one just like it."

"Anything else you remember?" I asked.

"License plate was a four, one something then a B. I didn't get a good look at the rest."

"Thank you, Mr. Brugess," Sully said.

"I can go now?"

Sully turned to Kalligan. "You have his information?"

"Yessir."

Brugess walked back to his car.

"One thing Inspector," Kalligan said. "Not that it's my business . . ."

"Go on," Sully said.

"Brugess mentioned that he didn't get a good look at the license plate but. . ." Kalligan referred to his notes. "It was cockeyed in the plate frame. Made me think the plate might've been switched from another vehicle. Like I said. . ."

"Good work, Kalligan," Sully said.

With the partial on the license plate, I contacted the Motor Vehicle Department for a list of Blue Dodge Coupes with registrations containing the numbers four, one followed by the letter B. We got nine hits on Dodge Coupes as far East as Antioch and North to San Rafael. Sully and I split up the list. Three days of knocking on doors turned up nothing.

Seven-forty that evening I returned to the Squad Room. Sully was already there.

"Anything?" I asked.

"Came up empty," Sully said.

"I thought we had this Gehern guy for sure."

"You'll find out that when something's that easy, it never works out," Sully said.

Desk phone announced a call.

Sully answered. "Robbery. Hold on."

Sully selected a pencil from a chipped coffee mug. "Okay, give it to me."

Sully began to write on a small notepad.

"Got it. We're on our way," Sully said, tearing the page off the pad. "Pawnshop on Mission robbed. Pockmarked face—wearing a blue-knit cap."

Crowd had gathered in front of the pawnshop. Two uniformed officers kept the crowd back, while the senior officer, Sergeant Brooks, interviewed the shop owner, Thomas Workman. As Workman described the robber, Patrolman Hanlon entered the shop.

"I got a man outside, you need to talk to Inspector," Hanlon said.

Sully gave me a nod. I followed Hanlon into the street.

"This is Mr. Donnati. He thinks he saw the robber."

Donnati, about fifty, short and stocky, spoke with an Italian accent.

"I crossa da street. Dis man, he run to the car, and whadaya know, he try'n run me down," he said blessing himself. "Drive-a so fast the wheels cry."

"Can you describe this man?" I asked.

"Kinda tall, maybe. Wear a fisherman hat."

"Knit cap?"

"Si. Knit cap."

"Mr. Donnati got the license," Hanlon said, handing me his notebook.

"I takea good look," Donnati said. "Seven—one C. Tree—tree… come ci dici…cinque.

Donnati held up five fingers.

"Five," I said.

"Si. Five."

"What make of car was it?" I said.

"Dodge."

"Are you sure?"

"Si, si. It had the whadayacall. . . sheep onna front."

"Ram?"

"Si! Ram."

I called dispatch to run the license. Car's registered to a Norman R. Ottley, South San Francisco.

Ottley's wife answered the door wearing a yellow print apron, wooden spoon in hand.

Sully flashed his buzzer and said, "Police officers ma'am. Is Mr. Ottley home?"

"Oh!" she said. "Police. You'll find him around back. You'll have to excuse me. I'm washing the dinner dishes."

"Thank you, ma'am," Sully said.

We walked around the side of the small gray framed house, found Norman Ottley filling trash cans with refuge on the side of the garage.

"Norman Ottley?" Sully asked.

He turned. "What can I do for ya?"

"Police officers."

"Oh! Did you find them?" Ottley said.

"Sir?" I said.

"My license plates!"

Sully and I exchanged looks.

"License plates?" I said.

"Best I can figure, they were stolen sometime between work and home last week. I didn't notice 'em gone until I washed the car Saturday."

Ottley moved to the front of the garage, pulled up the door. Inside, a dark green Plymouth sedan, license plate frame—empty.

"I park the car in the garage when I get home, so it was stolen at work or at lunch."

"No one could get into your garage?" I said.

"I lock it when I get home."

We told Ottley that we were following up on a lead. The department would be in touch. We headed back to the Hall.

"You two turn up anything?" Rickman said.

"Looks like this guy has a collection of plates he's usin'," I said.

"This case has got us chasin' our tails," Sully said.

"I want this wrapped up. And soon!" Rickman ordered.

I had an idea.

"I was thinkin'," I said.

"Christ! We're in trouble now," Rickman said.

"This guy's pretty clever. He steals a car. Owner of the car reports it stolen. It's on the hot sheet, but we don't see it because he's exchanged the plates. It could have been at least a week before Ottley realized his plates were missing."

"Yeah," Sully said. "Gives this guy some leeway."

"We should have Motor Vehicles get us a list of anyone reporting their plates stolen."

"It's worth a try, Lieutenant," Sully said.

"Do it!" Rickman said.

Watch cap bandit hadn't hit another establishment for nearly a week. We had exhausted all our leads. Seven-thirty-five Wednesday morning I arrived at the Hall. Sully came in several minutes later. We reviewed all the information we gathered so far on the robberies when Sully got a message from Motor Vehicles.

"Bingo!" Sully exclaimed as he read the slip of paper.

"Whadaya got?"

"Two license plates reported stolen in the last week," Sully said, picking up the phone. "Get me dispatch."

By eight o'clock, the stolen vehicle hot sheet listed the two license numbers. It was just a matter of time before a patrol spotted one of these numbers. That evening we finally got the break we needed. Patrol car spotted one of the stolen license plates on a Dodge coupe parked at the twenty-seven hundred block of San Bruno Avenue. We radioed the officers to stakeout the vehicle until we arrived.

A quick scan of the neighborhood revealed retail shops and two cafés within a short walking distance from the Dodge coupe.

"Let's try the cafés first," Sully said. "Since it's dinner time."

"Right," I said.

"You two stay here and cover the car," Sully said to the officers.

We checked the nearly half-full TJ's Café and came up empty. Lam's Chop Suey, two doors down, was teeming with diners. We approached the front counter. The hostess, a young Asian woman, greeted us.

"Good evening, gentlemen. Table for two?" she said.

Sully held his badge to the side of the counter so only she could see it.

"We're looking for a man. Brown hair. Marks on his face. Wearing a blue-knit cap."

The woman turned to the rear of the restaurant. At a table near the kitchen, a man looked up, then dropped his head trying to conceal his face.

"In the back," I said to Sully.

Sully and I started toward the back of the café. The man jumped up from his seat knocking dinnerware off the table. He grabbed his cap and bolted for the rear, Sully and I in pursuit. He crashed through the rear door that opened into an alley. Sully got through the door first and looked right. I went left.

"*This way!*" I yelled.

As we ran down the alley, the suspect stopped suddenly and fired a shot. I ducked into an alcove on the left, Sully behind some trash cans. I fired a shot but missed. The suspect continued running down the alley, coming to a wood fence about five-feet high. As he boosted himself up, I fired again.

"You tagged him!" Sully said.

Suspect fell to the ground as Sully ran towards him. He rolled over on the ground and got off another shot, hitting Sully in the leg. Sully went down in a heap.

Suspect dragged himself to his feet in an attempt to climb the fence. I went to Sully's aid.

"I'm okay," Sully said. "Don't let that bastard get away."

I raced toward the suspect until I was ten feet away.

"Drop the gun or I'll shoot!" I said.

The suspect turned, revolver still in hand.

"Drop it! It's your last warning."

Suspect let the gun fall from his hand. Patrolman Martinez arrived at the scene.

"Turn around. Hands up against the fence," I said.

"I'm shot," the suspect said.

"You'll live. Cuff him!"

Martinez secured the suspects hands behind his back. "Officer Dean's in the cruiser callin' an ambulance."

I went to pick up Sully the following morning. Doctors removed a .38 slug from his thigh. They kept him overnight for observation. He'd be on crutches for the next couple of weeks.

"Lyle Zangger's arraignment is this afternoon. Charged with robbery, assault on a police officer, attempted murder—drug possession. He'll be sleepin' on his belly for a while. I tagged him in his ass."

"What were ya aimin' for?" Sully said with a chuckle.

"Lower leg," I said with a shrug. .38 slug they took out of you matches the one from Hank's Diner."

"Got him off the street before he killed somebody," Sully said. "Our job is to find the truth. Not make a quick collar. Rickman likes to cut corners. If Zangger hadn't knocked over another gas station for a few months, an innocent man would've been sittin' in jail, maybe convicted of a crime he didn't commit."

"You're right," I said. "Lucky, he didn't kill you!"

"Gonna take a lot more than a punk like that to kill me."

I shook my head. Sully gave me a wink and a smile.

"Get me my pants so I can get the hell outta here."

I drifted off to sleep, running that case over and over in my mind.

Chapter 9

Sunrise the next morning revealed a cool marine layer over the city. I expected the cloud cover to burn off by late morning, just a typical San Francisco day. Lump on the back of my head had gone down. I was feeling better, the ringing in my ears had stopped but I was still a little tired. I had a light breakfast and a pot of coffee sent up to my room and rested until I got a call from my answering service at 10 a.m. I was to call Claire at her home number in an hour.

I picked up a couple of the newspapers in the lobby and lounged around my room, reading and trying not to think too much about the case, as it would give me a headache that aspirin wouldn't fix. I made myself a stiff drink then had the hotel operator put the call through to Claire. Her line rang twice.

"James?"

"Yeah, it's me, hon. Call me Jimmy—that's what my friends do."

"Got some information for you," she said, in a low tone, as though she was trying to hide her excitement. "Can you meet me at that café on Union Street in twenty minutes?"

"Sure thing. You're at home, right?"

"Yes, I am. Why?"

"You sound like someone might be listening in."

"It's just that I've never done anything like this before. You know—detective work?"

"Got it. Just relax. Everything's gonna be fine. See you in twenty." I hung up the phone.

I'd only been seated a couple of minutes at a sidewalk table when Claire got out of a cab two doors down from the café. She paid the driver then casually walked toward me. I rose and held a chair for her as she approached. She looked up and down Union Street then cautiously sat down.

"Are you sure it's okay if we sit outside? Someone could be watching."

"We're okay. I cased the joint when I got here."

She wiggled with excitement in her chair, covering her mouth with her hands.

"What?"

"You cased the joint. That is so . . . so . . . detective—ish."

"You read too many of those novels."

A waitress appeared at our table. I ordered us coffee.

"I was able to slip into the manager's office this morning. I went through sales records and came up with this," she said, reaching into her purse and sliding a canary yellow sales receipt across the table. "It's a receipt for a clay-fired urn. Over two hundred years old, from Italy, I believe."

I took the Westrom contract from my inside jacket pocket. Putting the receipt and the contract side by side it was easy to tell that both papers were signed by the same hand.

"It's the same handwriting alright. It looks to me like she's Irene—"

"Talbot. I also found this," she pulled out a red tag from her purse.

The waitress returned with our coffee. Claire held the tag tight against her chest until our waitress walked away.

"Adrian Schofield had been in the day before. The urn was still in the crate because of a late delivery, so he had one of the floorwalkers tag it. Irene picked it up the next day."

"You did good, angel."

She wiggled with excitement again.

"Schofield is some kind of art collector. He's always coming around looking for European artifacts and such," she said. "This Irene would come in often with Mrs. Schofield. Deidra's the wife's name."

"Things are starting to make sense in this fanciful tale. I'm beginning to think that she was interested in getting in ahead of Schofield and get hold of those statues for herself. She hired me to purchase them so she wouldn't be seen in Brooklyn's. The strange part I can't seem to figure is that your man Pitts told me the statues weren't alabaster, but ceramic and only worth three or four hundred dollars." I thought for a moment, then asked. "Has anyone inquired about the statues since?"

"No one," she answered. "What are you thinking?"

"If the statues weren't what they were supposed to be, why did Irene go through all that trouble to get them? Unless it's not the statues themselves? They may just be a part of a puzzle."

"What'll ya do now?"

"Do some research. What I'd like you to do is keep your eyes and ears open. If Schofield enquires about any other art objects or purchases, you let me know right away." I added: "You workin' tomorrow?"

"Yes."

"Okay. Not a word to anyone about this," I cautioned, as I returned the tag and receipt to her. "Put these back where you found 'em."

"I can swing by the office now. I left my scarf at my desk, just in case I needed an excuse to return."

"Smart girl. I guess I need to put you on the payroll."

She flashed a smile I wouldn't mind seeing on a daily basis. I gave Claire cab fare, then drove to my apartment. I wanted to get a closer look at those statues stuffed in Mrs. Vee's closet.

Feelin' good about things right now, aye pal? Sully said.

I looked into the rearview. Sully pushed his hat back off his forehead.

"Startin' to," I said.

You're on a roll, Sully said. *Like a Vegas gambler when the dice are loving you, you ride the wave until it stops.*

"I feel like this case is about to crack."

Remember to watch your back. It's easy to get caught up in all the hubbub and forget the important details.

When I arrived at the apartment, pinned to Mrs. Vee's door was a note. She had to run an errand downtown and wouldn't return until 5:00 p.m. I checked the hallway for any activity, quickly picked the lock and quietly entered her apartment. Without making a sound, I retrieved the package and locked the door as I left.

In my apartment, I opened the box, sifted through the straw insulation, removing the two statues wrapped in brown paper. I looked the two items over carefully. Nothing seemed out of place. A flat oval wooden base had four metal prongs that attached each of the statues to their platforms. I took a screwdriver, bent back the prongs and removed the wooden bases. The bottom of the statues appeared smooth and solid. I shook each and listened for any noise or rattle. Nothing. The statues were heavy and solid. I reattached the bases, covered the statues again and returned them to the box. I didn't expect any more unwanted visitors to come by again so I stashed the box under the kitchen sink. I rang up Barb at the phone company and had her look up a number for Irene Talbot.

"No listing for that name, Jimmy."

"Dammit."

"Well, she has to live someplace," Barb said. "She'll need gas and electric."

"Tell me you know somebody," I said with hope in my voice.

"Kimmy Lin. She works at PG&E. I'll give her a call, you head on over."

"I owe ya, Barb."

"You do. And believe me, I *will* collect."

"One more thing," I said. "Got a number for a Schofield, in Atherton?"

"Hold on," she said. Barb was back on the line a minute later. "I have the number. Beachwood 4-3735. Shall I connect?"

"Sure."

Barb connected me with the Schofield residence. Their housekeeper answered the phone and told me the Schofield's were in Los Angeles and wouldn't return until Wednesday. I hung up and left for the gas company.

Fifteen minutes later, I was in front of a receptionist. I gave her my name and asked if I could see Kimmy Lin. I took a seat and a few minutes later Kimmy entered the lobby. She was a cute, compact, bubbly Asian woman. I could see her and Barb getting into a lot of trouble out on the town on Friday nights.

I stood and said, "James Wolf."

I extended my hand. She took mine in hers. Her hand was surprisingly cool and held a small piece of paper. I palmed it.

"You're cute," she announced.

"Yeah, I know. It can be a curse."

"So. . . you're a friend of Barb?"

"Yes."

"She wanted me to make sure I took good care of you," she said with a smile. "Anyway, what you'll need to do is fill out an application for services." She gave me a wink and nodded toward the receptionist. "A deposit is required for first-time customers," she stated and handed me an application.

"Thanks so much."

"Tell Barb I said hi."

"I will," I responded with a sly smile. "You've been very helpful."

When I got out of the building, I gave the slip of paper a look. 467 Fell Street it read in an attractive even-handed script. I got into my car and headed across town to Fell. The house was an old converted Victorian. From the mailboxes at the front entrance, I could see that there were only six apartments in the building. Talbot was apartment three. I rang the buzzer to three but didn't get a response. I tried the entrance door and it was unlocked. I made my way to Irene's apartment and knocked on the door. No answer. The lock above the doorknob was one of those with a spring lock. You wouldn't need a key to lock up. Just flick the button on the inside and shut the door. It'd take me three seconds to outsmart the device. I was about to when I heard a

door down the hall open. A chinless woman poked her head out.

"You want something, mister?" she called in a rough raspy voice.

"I'm looking for Miss Talbot. She doesn't seem to be in."

"You a friend?"

"Not really. I have some money I needed to return to her," I said as I walked to the woman's apartment.

"Haven't seen her since Friday, I think it was. Come on in."

On her door was a plaque that indicated this was the manager's apartment. She introduced herself as Mrs. Ella May Hurlbut. Ella May was a large woman—well, large doesn't do the circumference justice. She was enormous, around forty years of age, with bleach blonde hair. She waddled over to a well-worn stuffed chair and hovered over it for a few seconds, positioning her girth for a successful landing. It was like watching the docking of the Graf Zeppelin in person. Her landing was about as gentle as a bowling ball dropped from a great height onto a hardwood floor. When her huge body finally settled into its resting place, any discernible evidence of the chair beneath her had vanished.

"Wanna beer or somethin'?" she grunted as she plucked a can of brew from the table next to her.

She took a generous quaff of the liquid and let out a soft belch.

I cleared my throat. "No, thank you. I would like some help, if you could see your way clear," I said as I fished cash out of my pocket and selected a ten-dollar bill.

She started to lean forward to take it from my hand and I quickly moved toward her. The last thing I needed was to have her fall out of that chair. There wasn't any way I could get her back into it without a platoon of Marines and a skip loader.

"What kinda help?"

"I'd like to get a look at her apartment," I answered and showed her my P.I. License. Last thing I needed right now was this nosy broad to catch me picking the lock.

She bent forward and squinted at my identification for a moment.

"Private Dick, huh," she commented and sat back into her chair. "Art!" she called.

There were several seconds of silence before she turned her head to the side. "ART!" she screamed in a tone reminiscent of a sea lion's bark.

"*What?* I'm doin' somethin'!" a male voice called back.

"GET IN HERE!" she yelled again at the top of her lungs.

I thought the windows would shatter from the sheer force of her voice, when from somewhere in the back of the apartment Art emerged. Bald and dressed in a dirty white T-shirt too small to cover his potbelly with greasy gray slacks, cinched below the bulge. Art had given up on life years ago. Now he was just Ella May's servant or gofer and he didn't care which.

"What's with all the yell—who's this?" he pointed a dirty forefinger at me.

"Shut up and get the key to number three."

"What do I need to do that for?" he whined.

Ella May snapped back. "Just get it!"

Art disappeared for a few moments, then returned with a key attached to a round metal and paper disk, the number 3 written on it.

"Give it to the gentleman."

Art handed me the key.

"You can go back to what you was doin'," she said.

Art turned and left the room mumbling something I couldn't quite make out.

"Don't know why I married him, good fer nothin'."

"Well, thanks. I'll bring the key right back."

I slipped the key into the lock of apartment number 3 and entered. Flimsy lace curtains covered the bay windows. It was apparent that this was once a sitting room. Neat and cozy.

Kinda place that would make you feel comfortable—if you like attractive but dead blondes lying in the middle of a room. I took the handkerchief I had in my jacket pocket and carefully closed the apartment door.

I went to the body on the floor. She was the woman who came to my office and told me she was Elizabeth Westrom. She had a surprised look on her face. It appeared as though her position on the floor was peculiar. Looked like a child's baby doll with its head twisted into an unnatural position, her neck clearly broken. I'd seen this before. The Selma Morris murder. There was no mistaking it. Irene Talbot was strangled by a man with large hands.

Chapter 10

The Selma Morris case. Promoted to Inspector only two months earlier it was my first case I worked alone. It was a cloudy Monday morning as I remember. Sully had strained his back. Needed a few days to recoup. Officer Davis responded to a 415. Disturbing the Peace. Loud radio playing. He radioed in that he was unable to raise the tenant, Morris, in unit E and requested assistance. I drove out to the Sunset District. Met Davis on the second floor.

"I tried knockin', Inspector," Davis said.

I could hear loud music from behind the locked door. Memphis Slim was Rockin' the Blues at an earsplitting level.

I banged on the door.

"POLICE!" I shouted. "OPEN UP!"

No answer. I quickly picked the lock and stepped into the room. Across from the small fireplace sat a yellow print couch. Next to the fireplace on a square table rested the blaring radio. I turned the instrument off and called out to the rest of the apartment.

"Hello! Police!" I hollered. "Anyone home?

"Check the kitchen, Davis."

"Yessir."

I moved to a closed door on the other side of the room. It led to the bedroom. On the far side of the bed, I notice two feet protruding. Left foot, covered by a black low-heeled shoe, right only in a nylon stocking. I moved to the bed. Miss Selma Morris lay there next to the closet. Head twisted in a grotesquely obscene position. My stomach heaved, but I held back the urge to vomit. I checked for a pulse—none. Her body felt cold. She had facial bruises. Her neck broken, she looked surprised, eyes wide, eyebrows arched. She was an attractive woman, between thirty and thirty-five years. Short stylish dark brown hair.

"Davis!" I called.

Davis poked his head into the room. "Yessir?"

"We've got a homicide. Call it in."

I bent down to get a closer look. Bruises on her neck indicated a large man had strangled her. Fat, sausage-like fingers snapped bones like toothpicks. The brute obviously didn't know his own strength.

Fingerprint team arrived. I left them to their work and canvassed the apartment house. No one heard or saw anything suspicious. I checked with the neighbors in the adjoining buildings. Nothing. Searching her personal effects, I found an address book. She worked as a clerk for The Emporium. Lived alone, from what the neighbors told me. She moved-in six months ago. She'd filed for a divorce, according to the neighbor across the hall, a Mrs. Bancroft.

Bancroft, 60 plus years, held a handkerchief over her mouth. Her gray hair piled on top of her head in a bun, held there by what appeared to be a small knitting needle. Looked like she'd posed for the Mother's Cookies label. Her voice quivered when she spoke.

"She was quiet, kept to herself—mostly," Bancroft said. "She always had a pleasant word for you. I had a terrible cold last month. She brought soup—"

"Yes, ma'am," I said. "Did she have any visitors?"

"Well! Her husband—soon to be her ex, came over last week sometime. I think it was Wednesday. Yes,

Wednesday. On Wednesday afternoons the quilting club gets together. We meet at a different lady's house each week—"

"This was last Wednesday?"

"Yes. When I returned home, it was about one o'clock, I believe. I heard loud voices coming from her apartment. I had just unlocked my door when Mr. Morris came out of her apartment and stormed off in a fit. That poor woman, having to deal with that man."

"Did you hear what they were yellin' about?"

"No. He'd come by before. It always ended in shouting."

"Did she have any other visitors?"

"A man did come to visit. I thought it may have been the husband, but they left together. Looked to me like he picked her up for a date. I never saw his face or anything."

"Can you describe him?"

"On the tall side. Same as the husband. Hair was dark."

Thomas J. Morris, thirty-eight years old, five-foot-ten inches, black hair, brown eyes, 160 pounds according to DMV records, works in a machine shop off Third Street. I found him working a grinder. It looked to me like he'd gained ten pounds since he renewed his license. He'd just shut the machine down, as the shop broke for lunch.

"Thomas Morris?" I asked.

"Yeah, I'm Morris."

"Police officer," I said, showing my badge. "Inspector Wolf. Is there somewhere we could talk?"

A curious look crossed his face. He glanced around the shop then said. "I suppose we can use the office."

He removed his work gloves. Hands were large and callused. I followed him to the end of the work area through a door. In a large room were desks and file cabinets. Off to the side of the room, a door with a glass window marked PRIVATE in block letters.

"We can talk in here. Everyone's gone to lunch. What's this all about?" We entered the office. Morris closed the door behind me.

"Wanna have a seat?" I said.

"What's goin' on? I have a right to know."

"When was the last time you saw your wife?"

"My wife!? What's she got—"

"Would you answer the question?"

"It was last week. Why?"

"You remember what day?"

"Wednesday. She works the afternoon to evening shift on Wednesdays."

"I understand you had an argument that day?"

"That's usually the case," Morris said, shaking his head. "I wanted to try one last time to stop the divorce."

"You haven't seen her since?" I said.

"No! What's this all about?"

"I'm sorry to have to tell you. Your wife is dead."

"Dead!" Morris said as his knees buckled. "Selma's dead?"

He leaned against the desk to keep from falling.

"You wanna have a seat?" I said.

Morris collapsed into a chair. He dug into his shirt pocket for cigarettes. Fumbling the pack, the smokes dropped to the floor. I offered him a smoke.

"I can't—how did it happen? Accident or somethin'?"

"We believe she was murdered."

"Murdered!"

His lips moved but no sound came out. The cigarette between his fingers fell to the floor. "This can't be happening," he said.

"You haven't seen or talked to her since last week?"

"Yeah. She wouldn't consider dropping the divorce. I just figured we were through."

"Were you aware that she was seein' someone?"

"No. She never said anything."

"You weren't jealous or—"

"Hold on! I had nothin' to do with this. I loved her. I wanted to get back together."

"Where were you last night?"

"In my apartment. I live on Dolores."

"Can anyone vouch for you?"

"I went to a café down the street for dinner around seven. Back home after eight. Ran into my neighbor on his way out. We chatted for a little while."

I questioned Emporium employees who described her as efficient. Well-liked by management she had received a promotion in less than a year, with a pay raise. Her immediate supervisor informed me that Selma Morris would often lunch with one employee in particular, a Sheila Dodd. It was Dodd's day off. I got her address and went by her apartment. No one home, I returned to the office. The preliminary coroner's report indicated the assailant was male. Between five-ten to six-feet tall. Had large hands. Husband was still my number one suspect. I had an early dinner, then tried Dodd's apartment again. She answered the door, it was apparent she'd been crying.

"Sorry to bother you, Miss Dodd. Inspector Wolf, San Francisco Police," I said.

"Please come in," she said. "I'm sure you have questions for me."

"Yes, thank you."

I followed her into a small neat living room. Magazines arranged in a fan on a walnut coffee table in front of a light blue couch. Furniture all looked relatively new. Two to three years old maybe, showing little signs of wear.

"Please, have a seat," she said. "I was about to have a cup of coffee, may I fix you a cup?"

"Sure. That would be fine. Black please."

Dodd returned with two cups of coffee.

"I received a call from an associate from the store. They told me what happened to Selma. It's hard to believe."

"Did you know her very long?"

"We met the first week she started. About a year ago. We kinda hit it off, you know. She told me about her marriage problems. I helped her move into her apartment six months ago."

"Her neighbor thought she was seein' a man recently."

"I believe so. She told me she was interested in someone. I was happy for her."

"Did you ever meet him? Did she mention a name?"

"I think she said his name was Chris. She was determined to take it slow. I know she didn't want to repeat the mistakes of her first marriage."

"She talk about that much? Her mistakes."

"Only that he drank. Couldn't hold down a job. They were always in debt. Selma liked the finer things."

"Did she seem worried lately? Concerned about anything?"

"No. She never said."

"Did you ever see this, Chris? He ever come around the store?

"Never saw him," she said, shaking her head.

"Thanks for your time," I said.

"You will find out who did this?"

"We will. You can depend on it."

I returned to the office. Had Morris put under surveillance. Went through Selma's personal things, date book, letters—anything that would lead me to the identity of a man named Chris. Following morning, I received the coroner's report. Selma Morris died from a crushed windpipe.

Bones in her neck were shattered, indicating an enraged attacker. Several bruises and facial lacerations were postmortem. Her killer had a vicious temper. For the next three days, the surveillance on Morris garnered nothing. He went about his daily tasks. Worked at the shop. Dinner out one night. Stayed in his apartment the other nights.

Among Selma's effects, a letter from her mother. Pleased that she had filed for divorce. Ruth Edmonds lived in Tempe, Arizona. I telephoned Mrs. Edmonds and informed her of her daughter's death. Mrs. Edmonds would make arrangements to travel to San Francisco to claim the body. Mrs. Edmonds arrived on the 3:35 train the following day. I picked her up at the station. We didn't talk much on the drive to the morgue. She identified her daughter. I took her to an office to give her time to compose herself before questioning her.

"Was it Thomas who did this?" she asked.

"We're not sure yet, Mrs. Edmonds. Did your daughter ever mention a man named Chris?"

"She told me about a Chris in a letter. She met him. . . it must have been a month ago. Christopher. . . I can't remember his last name. I'd have to find that letter."

"That's fine, Mrs. Edmonds. If you could, it would be helpful. We are doin' everything we can to find the person who did this. We'll let you know as soon as we find anything. I promise you. I'll take you to your hotel."

"Thank you."

She got up from the chair.

"Christopher Mayflower!" she said. "That's his name! No! Wait. I remember now. It's Christopher Mayfield."

I ran a make on Mayfield. Had two assault charges against him, one six months ago. Last known address— 935 Clayton Street. Mayfield had moved more than six months ago. A check with the DMV, no driver's license or vehicle registration issued to Christopher Mayfield.

South San Francisco resident Donald Hamerhill, Mayfield's assault victim, answered his door in bedclothes. It was 5:04 p.m.

"Donald Hamerhill?"

"Yeah. What do you want?"

"Inspector Wolf," I said, showing him my identification. "I'd like to ask you some questions about your assault complaint?"

"Thought that was settled?"

"Routine follow up."

"You might as well come in."

I stepped into the entryway of the small frame house at the top of the hill.

"I'm sorry to disturb you, but this is important."

"I'd just gotten up," he said. "I work nights."

I followed him into the small kitchen.

"Have a seat," he said. "Can I get you a cup of coffee?"

"No thanks. This won't take long. Tell me a little about the assault."

"I bartend. Joint on Market. Mayfield's a regular—used to be a regular. This one night he gets into some discussion. . . sports I think. . . with another guy, never saw before. Mayfield's a hot head. Tried to break it up, ya know—before they start tearin' up the place. Mayfield ain't havin' it. He shoves Tina—one of the waitresses, knocks her down. I try to throw his ass out. The mug grabs me by the neck—chokin' me. I nearly blacked out. Coulda' killed me! Had to go to the hospital."

"He attacked a waitress?"

"Tellin' ya. He's a hot head. He hit a girlfriend once, I was told."

"You've been helpful. Thanks."

"Guy should be locked up before he kills somebody," Hamerhill said.

"Yeah—before he does."

I called on Sully. It was nearly one in the afternoon when I tapped on his door.

"It's open!" Sully called.

"How you feelin'? I said closing the door.

"It's gettin' to me," he groaned. "Spasms come along all of a sudden."

"Brought you sandwiches and coffee."

"I'm starved."

"Corned beef or turkey?"

"Corned beef, whadaya think?"

I ran down the case as we ate lunch.

"Number one! Suspect the husband," Sully said.

"After talkin' with him, I'm not so sure."

"You're learnin'," Sully said. "Your second suspect, this Mayfield. No car. Uses public transportation. Maybe cab sometimes. Check with the cab companies."

"I'll work that angle."

After lunch, I went back to the apartment house to question Selma's neighbors. No one could pin down a day or time that she had a visitor who took a cab to her address. I canvassed the surrounding buildings adjacent to her apartment—came up empty. Tenants in three of the apartments I assumed were at work. I waited for them to return.

5:38 p.m., a man, medium build, in his forties, climbed the steps to the apartment house directly across the street.

"Pardon me, sir. Police officer," I said showing my identification. "I'd like to ask you a few questions?"

"Is this about the woman across the street?"

"Yessir. Did you happen to see anyone come by the apartment on Monday evenin'?"

"Cab dropped a man off. Close to six o'clock," he said.

"You ever see him before?"

"A few times."

"Did you see him leave?"

"Didn't see him leave, no."

"Notice the cab company?"

"It was the white and blue one."

"City Cab?" I said.

"Yeah. City Cab."

6:34 p.m., I met with the night manager William Grant in his office at the City Cab garage.

"Monday night, between five thirty and six o'clock, is that right?" Grant said.

"Right."

"Let's see. That was city seven-nine. Dropped a fair at that Parkside address. Seven-nine is Harry Brennan."

"Know where he is right now?"

"I'll find out. ALICE!" Grant yelled.

"Yeah!" a voice replied from the other room.

"Get city seven-nine to call the office," he said.

"Okay." Alice said.

A few minutes passed. Alice called from the other room. "Harry's on line four."

"Harry. It's Bill. Got a police officer here. Wants to know about a fair Monday night. 2420 Parkside."

"Where did he pick up the fair?" I said.

"Wants to know where you picked up the fair. Yeah."

Grant plucked a pencil out of a juice can, began to scratch the pencil across a small pad.

"Got it," he said, returning the receiver to its cradle. "Lou's Gym. Mission and seventh. Dropped him at Parkside around six o'clock."

Mayfield worked out four times a week according to Louis Younger, owner of the gym.

"Yeah, keeps himself in shape. Got cut from the L.A. Dons end of last season. Lookin' to get back in the game."

"Football?" I said.

"Fullback."

"He come in today?"

"Nah. I think he's got a tryout with the Seattle club. That's what he said yesterday."

"Gotta address?"

"Last I heard, Hotel Majestic."

The Majestic wasn't a joint I'd visit without some backup. I went back to the Hall, found Sully in the Squad Room.

"Didn't expect to see you," I said.

"Had enough bein' cooped up," Sully said. "How's the case comin'?"

I ran down the particulars. Sully put on his hat and coat and said, "Let's see what this Mayfield has to say for himself."

It took a little over ten minutes to negotiate traffic before we parked across the street from The Majestic on Third. Built before the turn of the century the building showed its age, but the rent was cheap.

"Christopher Mayfield," I said to the sleepy-eyed desk clerk.

The clerk turned in his chair, scanned the Pigeon-hole rack behind him and said, "Looks like he's in."

"What room?" I asked.

"Room eight, second floor."

We took the stairs to the second floor. Halfway down the dark hall, light leaked from under the door to room eight. I knocked.

"Who is it?" a deep voice called.

"Police officers," I said. "Like to ask you a few questions."

The door swung open.

"Cops?" Mayfield said. "Whadaya want with me?"

"Mind if we come in? We don't want to do this in the hall."

"Yeah, I guess."

Sully closed the door behind him.

"You know a Selma Morris?" I said.

"Yeah, I know her. We useta go out."

"When was the last time you saw her?"

Mayfield pinched his bottom lip with thumb and forefinger.

"I don't remember the day. . . coupla weeks I guess."

"Two weeks?" I asked.

"Yeah. I told her I was movin' to Seattle. We wouldn't be seein' each other no more. What's with the questions about Selma? We just went around for a few laughs, nothin' serious. Why all the questions?"

"There's been an accident," Sully said.

"Accident!" Mayfield exclaimed.

"Yeah," Sully said. "We'd like to have you come downtown. You may be able to help."

"Right now?"

"If you don't mind," Sully said.

"Yeah, sure. If I can help."

Mayfield sat quietly in the back seat of the car. Didn't speak. Stared out the window. Once in the interrogation room, we offered him a cup of coffee. He requested water. Said he was in training—preparing for a tryout with the football club in Seattle.

"Been workin' out a lot, gettin' in shape for next week."

"You played professionally?" I said.

"Yeah, in Los Angeles. Fullback for the Don's. Didn't get a new contract."

Mayfield was confident. Spoke freely but would go off on tangents from time to time. As the questioning went on, he became agitated.

"You know of anyone who'd want to hurt Selma?" Sully asked.

"Hurt her? Thought you said it was an accident?"

"Well we think that someone was with her at the time," Sully continued. "They may have had an argument that got out of hand."

"But you said she's in the hospital."

"Yeah, we're waitin' on a call. Hopefully she'll regain consciousness, so we can talk to her," Sully said.

"Then what do you need me for?" Mayfield pleaded.

"She may have told you something. She tell you about a new boyfriend?" I said.

"No! I don't see—"

"Let me get this straight," I said. "You saw Selma two weeks ago to let her know you were going to Seattle?"

"Yeah, that's what I said. You keep askin' me the same questions over and over."

"It wasn't last week?" I said.

"No!"

I looked at my notes and asked. "What about Monday?"

"I keep tellin' ya. NO!"

"What would you say if I told you that a cab driver identified you as a fair he picked up in front of Lou's Gym and dropped you at Selma's apartment house?" I said.

"Yeah, I took a cab. You keep askin' me if I saw her. I didn't! She wasn't home."

"What did you do when you found she wasn't home?" Sully said.

"I left. Got somethin' to eat at a diner."

"Take a cab?" Sully said.

"Bus," Mayfield said.

"There's a bus stop a block away. You take the next bus?" Sully said.

"Yeah. To downtown," Mayfield said.

Sully picked up the phone.

"Get me the desk," he said.

I gave Sully a look. I could tell he was up to something.

"Malone. It's Sullivan. She here?" Sully said. "Okay, good. Have her wait."

He returned the phone to its cradle, said. "Cab dropped you off around six o'clock. You got no answer at the door. You decide to leave, right?"

"Yeah," Mayfield said.

"You wait at the bus stop for the 6:25. Go downtown and have some dinner."

"That's what I said."

"There's a woman outside. Says she can identify you. Saw you board the 6:55 bus. Wanna explain that?"

"I don't know. I didn't keep track of the time."

"I'm just goin' by witnesses. You wanna try again?" Sully said.

Mayfield's face reddened. His hand shook as he sipped water.

I lit a smoke. Sully sat back in his chair. We both glared, not uttering a word. Tension in the room became unbearable.

"You wanna tell us, Chris? Why'd you kill her?" Sully said.

Mayfield dropped his head in his hands and sobbed. "It was an accident."

I began to write.

"Go on," Sully said.

"I wanted her to move to Seattle if I got signed, but she said no. She wanted to break us up. She started yellin'! I don't like it when people yell like that. The next thing I know she's on the floor. I thought for sure she was dead."

"She was, Chris," Sully said. "I'm arresting you for the murder of Selma Morris."

Before we left for the night, I had one question for Sully. How had he found the woman on the bus.

"I didn't," Sully said. "Mayfield's no killer. I figured he'd panic. Fastest way out was the bus. I figured he must have seen at least one woman on the bus that night."

Chapter 11

I took a close look at Irene Talbot's body. It was the same in the Morris murder. If Mayfield wasn't still servin' time in Quentin, he'd be my number one suspect.

You're lookin' for another big fella, Sully said. *Some kind of athlete I'd say.*

I turned. Sully was leaning against the door jam.

"Left cheek has bruises. Looks like fingers," I said. "A big hand covered her mouth. A big man yanked Zeke from the car. Ya can bet the farm they're the same."

Easy to see why no one in the building heard the struggle. She wouldn't have been able to make a sound.

"She has a cut on her forehead."

Blood had dripped from the cut and formed a small pool on the wood floor. It was dry. "She's been dead for a while. From the looks of the place, she knew the killer. Nothing disturbed."

I went down to one knee. Lifted her left arm by the wrist. Nothing under fingernails. Same with the right.

"Clean," I said. "She wasn't expecting it."

I glanced around the room. Resting on a table in front of the couch, two glasses. I bent down to get a closer look.

"Lipstick on one of these glasses," I said.

I looked down at Irene's body.

Same shade, Sully said. *So, Irene gets a visit from a guest, or guests. Pours a drink for herself and at least one guest.*

"Yeah," I said. "She must've hit her head on the edge of the table."

She's expectin' a delivery. Opens the door and lets 'im in.

"This big guy was the party I was to deliver the package to, I reckon."

Package never arrived. They wanna know what happened.

"She gives 'em my address. They come up empty. Smellin' like a double-cross . . ."

They're back with questions.

"And Irene didn't have the right answers."

Taking particular care not to disturb anything that may be important to the police, I searched the premises. Rickman can be a real pain when it comes to things like that. The small apartment consisted of a living room and bedroom with adjoining bath. The place had an almost lived-in look—but not quite. I found the usual things one would find in a single woman's furnished apartment except for one thing: photos. There were no pictures of her or any friends or boyfriends.

In the bedroom, in the top drawer of a small four-drawer dresser, I discovered a couple of paystubs from Golden Gate Realty and not much else. Diary in a small table next to the bed. One page had a list of numbers corresponding to dates.

L-4590 July 12

L-3528 Aug 4

L-1135 Aug 20

Next to some of the numbers were check marks. On another page notes:

CALL BAILEY – GET MONEY FROM NC

My office phone number and apartment address with the initials JW at the top were on another page. I finished my search, returned to the manager's apartment and tapped on Ella May's door.

"Who is it?"

"It's Wolf. Need to use your phone."

"Door's unlocked."

I entered.

She pointed to a small round table against the wall, said. "Phone's over there. You find what you're lookin' for?"

"More or less. I found Irene."

"That's funny. Why didn't she answer her bell?"

"Couldn't" I said, as I dialed police headquarters. "She's dead."

"Dead!" she said, nearly dropping her can of beer. "Jeez."

She tried to rise. I signaled her to stay put—the strain of getting out of the chair and the shock of seeing the body might give her a coronary. Didn't want two dead bodies on my hands.

"Murdered," I added, as dispatch answered.

"Art. That Talbot girl is dead!" Ella May called out.

"Yeah, Vance," I said into the phone. "James Wolf. Put me through to Rickman please."

"Dead?" Art exclaimed as he came in from the kitchen. "Well, I'll be. . . "

The phone buzzed in my ear twice. There was a click on the other end of the line.

"Rickman."

"It's Wolf, Rick," I said. "There's been a murder."

I gave Rickman the address. Figured I'd have at least fifteen minutes before they showed. Back in Irene's apartment, I copied down the phone numbers and notations in her diary. I lit a cigarette and waited in the hallway for Rickman and his boys to show up. I finished my second smoke, checked my watch. It'd been thirty-five minutes since I spoke with Rickman. I was about to light another when Sergeant McNabb came lumbering down the hall, Rickman close on his heels.

"Sure didn't break any speed records gettin' here," I said, pushing Talbot's apartment door open.

"Took your word she was dead. Didn't see the need to rush," Rickman said. "What have we got here?"

"Irene Talbot's the name. My client. Was anyway. Hired me to run an errand. I needed to talk with her. When I got here, I found her like that. Neck broken."

"We're not going to find any of your prints are we?" Rickman asked.

"Only on the door knob. I was very careful," I said with a smirk.

Rickman began to search the room. He went to the dresser, slid the drawer open.

"Where's that fingerprint team?" Rickman ordered.

"They've just pulled up, Lieutenant," McNabb said. "Coroner's on the way."

"I want this place gone over with a fine-toothed comb," Rickman said looking at the paystubs.

"Golden Gate Realty," I said looking over Rickman's shoulder. "Sounds like a good place to start."

"Just hold on a second. I'll be heading over there in a few minutes. I have questions."

He may have had questions but honestly, I couldn't answer many of them. They were the same questions I was asking myself about this dizzy affair.

Rickman gave me a probing look and said, "Just what are you working on?"

"If I tell ya, you'll be stomping all over town with your big flat feet scaring all the rats back into their holes."

"Why did you have to see this Talbot girl?"

"She'd paid me cash up front and I owed her some money."

Rickman snorted and said, "You're telling me that you—"

"Yes!"

"James Wolf, came here to give this woman a refund?! Now I've heard everything."

I shrugged.

"What's this world coming to?" Rickman said.

"I'm heading over to the realty company. I'll meet you there," I said as I put on my hat and headed for the door.

"Don't do anything until I arrive, you read me?" he said as I left the apartment.

I got in my car and drove down Fell Street for about four blocks before I came to a drug store on a corner. Went in, found a payphone and called the number for the realty company in Talbot's diary.

"Golden Gate Realty. Can I help you?" sang a high-pitched man's voice on the other end of the line. Sounded a little light in his loafers—but hey, takes all kinds, right?

"Yes. My name is Mr. Preston. I'm planning on moving into the area and a friend of mine lives on Paloma. He told me you have a rental property just down the street. Small frame house— green?"

Rustling of papers through the receiver.

"Yessir. That house is for rent, but it is in the process of cleaning and painting. Our last tenant moved out two weeks ago. He moved to San Luis Obispo for work. We should have it ready for viewing in the next couple of days if you'd like to leave your phone number."

"No thanks. That'll be fine. I won't be ready to look until next week. How long did your last tenant live there?"

"Mr. Delback? He was there for over five years. Got a promotion with his company and had to move. He really hated to leave the place. Two bedrooms, one bath with a great floor plan. In a really nice neighborhood too ya know."

"Yes, I know. Thank you so much. I'll be in touch."

He started to say something about the convenience to shopping, but I hung up before he could finish.

I looked up Golden Gate Realty in the phone book. It was on Fulton Street. I parked across from the office and waited for Rickman to show.

Played a hunch and it paid off, Sully said.

Startled, I looked into the rearview mirror. "Jesus Sully. Don't creep up on me like that. I nearly had a heart attack."

Sorry. That explains how she had access to the vacant house to set up the meeting. It all fits together.

"There's something I can't figure though."

What's that?

"Why?! Why was she posing as Elizabeth Westrom? Why did she need that drop-off site? Why was she interested in those statues in the first place and why did she end up having her neck snapped?"

You got a few problems there all right.

"This case has more problems than an algebra class." I lit a cigarette. "I'm beginning to think that this Irene dame didn't just pick me out of the phonebook, you follow. She must've had me in mind for some . . . "

I glanced in the mirror. Sully was gone. All this talk about my problems with this case must've been boring him to death.

"Bored to death. That's kinda funny," I said to myself with a chuckle.

I finished my smoke and listened to a comedy show on the radio for the next half hour. Rickman's car finally pulled up in front of the realty office. I got out and met him at the curb.

"Coroner figures this Talbot dame's been dead for a couple days," Rickman said. "He'll know more when he does a full exam."

"Let's see what her employer has to say," I said.

"I'll do all the talking," Rickman said, moving to the entrance of the building.

"Don't introduce me, I'll just lay back and observe."

"Observe all you want, just keep your mouth shut."

A young sandy-haired man sat at a desk just inside the entrance to the office, dressed in a starched white shirt and blue striped tie. He was in his mid-twenties and thin in build. You could tell he was lanky even from a seated position as his shirt was more or less covering him rather than him wearing it. He looked up as we entered and smiled.

His voice squeaked as he spoke, confirming my earlier suspicions when I spoke with him on the phone. In five years, he'd be an interior decorator. "Can I help you gentlemen?"

Rickman flashed his badge.

"Police! Your name?" said Rickman in his best police officer impersonation as he flipped open his notebook.

"Thomas Dumont. What's this all about?" he uttered, blood draining from his face. He nervously adjusted his tie.

"Do you know a woman named Irene Talbot?" Rickman inquired while jotting down notes.

"Irene? She worked here, but she quit a couple of months ago," he said as the frosted glass door to the adjoining office opened.

A man in his mid-thirties came into the reception area dressed in a light blue shirt and red tie. His sleeves rolled halfway up his forearms, mug of coffee in his hand. A puzzled look occupied his face.

"Is there some problem, Thomas?" the man inquired in a calm monotone.

"These gentlemen are from the police, Mr. Shortt," Dumont responded with a flutter of fingers. His voice broke on pronouncing the word police. "They're asking about Irene."

"Irene? What about her?"

"I'm Lieutenant Rickman. And you are?"

"Bailey Shortt. I'm the branch manager. What's going on here?"

"Irene Talbot was found dead this afternoon," Rickman stated flatly. "Murdered."

"Murdered!?" Shortt's self-assured composure collapsed as the coffee mug slid from his hand and shattered on the floor. A chunk of ceramic landed next to my foot. Thomas rose from his chair, shocked look on his face as he fumbled for something to clean up the mess. "How. . . what. . . I. . . ?" he stammered. "I can't believe it!"

Thomas started to collect the broken pieces of the cup.

"I understand she no longer works for you," said Rickman.

"She worked here up to a couple of months ago," Bailey Shortt responded, apparently still in shock.

"She work here very long?"

"Ahh. . .umm. . . Yes. She was with us for almost a year."

"Did she give a reason why she quit?" Rickman asked as his pencil scratched across the notepad.

"She just gave her notice one day."

Shortt swallowed hard. His face went pale.

"Did you know her very well? Do you know what she might have liked to do in her spare time? Who her friends were?"

"Not really," said Shortt. He steadied himself on the edge of Thomas' desk.

I wondered if Bailey Shortt might faint. Thomas continued sweeping up ceramic shards of coffee cup with one eye on Shortt, apparently thinking the same thing.

"I see. Do you know if Miss Talbot had any enemies—angry boyfriend stalking her?"

Thomas went to a supply closet, retrieved a towel and started to wipe up the spilled liquid.

"No. She wasn't seeing anybody as far as I know," Bailey said, somewhat distracted, causing Thomas to pause for a moment in the middle of his cleaning.

Bailey glanced in Thomas' direction. Thomas averted his eyes. I made note of that pause.

"So you can't think of anyone that may have wanted to harm her?"

"No, not at all."

"And you, Mr. Dumont. Can you think of any reason?"

Thomas, still in shock, rapidly shook his head.

"No," he uttered, barely a whisper.

"We believe she was killed sometime late Friday night," Rickman said looking down at his notebook. "Where were you Friday night?"

"I had dinner with potential investors," Bailey said.

"What time was this?"

"I left the office between six and six fifteen. I had to run an errand. Had reservations for seven."

"And this was where?"

"Tadich Grill," Bailey said.

"What time did you leave?"

"Sometime after nine. After that one of the investors and I went to Dante's for drinks."

"When did you leave there?" Rickman said.

"It was almost one. By the time I got home it was 1:45. I went straight to bed."

"Do you know of any family she has living in the Bay Area?"

Both indicated they didn't.

Rickman let out a breath. "Any idea of who might have wanted to harm her? Ex-boyfriend?"

"Not that I know of," Shortt said.

"And what about you, Mister. . ."

"Dumont. I left the office at five-thirty. Met some friends at O'Shea's. A group of us tend to meet Fridays for drinks. You know—end of the week. Four of us went out for dinner on Geary. After dinner two of us went to a show at the Orpheum."

Dumont and Shortt gave Rickman a list of witnesses.

"I'll leave my card. If you think of anything else, please call me," Rickman stated and placed two of his cards on the desk.

"Yes Lieutenant, I will. I don't know why anyone would want to harm Irene, she was. . ." Bailey said, his voice trailing off.

"Thank you for your help," Rickman said, putting on his hat and turning for the exit.

We left the office and walked to Rickman's car. Sully was leaning against the front fender, visible only to me of course.

Shortt is lying, Sully declared emphatically.

"I know," I said, without thinking.

"What did you say?" Rickman asked.

Sully vanished. I could've kicked myself. "I was about to say I know Shortt is lying."

Rickman got into his car and I shut the door for him and then leaned in.

"He was in shock from the news. Nothing more than that," Rickman said evenly.

"I don't know why he won't say, but he knows exactly why Irene quit," I went on. "You couldn't see, but Thomas reacted to the boyfriend question. I think Shortt and Irene were carrying on a little love affair and he doesn't want anyone to know."

Rickman thought this over for a moment then said. "You think Shortt has a wife or something?"

"Could be. You might want to check this out right away," I said, as I slipped Rickman my handkerchief with a piece of the coffee mug Shortt had broken in it. "I lifted it when no one was looking. You might get some nice prints from it."

Rickman looked at the chunk of mug. "You're a pain in the ass but every now and then you knock in a run. But don't think this lets you off the hook. I need to know what this Talbot dame hired you to do? And don't tell me you were there to give her a refund. How stupid do you think I am?"

"I don't think you're *that* stupid," I said.

"There's been a murder and I need to know why. You read me?"

"Let me know what you find on that chunk of mug."

Rickman muttered some remark under his breath that I couldn't hear, started his car and pulled away from the curb with a squeal of the tires. As I turned to cross the street to my car, I could see Shortt watching from the window of the office.

Nice move coppin' the piece of coffee mug, Sully quipped.

"I have my moments," I said, as I crossed the street to my car. "Irene gave those two thugs my address. They staked out my flop. When my car pulls up. . . "

Zeke takes a beatin' meant for you.

From Shortt's vantage point, I looked like a guy who talked to himself. Nice.

Stopped at a liquor store on my way back to the hotel and picked up a pint of bourbon. When I got to my room, I called the desk and had them send up a bucket of ice, syphon of soda and a pastrami sandwich. I was going to need more than one drink to put this lousy day behind me. My client was dead. My old friend confined to a hospital bed and I didn't have a lead that amounted to squat. Felt like an ignorant child. Hell, if ignorance were music, I'd be Guy Lombardo right now.

Couple of hours later I had the sandwich eaten and half the pint gone. I lay there, eyes focused on the ceiling, brain swimming in alcohol. Not all the pieces I had were enough to form any kind of picture. I was lost, like a polar bear in the Sahara.

Chapter 12

Daylight from the hotel window woke me the next morning, still fully dressed. My head hurt and my tongue felt like Bill "Bo Jangles" Robinson had tap-danced on it all night long. Pealed myself off the bed, threw my clothes in a corner, crawled into the shower. First hot water, then cold, to get the blood flowing again, then back to hot. The shower made me feel better but I was starving. I shaved, dressed, had breakfast at French and Lou's Diner. After ham, eggs and a pot of coffee I began to feel human again. With breakfast finished, I checked with my service. Rickman had called and wanted to see me at 10 a.m. It was 9:45 when I looked at my watch. I had my girl call Rickman back and tell him I'd be there with bells on.

It was exactly ten o'clock when I stepped into Rickman's office. He was going over stolen car reports when I entered.

"Grab a seat!" he barked. "I want to know how this murder fits in with your case."

"Up half the night tryin' to answer that myself. Told you: I only saw that Irene dame one time."

"You were only hired to make a delivery?"

"That's what it amounts to," I said.

Rickman glared at me for a long moment. "So what happened?"

"Car trouble. Missed the appointment time. Went to her place to make things right. When I got there, she was dead.

No idea what her angle was, only that she needed me to represent her."

"What else?"

"That's it."

"What were you supposed to deliver?"

"I was to find a certain item, from a certain place, then bring it to her. . . well not her exactly," I droned.

"What exactly, then?"

"An address. All I had was an address."

"Then what?" Rickman said.

"Car broke down. Was an hour late. When I got to the place, no one was there. It was that simple," I said. "Next thing I know, a coupla mugs show up at my place. Mistook Zeke for me when he showed up at my place in my car. I figure as long as I got the item, I've a good chance of getting the person or persons who went after Irene and Zeke to come after me. I at least owe her that."

"What was the item," Rickman said.

"The item is a semi-valuable piece of art."

"Hand it over," Rickman said.

"For what?"

"It's evidence!"

"Evidence my ass. I was the only one who even touched the dingus. How can it be evidence?"

We went back and forth for a little while longer, with Rickman pressing me to tell him exactly what item she hired me to deliver. I continued to press Rickman for anything he'd uncovered. It was a little ballet of evasion, negotiation—I'm never keen on divulgence. I respect client confidentiality—especially when they're dead.

Rickman determined that Irene had rented the apartment six weeks ago. She'd leave for work every morning and return in the evening. Never had any visitors according to the landlady and neighbors. Rickman said he had Sergeant McNabb going over evidence collected at the apartment.

"Any prints off the chunk of mug?" I probed as I helped myself to a cup of stale coffee.

"Two good ones. Thumb and middle finger. Still waiting on results."

"What about the Packard?"

"There are three that meet the description. All black, with either HI or HL in the license. One stolen nearly a week ago from a man in San Jose. I've contacted the San Jose PD and they're looking into it. Also, a blue Packard we came across, license was AE." Rickman handed me the list. "Looks like we'll need to find that stolen car. Maybe lift some prints. The other two and the blue Packard are all accounted for. One is located in Sacramento, one in Bakersfield and the blue one in Daly City."

I looked at the report and noticed one thing: owner of the blue Packard was Mrs. Agnes Forge. Only dark color Packard in the immediate area. It was a lead. Razor thin—but a lead. I made a mental note of the address.

"You get a good description of the guys who worked over Zeke?" I said.

"We canvassed the neighborhood. No one got a good look."

"If I get my hands on anything concrete, I'll let you know," I said as I left the office.

I heard Rickman say, "You goddam better let me know or I'll. . ." I was too far down the hall to hear the rest.

Before heading to Daly City, I swung by the Coroner's Office. Dr. Ridgefield had just wrapped up an autopsy. Victim of an industrial accident.

"Hey, Doc," I said entering the crime lab. "How's business?"

"Jimmy Wolf! Long time," he said. "People just dying to get in."

"You need some new material Doc. Whatcha workin' on?"

"Poor slob got his chest crushed. Back-Hoe flipped over on 'im. Nasty business. What brings you here?"

"Wanted to get some information on a homicide."

"You workin' a case? Thought you specialized in divorces."

"I'm branchin' out," I said. "Name's Irene Talbot. You do the work up?"

"Yeah. Pretty blond. Hair was a chestnut color at one time. Think she bleached it a month back."

"Wanted to change her appearance?"

"Who knows," Ridgefield said. "Maybe her boyfriend tired of the dark color. She *had* a boyfriend by the way."

"That so?"

"Recent sexual activity. I'd say two days ago."

"What about cause of death?"

"Crushed windpipe. Killer grabbed her from behind. Left hand across her mouth. Bruise marks on her cheeks. Squeezed pretty hard. Right arm across the neck, like this," Ridgefield said, bringing his right arm up. "You'll notice I have the second knuckle of my thumb against the laryngeal protuberance."

"In English, Doc," I said.

"Adams Apple."

"I thought women didn't have an Adam's Apple?"

"A misconception, Jimmy. In women the larynx tends to be smaller in size. So, the bump caused by the protrusion of the laryngeal protuberance is less visible or even non-discernible in some cases."

"I think I follow, Doc. Just barely."

"At any rate, I would say the sequence went something like this. Killer twisted the head to the left with great force, while simultaneously crushing the windpipe with the right hand pulling tight against the neck."

"Final summation?"

"She died almost instantly. My guess she was focused on something, or someone, in front of her. Killer came up from the rear. It all happened within a few seconds."

"Time of death?"

"Forty-eight hours, give or take. Late Friday."

"Thanks, Doc," I said.

"Shame," Ridgefield said. "She sure was a pretty girl."

Sully was in the back when I returned to my car.

"Coroner says Talbot was killed late Friday."

Turns things around a bit. You didn't show up for the meet, Sully said. *Irene gets a call from her boys. She gives them your address. They stake out the place.*

"Yeah. She gave 'em my entire rap sheet for cryin' out loud!"

Right down to the car you drive.

"They don't get the package. Head straight back to Talbot. Christ! What a sap I am."

Take it easy. What's done is done. You need to track down that Packard.

I started the car. Pointed it south for Daly City.

Forty-five minutes later, I pulled up to the Daly City address of Agnes Forge. Garage door was open and there inside sat a dark blue 1945 Packard Clipper. The Daly City house was in a well-kept neighborhood. Mrs. Forge's house was one probably built in the late twenties. I walked up to the front door and pressed my thumb against the doorbell button. From the outside, I guessed the home was a two-bedroom variety. I pressed the button again.

"I'm coming," said a woman's frail voice from behind the door. The door swung open and a short round woman, with neatly coiffed grey hair, wearing a print dress smiled a warm smile. "Can I help you young man?"

"Good morning. My name is James Lupo. I was driving by and saw your car in the garage. That's a 1945 Packard, isn't it?"

"Yes it is. It was my late husband Arthur's car. He passed away last year."

"I'm sorry to hear that. It certainly is a beauty."

"It is, isn't it? Arthur was so proud of that car."

"Do you drive it often?"

"Oh no. I don't drive. My nephew drives me where I need to go. He's the one who takes care of the car for me. Keeps it washed and polished."

"Would you mind if I just take a closer look. I'll be very careful."

She smiled and said, "Go right ahead."

"Thank you. I'll only be a minute and I'll be on my way," I replied, tipping my hat and heading for the garage.

The car was Navy blue, but at night there'd be no doubt that someone would describe it as black. Carefully making my way around the car, I inspected every detail. Looking closely at the rear plate, I noticed mud caked on the top of the letter "A". From a distance, the "A" would look like an "H". The letter "E" also had mud caked to it. From a distance, you'd guess it was an "L".

"Looks like that was done intentionally."

Maybe. But you better make sure, Sully said.

"I'll bet the farm the nephew was the wheel man on this job."

Could be. Just don't jump to a conclusion before you get the facts.

"You're right," I said.

"You say something, Mr. Lupo?"

"I was just tallkin' to myself. Your nephew does a fine job takin' care of the car."

"He loves taking care of cars. Would you like a cup of tea?" she asked. "I have a pot on."

"No, I'm fine. I was wondering if he'd be interested in doing the same for me. I would be willing to pay."

"I'm sure he would. I'll get you his phone number and you can ask him."

Agnes disappeared for a minute or two and then returned with a slip of paper in her hand.

"You can reach him at this number. They'll take a message."

I took the paper and thanked her.

When I got to my car, I looked at the paper. Agnes had written MANNY STRUPP in block letters and the phone number. BA-5-2564. I stopped at the first payphone I saw and dialed the number. It rang maybe ten times before a man's voice came through the line.

"Tic-Toc Club."

"Can I speak to Manny Strupp, please?"

"Hold on," he said. "*Hey!* Is Manny *here!?*" he called, as a chorus of voices in the background returned with a cacophony of responses. "He's not here. Take a message," the man said.

"I'll call back."

Manny was using the club as his answering service, but he was still a strong lead. It seemed obvious with the mud employed to change the letters on the license plate. When I returned to my car, Sully was in the back.

"I'd wager that Agnes had no idea that Manny had borrowed her car Friday night."

First thing! Find out who the hell Manny Strupp is. Second, find that connection to you and Irene Talbot, if any, Sully said from the back seat.

"If any?" I said.

You still don't know for certain how Manny fits in. He's your only lead to the big guy. Dig a little deeper.

"Oh, I'll dig all right. But first I'm gonna take a closer look at those statues."

Back at my joint, I checked the lock mechanism carefully before entering. No new scratches, I went directly to the kitchen to retrieve the items in question. I placed the two figurines on the table and began a thorough inspection. I removed the wooden base from each and probed them with my pocket knife. The bases were solid wood. Next, I worked on the old man statue, the larger of the two. I scraped away some of the paint that decorated the item. The paint flaked off to reveal smooth, white ceramic. I tried several places around the statue with the same result. Did the same with the old woman statue. Nothing appeared to be out of the ordinary. There were four water buckets with something like woven hemp representing handles. The buckets seemed painted with the same sort of paint as the figurines.

I sat, staring at the two pieces of art for more than twenty minutes. The person who hired me to purchase them was dead. She may have been representing the art collector Schofield. Then again, she may not have. She may have been working on her own.

I picked up the old woman figurine and hefted it in my hand. I turned it upside down and inspected the bottom. The bottom of the piece was unpainted. I started to poke at the thing with my knife. I was able to chip away pieces of ceramic. Just under the outer surface, the material was soft. As I picked, more and more of this white grit crumbled onto my table. The white grit then changed to a tan color. Similar to fine sand. I continued to chip away until I removed enough ceramic material to create a tiny round hole.

I turned the statue upright and shook it. More sand leaked out of the hole. I continued to chip away more and more material. Sand started to cover my table then it suddenly stopped. I was only able to get the point of my knife a fraction of an inch into the bottom of the statue. I began to twist the knife to remove more ceramic. The more I chipped away the larger the hole became. When I finally got the hole to approximately the size of a quarter, I took my flashlight and shined it in the hole. I could barely make out what looked like white cloth inside the hollow figurine. I worked feverishly with my knife, enlarging the hole until it was nearly an inch and a half in circumference.

I wedged my thumb and forefinger into the hole and after some wiggling and twisting. I had a firm hold of the fabric and began to remove it. Inch by inch the fabric slid out. Once on the table, it appeared to be a cotton bag or sock, stitched on both ends. I cut one end of the sock with my knife and out fell diamonds, rubies and emeralds.

Chapter 13

I honestly don't remember the four-letter word that shot out of my mouth when those jewels cascaded across my table. My head started to spin.

Was Irene a smuggler? Did Manny Strupp have something to do with this? I needed a drink. I started to rise from the table and then it hit me—that old Chinese gentleman was glaring at me. I reached across the table and brought the sculpture to my lap. With my knife, I started the same procedure, this time with trembling hands. I chipped away at the bottom, suppressing the urge to smash the thing with a hammer. As the hole grew, out came the fine sand. I kept chipping and scratching until the hole was over an inch in diameter. I could see a fabric bag inside. I shook the statue and the bag moved. I was able to get my fingers inside, just enough, to wiggle the bag out of the hole. I had to chip away a little more of the ceramic before the bag slid out. I cut one end and out came another pile of gems. I really needed a drink now.

Pacing back and forth in front of the table sipping on my second bourbon and soda it dawned on me that maybe this was some kind of con. The gems looked real enough—but were they? I picked up one of the diamonds, held it firmly between my fingers and ran it down the side of my glass. It scored the glass as easy as you please.

They're real all right, Sully said. *Looks like you hit the jackpot.*

"They must be worth a million!" I exclaimed as I poured the rest of my drink down my throat. "This is starting to make more sense now. Irene needed a patsy to transport stolen gems. Perfect set up. If anything happened, I would be left holding the bag."

Literally holding the bag, Sully said.

I fixed myself another drink.

If this Strupp character turns out to be a big ape, you've got your murderer.

"With a clear motive."

What's your next move, Jimmy? Sully asked.

"I need to find out where these statues came from. This is the best lead I've had so far. Claire should be able to find that out for me. I'm gonna hide these first." I said, pointing to the pile of precious stones covering my kitchen table.

Coffee can, Sully suggested.

"Bingo!" I exclaimed.

I opened my two-pound can of Hills Brothers, dumped the contents into a bowl. Put the gems into two small paper bags and placed them in the bottom of the can. Poured as much ground coffee back into the can as would fit. Next, I went around to the back of the apartment building and scooped up a bucket of stones and gravel that trimmed the walkway of the rear entrance. I refilled the cloth sacks with the stones and stitched them up the best I could, stuffing the sacks back into the statues. A quick trip to the hardware store for a bag of Plaster of Paris and within forty-five minutes I had the statues sealed. As soon as the plaster dried, I attached the wood bases. My heart was pumping like a bilge pump on a sinking ship. I made myself a ham sandwich, fixed another drink and tried to calm down before I called Claire.

I washed up and put on a clean shirt and tie before calling her. I told her to meet me at Jax, this dark little joint on California Street. When I arrived, I got myself a booth in the back. Only a few people were in the place when Claire walked in. She came to the back and slid into the seat across from me. She looked good.

"I need you to do something for me."

"I'm fine James, how are you?" she said sarcastically.

"Sorry. I've got a lot on my mind. Would you like something to drink?"

"Manhattan, please."

"Manhattan for the lady, Sammy," I called to the bartender. "I need you to do something for me, it's very important."

"Is this another assignment?" she said, excitedly.

"Yeah. I'd like to find out where those two water carrier statues came from. I have the lot number."

I slid a sheet of paper with the lot number on it toward Claire.

"That will be simple enough. What's going on?" she said.

"These statues have more to do with this case than I thought. Thanks Sammy," I said as he delivered the drink. "What do you know about this Schofield character?"

"Not much really. I've only seen him once, I think. Mrs. Schofield is the one who usually comes to the business," she remarked and took a sip of her drink. "I almost forgot, I saw that Irene girl, maybe two weeks ago. She was at John's Grill having lunch with this man. They looked very cozy. I thought it must have been a boyfriend."

"Have you ever seen that guy before then?"

"Nope. I just remember that I recognized her from coming into the shop, that's all."

"What did he look like? Short, tall, on the skinny side?"

"I'd say, five-foot-nine, dark hair. Slim build. Nice looking. Businessman type," she said.

"Businessman type?"

"Yeah. He was wearing a nice suit and tie."

"Sounds like this Real Estate broker Irene worked for."

That confirmed Bailey and Irene were an item and he didn't want anyone to know. Only person who could fill me in on this was Thomas Dumont. He knew the skeletons in Shortt's closet. Feeling like a one-armed prizefighter, I needed to get some help.

I left Claire and headed over to this dive in the Tenderloin. It was still early in the evening so I was reasonably sure I would find Dr. Percy Haladae, still with his wits about him. About to start my car when I heard a familiar voice come from the rear seat.

You're taking a chance with Doc. Too much drink and—

"Just about the only person left I can trust," I said interrupting. "If he gets too drunk he won't remember what I asked him anyway."

"*Squint Millet,*" Sully said.

Chapter 14

Leo Millet—everyone called him Squint. His rat-like beady little eyes gave him a perpetual squint. Burglar by trade, Squint would steal the dentures off the Pope's bed-stand if he could make a buck. Knew who was doing what and where they were doing it. We kept a close eye on Millet. He was making the rounds, circulating counterfeit twenty-dollar bills once. Sully and I got lucky, caught him in the act passing the stuff at Golden Gate Fields. We struck a deal. If he agreed to be an informant, we wouldn't turn him over to the Feds.

"That's the deal, Squint," Sully said. "Take it, or leave it."

"You boys drive a hard bargain."

"You're lookin' at a heavy Federal wrap," I said.

It didn't take long for Squint to think it over. A month later, he proved to be a valuable asset, within limits mind you.

It was Thursday morning, 10:33 a.m. when Sully and I met with Captain Zamora, Chief of Homicide.

"Wanted to see us, Skipper?" Sully said.

"Close the door, have a seat," Zamora said.

"Sounds serious, Skip," I said.

"It is. Shooting at the Hotel Compton, about an hour ago. Victim: Bruce Edward Danner. He's at General. Docs give 'im a fifty-fifty chance of pullin' through. Danner was in Federal custody. Witness in an organized crime trial. Federal officer Derick Ryan wounded. Should pull through."

"If this is a Fed case, how are we involved?" Sully asked.

"That's just it. Only the Feds knew that Danner was here in San Francisco. Someone leaked his whereabouts."

"We got a guard on 'im?" Sully asked.

"Yeah. As soon as he's stable, we're planning on moving him under a John Doe to another hospital."

"Whadaya want us to do Cap?" I said.

"I want you two to head up an investigation. Keep it on the QT. No one in the department is to know that we're helping. You two only answer to me. Got it!"

"Got it, Skip," Sully said.

"You only check in with me. Personally! No messages. We meet outside of the department. That's all for now. Oh! By the way, check with narcotics. I've arranged for some pocket money to move things along. Spend it wisely."

We left the Hall and hit the streets. Three solid days of canvassing the seedy parts of the Bay. Every back alley—dive bar—pool hall—anywhere an informant would likely hang out we checked. We came up as empty as a burlesque hall on Easter Sunday.

It went that way for over a week. Agent Ryan was out of intensive care by this time. It was still touch and go for Danner. Sully and I had lunch at the Pig 'n Whistle next to City Hall.

"We should see what Squint can come up with?" I said.

"Squint drinks too much. He's a liability," Sully said.

"We'll tell 'im to keep his ears open, you know. If he happens to hear somethin'."

"I don't know."

"I'll get a message to 'im. Never know what he might run into."

We walked back to the Hall. I put out the word I was looking for Squint Millet.

I received a message around three o'clock that afternoon. I was to call a phone number in an hour. It was exactly 4 p.m. when I dialed the number.

"Wolf?" the voice on the other end of the line said.

"Yeah."

"Squint. I've got somethin' fer ya. Meet at Pier 29 in an hour. Make it look good."

"We'll be there," I said.

We rolled up to Pier 29 at 5 p.m. Squint leaned against a lamppost, cigarette dangling from his lip.

"Whadaya say, Squint?" I called getting out of the car.

Squint had a look of surprise. Sully jumped out and came around to the other side of Squint.

"Now fellas," Squint said pleadingly.

I grabbed him by his collar and pushed him towards the car.

"Hands on the hood, Millet!" Sully commanded.

He put his hands on the hood.

"You got nothin' on me. What's this all about?"

I patted him down and said, "He's clean."

"Empty your pockets," Sully said.

Squint took a wallet from his jacket pocket. Comb from his pants hip pocket. An assortment of coins and a watch, silver colored metal band. He placed them on the fender of the car.

"Lemme see your wrists!" Sully ordered.

He slid his sleeves up. He wore two watches, one with a leather band the other with a silver metal band.

"You keepin' track of Mountain Time, Squint?" I said.

"It ain't against the law to own two watches is it?"

"If it's from a burglary it is," Sully said. "Cuff 'im."

I cuffed Squint, assisted him into the back of the car. A small crowd had gathered several feet away.

"Keep it movin' here people," Sully said to the bystanders.

We pulled away from the curb.

"Jeez, Wolf. You put these on a little tight," Squint said.

"Gimmie," I said.

Squint reached his hands over the front seat. I unlocked the cuffs and put them back in my pocket.

"We're lookin' for an out-of-town torpedo," I said. "Tried to ice a federal witness. What's the word on the street?"

"All's I know is maybe a gunsel from back east pulled the trigger."

"We need to get a line on this guy," Sully said. "It's worth a sawbuck?"

"I'll do some nosin' around," Squint said.

"Don't stick your nose out too far. This mug is dangerous," I said.

"I'll be in touch," Squint said.

We dropped him off a few blocks away. Headed back to the Hall.

We got a call from Squint around eight-thirty that evening. He'd be at the Shanty at ten o'clock. When we arrived, Squint occupied a stool at the far end of the bar. We ordered beers. Squint gave us the high-sign. Moved off his stool. Headed to the washroom. We waited a moment. Then followed.

"Coupla heavies in town," Squint said. "Detroit, I think."

I looked under the stall door in the rear.

"It's clean," Squint said. "I checked."

"You said two?" Sully asked.

"Yeah, that's what I hear. Bad too. Word on the street is they's in town on a job. Things didn't work out. Stuck here until they get it done, know what I mean? Maybe it's the mugs you're lookin' for."

"Got names—description?" I asked.

"Nah. Thought, youz guys'd like the tip, so I brung it. I mean these two are really bad. Beat up some sailor over a pinball game."

"Thanks for the tip, Squint. Keep your eyes open," Sully said.

"Find out anything you can on those two," I said, handing Squint a ten-dollar bill. "It'll be worth it to ya."

Squint snatched the bill from my hand.

"You get us information where we can find these guys, there's a nice reward comin' to ya," Sully said.

We met up with Captain Zamora. Gave him the rundown. Continued our canvassing. Soliciting any information on muscle from Detroit.

We were able to put bits and pieces together over the next week but nothing concrete. Friday 10:30 p.m. we received a radio call from dispatch.

"Five-Henry-Twelve, call HQ. Five-henry-twelve, call HQ."

"That's us," I said. "Five-henry-twelve, ten-four. There's a drug store—middle of the block."

I called headquarters. We had a message to call Brunswick 2-6682. I hung up and dialed the number.

"Yeah," the voice said.

"It's Wolf."

"Squint here. Meet me at Luke's."

"Be there in ten minutes."

Friday night we expected Luke's to be crowded. It was. We found Squint in the rear of the place watching a couple of drunks attempt a game of eight ball. Squint spotted us and signaled with a head nod to meet him in the back alley.

"You got somethin'?" Sully said.

"Yeah, it's about the Detroit muscle. Gettin' antsy hangin' around town with nothin' to do."

"Get to the point," I said.

"They's lookin' fer somethin' to take the edge off. If ya know what I mean."

"We can guess," Sully said.

"Soz this guy I knows hits me up if ya know what I mean. Knows I got connections. See what I'm sayin'? I toll 'im it'll take a day or two but I could hook 'im up, for sure. I asks 'im if these friends of his are on the square. Ya know? If they's straight shooters, ya see. He sez yeah. Tells me, they's from Detroit." Squint said with a laugh. "From Detroit. Straight shooters, get it."

"Yeah, go on," Sully said.

"I figures these guys are the muscle youz lookin' fer. I tell this friend I'll set it up. He gives me a number."

"Gimme the number," Sully said.

Squint had it on a slip of paper. Sully took it.

"He wrote down Vince. Ask for 'im. You gotta tell 'im Squint sent ya."

Sully stuffed the paper in his pocket, took out his wallet from his jacket and opened it. "We'll take it from here," Sully said. He pulled out two twenties. "This is for now. There'll be more if this works out."

We went over the plan with Zamora. It was simple. One of us would impersonate Squint's drug connection. Call the number, set up the meet. If both gunsels showed up it would be a bonus, but at least we'd get one of them off the street.

"Wolf. You play the part of the drug dealer," Zamora said. "Somehow, I don't think Sullivan looks the part."

"I'm not sure if I can take that as a compliment, Cap," I said.

"I don't have to tell you to be careful. These two are dangerous. You're not to take any chances. Anything feels hinkey. . . you get out of there. That's an order!"

We set up a detail for the buy. Two cars would work in tandem to follow me to the meet. Once all was coordinated, I made the call. It was 2 p.m.

"Yeah," the baritone voice said in my ear.

"Squint told me to call. Askin' for Vince."

"Whatta we lookin' at?" he said.

"Double sawbuck. Where you wanna meet?" I said.

"There's a little park. Kearney and Clay. Nine o'clock," he said and clicked off.

At 8:55 p.m. I parked on Kearney and walked into the park. Made my way to the middle, quickly scanned the area. No one there. Found a place on a bench that gave me a wide view. If anyone entered, I was sure to see. Lit a smoke, checked my watch. It was 9:01. An elderly Asian man entered. He had a small dog on a leash. They passed through without stopping. 9:10, no one entered the park. 9:15, still no one. 9:30 I made my way across the street to the phone booth on the corner. I called Headquarters. There were no messages. I guessed this may have been a dry run, so I drove back to the station making sure I wasn't followed. Sully met me in the garage.

"Didn't figure on a no-show," he said.

"Maybe they were testin' me."

"Sure no one followed you out of the park?"

"Was careful."

"Let's check with Squint," Sully said.

Back in the office, we checked in with Zamora then called Squint's number. No answer. We went back to the streets checking his usual hangouts. No one had seen him. We called it a night. I went home. I had a bad feeling gnawing at my insides. It was my idea to get Squint involved.

The next morning, we made the rounds again. We wore out shoe leather until 1:15 p.m. Still no sign of Squint. 1:22 p.m., we stopped at Tommy's Joynt for a sandwich and coffee. Halfway through our lunch a pimple-faced bus-boy approached the table.

"You Wolf?" he asked.

"That's me."

"Phone call for ya. You can take it at the front."

"Wolf speakin'."

"It's Martin. You're to call a Freddy at this number Bayside 3-6641."

"Thanks, Marty. Will do."

"What's up," Sully said.

"That weasel Freddy Tumes called. Wants to talk."

"Heard we were payin' for information?" Sully said.

"Looks like."

We finished our lunch. I called Freddy. We arranged to meet at the Palace of Fine Arts pavilion in an hour.

We found Freddy along the walk next to the reflecting pond. A real smooth dipper. Once got grabbed picking pockets by a security guard at the ballpark. Put Freddy in a room with bars on the windows. Called the cops to pick him up. Thin and wiry, Freddy could twist his body in unnatural positions, like he was held together with elastic bands. By the time the cops got there he'd squeezed through the bars.

"Hear you've been lookin' for Squint," Freddy said.

"You hear right. Give!" I said.

"Can't tell ya where he is but I knows someone who seen him yesterday."

"Who?" Sully asked.

Freddy rocked on his heels, twisted his face in a crooked smile, revealing uneven yellow teeth. I peeled off a fiver. He snatched it from my fingers.

"He was seen with some skirt. Names Audrey."

"Gotta last name," I said.

Freddy rocked on his heels again.

"Jesus, Freddy!" I said peeling off another five-spot. This time holding on tight. "This better be—"

"Audrey Golladay," he said.

"Where can we find her?" I said.

"Don't know that," he said.

I started to shove the money in my pocket.

"Now hold on chief. I can tell you where to start."

"Go on," I said.

"She and Squint were at Shifty's. I saw him myself."

"Shifty's! Half Moon Bay?" Sully said.

"Yeah."

"What time was that?" Sully said.

"Sometime after eight. I was on my way out."

I gave Freddy the other five.

"Keep your nose clean," I said.

I called Captain Zamora's office to run an R&I on Audrey Golladay.

"I'll have that for you in thirty minutes," Zamora said. "Just got a call. Squint Millet's at General. Get over there right away. Ask for a Doctor Prentis."

Chapter 15

We approached Reception at S.F. General. Patrolman Sweeney met us.

"Whadaya got?" Sully said.

"A waitress, Miss Lang, went into the alley for a cigarette break when she heard a kinda moan comin' from down the alley. Checked it out. Found a man beaten pretty bad. Called it in. I searched him for ID. Leonard Millet."

"She didn't hear anything?" I asked.

"Restaurant's too noisy to hear anything outside. Canvassed the business along the alley. Nothin."

"Muggin'?" Sully said.

"Didn't figure. Millet had cash in his pocket."

"Thanks Sweeney," Sully said.

Nurse staffing the desk was on the phone. Sully and I showed her our badges. She nodded and held up her index finger. Name tag read D. Vaughn. Mid-forties. Light brown hair. Brown tired eyes.

"Doctor Hershman will return your call. You're welcome, doctor."

She dropped the phone onto its cradle.

"Police officers to see Doctor Prentis?" she said.

"That's right," Sully said.

"He's expecting you," she said and dialed. "Doctor Prentis, please."

A few moments passed.

"Doctor Prentis? Two police officers are here to see you. Yes doctor," she said and hung up the phone. "If you'll follow me."

We followed Nurse Vaughn down the corridor leading us to an examining room.

"Doctor Prentis will be right down."

I took a seat in one of the chairs. Sully perused the medical posters on the wall. Several minutes later the door opened. Doctor Prentis stepped into the room, closing the door behind him.

"I'm Doctor Prentis. I was the one that called."

Prentis was in his late twenties, tall, sandy blond hair. He looked tired as if he had just run a marathon.

"Inspector Sullivan, Doctor. This is Inspector Wolf."

"How do you do, gentlemen," he said, shaking our hands.

"Fine, sir," Sully said. "Will it be okay if we speak with Mr. Millet?"

"I don't think you'll get much out of him. He died just a few minutes ago."

"Jesus!" I said. "What happened?"

"Millet had several skull fractures. Hit numerous times with a blunt instrument about the head. We have no idea how long he was in that alley before someone called the police."

"Was he conscious at any time?" Sully asked.

"Barely. I'm not sure he knew where he was."

"Did he say anything?" I asked.

"He mumbled something about a church. He said church. Tell Sullivan—church."

"Anything else?"

"No," he said, shaking his head. "He slipped into unconsciousness. Never came out."

"Well thank you, Doctor Prentiss," Sully said.

"Wish I could have been more help. He took a vicious beating. I hope you catch the person who did it."

"We can promise you that Doc," Sully said.

Before leaving the hospital, we checked back in with Captain Zamora. Nothing on Audrey Golladay. We headed for Half Moon Bay.

I gazed blankly out the window as we drove south.

"It's not your fault," Sully said.

"I got the poor guy into this. Now he's dead."

"You warned 'im first of all. Second of all we're not sure who killed 'im."

"Yet!" I said. "Simple explanation is always the best. Isn't that what you've always told me? What did you call it?"

"Occam's razor."

"That's it. Simple explanation is. . . Someone tipped off the Detroit hoods Squint was workin' with us. Who else would have wanted him dead? He got drunk. Started shootin' his mouth off."

We didn't speak for the rest of the ride.

Just off a beach access road along Highway 1, you'll find Shifty's. Restaurant in front—dance floor near the bar— gambling in the back. All kinds of clientele frequent the joint, from the well-dressed San Francisco elite, to the down-to-his-last buck gambler hoping to get healthy. Out of our jurisdiction, flashing our tin wouldn't garner a second look, so we played it cool. Planted ourselves on stools at the end of the bar, ordering a couple of beers.

"Audrey Golladay come in often?" Sully said to the bartender.

"Who's askin'?" he said sharply.

Baldheaded waiter squeezed in elbowing Sully to the side.

"Pardon Mac," he said out of the side of his mouth. "Need two martinis, Pete. Make one dirty."

"Gotcha."

Pete could have been a circus performer in the past as he whipped around bottles of gin and vermouth like a juggler. A shake—a pour, olives on toothpick plunked into the glasses with a splash, the waiter was off again.

"About this Audrey," Sully said.

"Like I said before, Pilgrim. Who wants to know?"

"We're investigators. Insurance claim. She may have some information," Sully said, dropping a ten-dollar bill on the bar. Pete closed his fingers around the bill, slid it in his pocket.

"Yeah, she comes in most nights."

"She come in tonight?"

Pete looked around the bar area and said, "Nah. Not here right now."

"You expect her?"

Pete shrugged. "Could be," he said. "You can wait if you want."

"Two more," Sully said as he dropped a five-dollar bill on the bar. "Keep the change."

We nursed our drinks for nearly a half hour. The place was filling up. Pete collected our glasses. Sully was about to order another round when Pete gave him a nod. Walking into the bar was a woman, medium build, late thirties, brown hair that looked like she'd just got off the coaster at Coney Island. She had on a blue outfit. A fury scarf-like accessory long enough that she wrapped around her neck twice and still had some to swing in her hand. There was a time in the past she'd been a real looker, but years of alcohol and cigarettes had taken their toll. She headed straight for the bar.

"Hey, Pete! What's shakin'?"

Her voice sounded like a worn-out foghorn. She muscled her way between two men at the bar. "Scotch, ice!" she said.

She dropped her handbag on the bar. Fumbled an attempt to dig out her wallet. It was apparent she already had quite a few.

"I'll get this, Pete," Sully said, tossing some bills on the bar.

"Well thank you, mister," she said. "You're a real gentleman."

"Been waitin' for ya to come in," Pete said.

"Me! Do I know you or somethin'?" she said leaning in to get a closer look.

Her alcohol breath nearly knocked Sully off his stool.

"No, you don't know me. You know a friend."

"Who's that?"

"Squint Millet."

"You a friend of Squint? Nice ta meetcha."

"Heard you saw him last night?" Sully said.

"Yeah, yeah. We had a few drinks. He bought a coupla rounds for his friends."

Pete laughed. "He was everybody's friend last night. Throwin' around lotsa cash."

"Did he usually throw around money?" I asked.

"First time I seen it. Most times he's tryin' to get pals to buy him drinks," Pete said.

Audrey chimed in. "He was boastin' how he would come into more. Sellin' information. That's what he said, right Pete."

Pete snickered then said, "Workin' on a case. Some kinda big deal. Just the booze talkin'."

"What time did he leave?" Sully asked.

"Settled his tab just after ten," Pete said. "What's this got to do with insurance?"

"Squint didn't have any," I said. "Someone beat the hell out of him."

On the way back to the city, we tried to figure the church angle. Was Squint assaulted at a church, or near a church? Did it take place on Church Street? Then they dumped his body in that alley. All we had to go on was hit men out of Detroit and a contact named Vince.

Over the next three days, we ran up blind alley after blind alley. No one knew anything. No one heard anything. We searched Squint's dump on O'Farrell Street again, negative results.

"Maybe we need to take a different tact," I said to Sully as we walked back to the car. "This Vince character was lookin' for a drug buy. He must've scored by now. Let's start puttin' the heat on the dealers."

"I think you're onto somethin', Jimmy."

Zamora assigned us a four-man unit. We started pulling in all known drug dealers as far as South San Francisco for questioning. Our focus, anyone sold to a man named Vince. Anyone with information of two heavies from Detroit were to contact us. We offered a reward. Word started to spread. We followed up on a couple of leads but they didn't pan out. The third day of the operation we received a call from a Timo Ferarro.

"Meet me at Burt's Café in Oakland. 16th and Clay. Try not to look like a flatfoot on a holiday. I got a reputation," Ferarro said.

"How will we know you?" I said.

"I'll know you. Just be there in an hour."

We contacted Oakland PD. Ferarro ran a bookie joint. Several arrests, one conviction, moved around a lot. Vice had trouble pinning him down.

When we entered Burt's, a neatly dressed man approached us. He was round in shape, about five-foot-seven. Bushy eyebrows that came to a V at the bridge of his nose, gave him a sinister appearance. He gave us a nod. We followed.

He led us into a small room. A desk sat in the corner. Boxes of restaurant supplies piled along a wall. There was a door on the far end of the room. Behind it came the muffled sounds of phones ringing through the thick wall. He sat himself on the edge of the desk, rubbed his chin then the back of his neck.

"Well we're here," Sully said.

"Look! I don't like to get involved in other people's troubles," Ferarro said. "I'm stickin' my neck out. I mean really stickin' my neck out. Get me?"

"You got somethin' to tell us?" I asked.

"I'm doin' this for Squint. He was a friend of mine. Ain't never shoulda happened. Squint was a decent kinda guy. Heard you guys are lookin' for the mugs who done him that way."

"We are," Sully said.

"You didn't get it from me, understand. You didn't see nothin'! You was never here. That's the deal."

"We get it. The locals have no idea we're here and it'll stay that way," Sully said.

"All's I can tell ya. Squint was doin' a deal. I don't know what and I don't care. But I do know it was with a coupla thugs from Detroit. Church brothers. Larry and Vince Church. These guys are bad. Believe me. Somethin' wrong with their heads. Crazy. Know what I mean? They just as soon shoot ya as look at ya. And they're here on a contract. They get a whiff you been talkin' to me—"

"Nobody's gonna know," Sully said. "You know where the brothers are right now?"

"No idea. All's I know is, they ain't finished the job."

"Thanks for callin' us. City is offering a reward—"

"Forget it! I don't want nothin' savvy? I'll be outta this joint before you guys get across the bridge."

Ferarro crossed the room and opened the door. We left without another word.

We headed back to the office. Called Detroit and had them send us all they had on the Church brothers. We'd have their packages within the next 48 hours. Captain Zamora called a meeting.

"Forty-eight hours sittin' on our asses is not what this division needs to be doin'. Any ideas?"

"I was just thinkin' Cap," I said. "Why don't we bait the brothers to attempt another hit?"

"Go on," Zamora said.

"We leak some information. We say Danner's been moved. Safe-house—private hospital or something. I mean information got leaked before."

"I like that idea, Cap," Sully said.

"It's your baby. Be careful."

We let information leak about Danner's location at a private hospital in Burlingame. We were lucky. We found a new clinic that hadn't opened yet. We were able to staff the location with officers posing as doctors. Couple of policewomen volunteered to act as nurses. We sat back, waited. The following morning, we had some walk-ins wanting information, none fitting the description we received from the Detroit P.D. Following day was much of the same. A few walk-ins.

It was 5:47 p.m. when a tall man in a dark overcoat entered the clinic. From the description, this was Larry Church. Stationed at the reception desk, behind a sliding glass window was Officer Sheila Harris. Sully and I watched from a room off to the side.

"Can I help you, sir," Harris said.

"Can I see a Doc? I got this bad sore throat," he said, eyes taking in the vacant lobby.

"I'll need you to fill out this form," Harris said. "I'll be right back with the doctor."

Harris made her way to the rear of the building. Sully moved to the reception area. Gun drawn as he opened the door to the lobby.

"POLICE!" Sully yelled. "HANDS OVER YOUR HEAD!"

Church fumbled for his gun under his overcoat. Sully fired once, hitting him in the chest. Church staggered back, crashing into the small table. I burst into the room. Church's coat came open, .45 automatic came out. Sully fired again, hitting Church in the stomach. He doubled over then tried to raise his gun. Sully fired again. Church was dead before he hit the floor. Out in the parking lot, we heard gunfire. Two officers covering the outside were exchanging gunshots with Vince Church. He surrendered after being shot. One round in the arm and one in the thigh.

Now a sensible person would opt to keep Doc out of the spotlight. It was risky—but I was too set in my ways to start becoming sensible.

Chapter 16

My fourth stop searching for Doc. The Lucky Tap Saloon located on Mason Street. The "Tap" as a regular customer refers to the place, catered to the local hooligans. It only served rotgut liquor. If you weren't inclined to drink the stuff you could always use it to clear clogged drains.

I discovered Doc at the bar pontificating on some obscure philosophy from some Greek philosopher.

"Although Aenesidemus was a member of Plato's Academy, he disputed their theories and adopted Pyrrhonism. It is a fact."

The bartender nodded as though he actually understood what Doc was discussing. I slid onto the stool next to him.

"How are things Doc?" I said as I put my hand on his shoulder.

Turning he said. "Well, Giaco! It is indeed a special day when I get to lay these weary eyes upon you." Doc was fond of my Italian origins and often called me by my birth name. Giaco was his way of putting an arm around my shoulder.

"Yeah, good to see you too Doc. How about another for the Doc and I'll have a shot of bourbon."

"Ahhh. . . Jimmy, you know how to make an old friend feel welcome."

Percy Haladae was once a well-to-do practicing dentist in the city. Unfortunately, it was his love for the ponies which got him into financial trouble. From Tanforan to Bay Meadows, Doc spent more time at the track than his dental office. When his bookie threatened him with bodily harm, he made a deal to write phony prescriptions for his bookies drug dealing chums that got him jail time and the loss of his license to practice in the state. I think what drove him to drink was the constant ribbing he got with the Wyatt Earp and Doc Holladay connection. If Doc was drunk enough, he could fly into a verbal rage if someone even responded with an 'O.K. Corral' reference. These days he kept his head just above water by working in his dental lab making crown molds. Doc was just sixty years old but to look at him you'd think he was seventy. Despair and alcohol had added a decade.

"I'm workin' on a case and I think I need some help."

"I'm always at your service my lad. How can I be of assistance?" he roared.

"How about keepin' it down to just the two of us in this conversation? We don't need the entire Bay Area involved."

Doc shifted to a more subdued tone.

"You are correct, my friend," he said looking around the bar. "The night has eyes and ears."

What a goofball. I signaled the bartender for another drink for Doc.

"I need some information on a Manny Strupp. His phone number is the Tic-Toc Club."

"Ahhh, yes. I have frequented that establishment from time to time. I don't know anyone named Strupp though."

"I want you to go to the club. You know. Get into a friendly conversation with the barkeep—some of the regulars. See what you can dig up. But be careful," I said, slipping him a twenty. "This is for expenses. Got another for you when you come up with something."

Doc covered the bill with his hand.

"This will do nicely. Should loosen some tongues, indeed!"

"Good. You know what to do. Call my service when you have somethin'," I said. As I slid off the barstool, I patted him on the back. "Try to stay reasonably sober for a while. Listen. Be careful. This Strupp and his partner may have killed once already."

"Not to worry Jimmy. I will keep a sharp eye out."

"Good. Get on it as soon as you can," I said.

"I will traverse the boulevards of our fine community immediately and drag these weary bones to the Tic-Toc, post haste."

"Yeah."

I pulled a couple of singles from my pocket.

"Here—for cab fare. I don't want you draggin' anything."

"You are a gentleman's gentleman, Jimmy," he said as I fled the bar.

I found Thomas Dumont's address in the directory and headed to his apartment on Oak Street. It was 8:40 p.m. when I pressed the buzzer. Dumont's place was on the first floor of the two-story building. I waited only a few seconds before he buzzed me in. I entered and as I walked down the hall, a door opened on my right-hand side and Dumont stepped out into the corridor.

"Oh! Police. I was wondering when you would come around," he stated.

"Yeah, gotta couple more questions for ya. May I come in?" I asked as I removed my hat, stopping just a few feet from Dumont.

"Sure, come in," he said and indicated with a sweep of his hand for me to enter. "Make yourself at home."

I stepped in. He closed the door behind us.

"Can I get you something to drink?"

"No thanks. I won't be long. Sorry for the late call, but—"

"You want to know about Mr. Shortt and Irene," he interrupted, shaking his head. "Have a seat."

I plopped down on an olive-green sofa, holding my hat in front of my knees. "I have to confess. I'm not with the police. I'm a private investigator working on this case."

Dumont slowly sat down in an armchair across the sofa.

"Oh! I see," he said, puzzled.

"Shortt wasn't very forthcoming regarding his relationship with Irene was he?" I asked in a matter-of-fact tone.

"No. He and Irene were seeing each other for a while. It's not like they kept it a big secret or anything. They would see each other socially, dinners and movies. I kinda thought it would get serious."

"Can you think of any reason he'd lie about their relationship?"

"I can't. Irene told me she wanted to take this other job. She never told me what the job was, or anything like that. *But*! Mr. Shortt was fine with her moving on. That much I know."

"Do you know anything about the Schofields?" I asked.

"Schofields?"

"Yeah. That's where Irene went to work. She ever come around after she quit Golden Gate?"

"Never. I kinda thought maybe Irene and Mr. Shortt split up," he said with a shrug. "Mr. Shortt never talked about seein' her after she left."

I sat there for a moment trying to fit some of these pieces together. Irene had to know there was something important about those statues. Was Shortt running some kind of smuggling operation? Was Adrian Schofield the smuggler? Who was Manny Strupp working for and how did he fit into the puzzle? This case was knocking me around like a ping-pong ball in a windstorm.

Dumont finally broke the silence.

"There is something fishy going on at the office. I've had a feeling for a while."

"How do you mean?" I said my interest aroused.

"Mr. Shortt's been getting a lot of phone calls. I heard him tell a caller he needed just a little more time, that everything would be taken care of."

"You know what he was referring to?"

"No. It could be some of the investors he'd gotten involved in with a real estate project. I know that he had to pay some of them back. It was a large sum."

"How large, do you know?

"I don't. I do know that they were not getting what Shortt promised and they wanted to pull out of the deal. Shortt stalled them for as long as he could then paid them off."

"What kind of real estate project was Shortt workin' on?" I said.

Dumont shook his head. "Can't tell ya. Shortt was very secretive about it. Kept those papers in his briefcase."

"You said Shortt was able to pay these investors off?"

"That's right. Somehow, he came up with the money. I know he talked to his sister about money."

"His sister?"

"She lives in Monterey."

"What made you think the deal was fishy?"

"It's not how I've seen deals in the past. Shortt kept me in the dark. He was always gettin' calls on his private line.

He handled everything personally," Dumont shrugged. "You get a feeling about these things."

"You have been very helpful. Sorry for the inconvenience," I said and got up from the sofa.

"Not at all. Glad I could help."

Dumont rose and we shook hands. He had the tell-tale sign of nervousness regarding the circumstances. His hand moist and cold.

"I don't think I'll be around much longer at Golden Gate. As I said, something's fishy. It's not the kind of work atmosphere I'm comfortable with."

Thomas gave me Bailey's address before I left and I immediately headed over to his place. I tried his apartment buzzer several times, didn't get an answer. I found a drug store a few blocks from Bailey's place and phoned my service. Doc had left me a message to meet him at the Tic-Toc Club. He'd be at the bar for another hour. The call came in twenty minutes earlier so I headed right over to the club.

The Tic-Toc was one of those joints that served watered-down drinks at a cheap enough price that you didn't complain. Place had most of its tables occupied and half of the bar stools full when I entered. A four-piece band hadn't mastered the lesson on how to tune their instruments to each other as they were playing a song I could barely recognize. Three chorus girls did their kicks, trying in vain to keep time with the music. I looked along the bar and spotted Doc at the far end sitting on the last stool in the corner. I walked to where he was seated, tossed my hat on the bar and planted myself on the stool next to him.

"Nice work Doc. What've you got for me?"

"Enough to tell you to be careful my boy," Doc said as he leaned a little to his left and looked past me. "There's a young lady sitting with a coupla out-of-town jokers over by the bandstand. Viv Parker's the name. She goes around with Strupp."

I signaled to the bartender that I wanted a drink and got a quick look at the girl at the table in the process. I ordered a drink, turned back to Doc.

"Strupp is one of Nicolo Cappello's boys," Doc stated with a raised eyebrow.

"Nick 'The Hat' Cappello?" I said.

"Part of the Manzetti mob. Came out here from Kansas City."

"Wasn't Manzetti rubbed out by the Parone Gang?"

"Right. About four years ago. Cappello went to Philly, then came here. He's loan sharking, bookmaking and he's tough. Believe me. I've had a couple of run-ins with his bookies and have ascertained with much alacrity that I do not care to conduct any further business with the man."

"And Strupp?"

"Strupp is his minion. Short weaselly lookin' guy. Kind of on the dumb side, but he does what he's told. He's been throwing a lot of dough around lately, talking big. Got a big deal he's working on."

"Showing some initiative maybe?"

Doc gave a shrug. "Could be. Trying to impress Viv, maybe."

"Any idea where he's floppin'?"

"Couldn't get a line on that. He's got a deal worked out here. Calls in to check for messages."

"Anything on that pal of his? A big guy."

"Not sure about that one Jimmy. Strupp runs around with a guy. Could be this ex-boxer. Bruno's the only name I got."

I patted Doc on the back. "You did better than I could figure, Doc."

I slid a twenty in front of him.

"You get anything else you call me," I said, grabbing my hat.

"At your service, Jimmy."

"Thanks Doc."

I flipped a dollar on the bar and signaled the bartender with a tilt of my head to fix Doc another.

Got in my car and started to drive across town.

So, Nick 'The Hat' is behind this. Sully said from the rear of the car.

"It fits," I said. "I figure Bruno is the mug that's good for Irene's murder."

What's next?

"O'Scanlon's Gym on Third and Yosemite."

Edward Bordey, Sully said. *Smart move.*

Ed Bordey was an old pal of mine from my beat cop days. Ed was a boxer then, now he handled a few boxers as well as promoting bouts all over the western states. If anyone would know a boxer named Bruno, Ed was the man.

O'Scanlon's was an old warehouse that had been converted into a gym over fifteen years ago. A blind man would immediately know it was a gym. The unforgettable smell of old dirty socks hit you as you stepped through the entrance. O'Scanlon had a section of the building renovated and turned into a locker room with showers. Mickey O'Scanlon's office was up a staircase in one corner of the building. On the main floor were workout areas of heavy bags, weights and other various exercise equipment. Two boxing rings were located in the center of the gym floor, each surrounded by a string of benches where trainers and promoters could watch combatants spar. Place was humming with activity, as trainers were getting their charges ready for Friday night's fight card at the Cow Palace. I found Ed instructing a young fighter as he sparred in the ring farthest from the building's main entrance.

"What's the good word, Edward?" I said as I approached the ring.

Bordey was an imposing man of six feet, broad shoulders—long powerful arms. Born in Jamaica, been in the fight game since he turned eighteen. Fought as a heavyweight for eight years before an eye injury prevented him from getting into the ring again. Turned to training other fighters, then promoting his own events.

"Ahhh. . . my old friend James, the Wolf," Ed gushed in his distinctive Jamaican accent. "How are tings in the soft shoe bizz-nez?"

"Gumshoe, Eddy. Gumshoe."

"Move to de left mon!" he called to his boxer. Then he said to me, "I can never figure why you are a mon wid gum on 'de shoe."

I started to say it's not gum on the shoe, it's the soft— then thought better of it.

"Listen, I'm trying to get a line on a guy that was probably a boxer at one time. His name was Bruno. I don't have a last name."

"Bruno? Maybe someone who come here, most everybody does," Ed said to me turning back to the ring. "That's enough for today Rickey. Cool down and hit de shower." Then to me,

"Rickey 'Kid' Cashman. My best boy. I tink maybe we go upstairs and look to see if Bruno has locker here."

I followed Ed up the staircase to O'Scanlon's office. Mickey, pushing sixty, was behind a desk shuffling through receipts, puffing on a cheap cigar.

"Mickey!" I said as we entered.

"Shamus! What you doin' here? Lookin' for a cheatin' wife?" O'Scanlon said laughing.

"Want to look at de locker file, Mick," Ed said as he opened a cabinet set against the wall.

"Who you lookin' for Wolf?"

"Boxer named Bruno."

O'Scanlon shrugged, "Don't recall a Bruno off hand."

Ed sifted through the card file. "I tink this is the mon. "Bruiser" Durkin. Locker 226."

"Yeah! I remember him," O'Scanlon said. "Big dumb lug."

"Let me see," I said, as I took the card from Ed's hand. "1239 Turk Street. Thanks gentlemen," I said as I left the office.

I called the Hall from the pay phone in the gym lobby. Rickman had left for home so I decided to pay a quick visit to find out what he had on the Talbot murder. Rickman lived in an apartment house on the edge of Chinatown, corner of Clay and Mason. I pressed the buzzer to number twelve and a few seconds later I got a buzz back that unlocked the entrance door. I walked up a flight of stairs and tapped on Rickman's door. The door swung open and Rickman greeted me in shirtsleeves holding a sandwich.

"Oh it's you, Wolf," he said dejectedly.

"Expecting anyone?"

"No. Not really. Wanna drink?"

"Bourbon and soda."

"Have a seat. To what do I owe this visit?" he said as he disappeared into the tiny kitchen to fix my drink.

"I wanted to check with you on Shortt's fingerprints. Turn up anything?"

"Nothin'. He's clean. Several traffic citations, that's it." Rickman said as he returned with my drink. "He's not married, but I think he may have been stringing this Irene dame along."

"She could've been playing him."

"That's also a possibility. At any rate, there's nothing we can pin on *him*!"

"What about Dumont?" I said.

"What about Dumont?"

"He may know something," I said taking a sip of my drink

I wanted to keep what I found out from Dumont to myself for the time being.

"I doubt it. Shortt had nothing to do with the killing as far as we can determine. His alibi checked out. So did Dumont's. We've got other information to follow up on."

"Anything you can share, pal?"

"Not for you, *pal*," he said. "So just what was the errand you were supposed to have handled for this Talbot dame?"

"I told you before," I said.

"Tell me again."

"I was to deliver a package to an address. When I got there, whoever I was supposed to meet had gone."

"What was in the package?"

I shrugged. "I don't know. All I had to do was deliver it. You know the rest."

"Where's the package now?" he asked.

"It's safe."

Rickman, getting hot under the collar, snapped back. "I didn't *ask you* if it was *safe* or not, I asked you where it *was!*"

I downed my cocktail, rose from the chair and said, "You'll find out in due time."

"Listen, Wolf!" Rickman barked. "If you're withholding evidence you're gonna get yourself in big trouble and I won't be able to smooth things over with the D.A."

I opened the door and turned to Rickman.

"As soon as I've got something concrete, I'll let you know."

As I shut the door behind me and strolled down the hallway, Rickman let out a litany of expletives regarding my family tree and my country of origin. As I exited the front entrance, I stopped and let out a good laugh.

Chapter 17

The following morning, I sat with a cup of coffee and Danish at Pete's just a couple of blocks from my apartment figuring my next move.

Before returning to my apartment the previous night, I stopped by Durkin's Turk Street address and found no one home. I'd give Bailey's place another shot before trying Schofield's. I finished my breakfast and headed over to Bailey's. It was 7:46 a.m. when I arrived. I rang the buzzer to his flat and didn't get an answer. The box in the lobby, labeled B. SHORTT had a bundle of mail stuffed in it—an indication that Mr. Shortt hadn't been in his apartment for a few days. Drove over to the Golden Gate Realty office. At 8:04 a.m. I arrived at the realty office. Dumont was shuffling papers at his desk when I stepped through the door.

"Good morning," I said.

Dumont looked up. His face registered fake surprise and hidden concern.

"Oh! Mr. Wolf. Good morning."

"Bailey in?"

"As a matter of fact, he is not but I just got off the phone with him. Very strange."

"How's that?"

"I'd barely gotten to my desk when the phone rang. It was Mr. Shortt. He wants me to go to his apartment and pack a suitcase for him."

"Is that so? He's not at his flat?"

"No." Dumont picked up a note from his desk and referred to it. "He wanted me to get the leather suitcase from the bedroom closet and pack it with a change of clothes. Toiletries in a black shaving kit in the bath and bring it to him."

"Where is he now?"

"He said he's at the Victorian Hotel on 4th Street. Room 337."

"Can you get into his apartment?"

"Yes sir. He has a spare key in his desk drawer."

"Okay. Get the key and I'll drive you to Bailey's. I want to look around while you pack. Then I'll deliver the suitcase to Shortt."

I drove Dumont to Bailey's place and while he was packing clothes, I searched the joint for anything that would give me the pieces I needed to complete this nutty puzzle. I found names and phone numbers in a small notebook in a desk drawer. Some of the names had four or five- figure numbers next to them.

I noticed Sully standing by the window.

"Some of these names have lines scratched through them," I said. "Others noted with a star."

Prospect list, I reckon, Sully said.

A folder in another drawer contained printed sheets of vacant properties in the Bay Area, most were distressed.

"This must have something to do with that real estate deal."

"You say something, Mr. Wolf?" Dumont called from the bedroom.

"Talkin' to myself," I said. "You about done?"

"Couple more minutes."

I searched through his closet and every drawer in the place. It became apparent that the odds of me finding that lynchpin clue was about as likely as a three-legged horse winning the Kentucky Derby. Dumont finished packing Bailey's clothes and stepped into the living room. I called the Victorian.

"Victorian Hotel," said a male featureless voice.

"Yes. I'd like to leave a message for the gentleman in room 337."

"Three, three—"

"Seven," I interjected. "Mister. . ."

"Parker?"

"That's correct."

"What's the message?"

"Tell him Mr. Dumont called and I'll be on my way immediately."

"Dumont, you say?"

"Yes, that's correct."

"I'll slip it under his door right away," he said, blandly.

"Thank you," I said and hung up.

I drove Dumont back to the Golden Gate office, then immediately drove to the Victorian Hotel. I knew Bailey had to be scared. The Victorian was one of those old hotels that barely survived the quake in '06. It used to be quite the place back in the old days. The Vic offered rooms that were cheap but comfortable. It was nearly nine o'clock. I tapped on the door of 337. I could hear someone moving toward the door.

The voice behind the door was just above a whisper but I could recognize it was Bailey. "Who is it?" he said.

"James Wolf. Got your suitcase."

There was a moment where Bailey was deciding if he should open the door or not. I heard the lock click—a chain removed. The door slowly opened enough for me to slip through with the suitcase held in front of me. When I was completely in the room, Bailey peeked around the door and eyed the hotel hallway before he closed and locked the door.

"Just what the hell are you doing here?" a very agitated Bailey hissed.

"I'm a delivery man, didn't you know? People call me up all the time to deliver things."

"Cut the comedy act. What do you want?"

I took off my hat and moved to the only chair in the small hotel room. Bailey must've been there for at least two days. The room looked as though he hadn't once ventured into the hallway. Tray of dirty dishes on the dresser contained, at least, last night's dinner as well as this morning's breakfast. Squads of ants were battling over a piece of charred toast with jam, cemented to the chipped plate by a generous amount of egg yolk. I took a seat in the corner chair.

"I need some information and don't try to con me," I said.

"Whadaya wanna know?"

"What was Irene up to?"

"She was trying to help me get out of a jam," he said nervously pacing.

"Sit down, will ya! You're straining my neck."

Bailey sat on the edge of the bed rubbed his knees with the palms of his hands.

"Start from the top," I said. "What's this jam you're in?"

Bailey took a deep breath. "I was trying to put a real estate deal together. There are properties around the Bay Area that are available and for a low price. I was trying to get a block of plots together for an investment deal. It'd be a housing development."

"Sounds reasonable so far."

"I needed cash to option several plots, that way I'd have documents to show investors."

"Then, once the investors gave you their money, you'd skip town and all you were out were the option monies?"

"That's how it started. Then word got out that I had options on these plots. I was getting calls from an investor named Stevenson Grandley. Comes out here from back east, lookin' for land to build a housing development. He wanted in on the deal. I mean legitimately!" Bailey said excitedly. "Liked what I had to offer."

"What were you offerin'?"

"Hefty percentage."

"Lemme guess. You get twenty investors to buy in for a fifty percent share of the deal."

"Something like that," Shortt said.

"Yeah. Something like that. Go on."

"Then I got this call from an architect, who got my number from Grandley. He wanted to discuss his plan with me. After talkin' to the guy, his plans were perfect for the property I'd optioned. I realized that as a legit project, this could be worth millions."

"Okay, let me get this straight. Your sham project turns into a real goldmine. I fail to see how this gets you into a jam."

"That's just it. Grandley wanted to fund the whole project. He heads back east to make the arrangements. I only put a down payment on the thirty-day option, because I thought I'd have this wrapped up in two weeks. Another two weeks go by. No word from Grandley. Next thing I know, I need to come up with the rest or lose the option. I was given twenty-four hours to come up with five G's or the whole deal would fall apart."

"Then what?"

"I took five grand from the company bank account. There were more delays on Grandley's end. Three weeks later I get notified of an audit."

"You needed to put the five-G's back."

"Yeah. I told Irene about it. She told me she knew this Nick Cappello and he could get me the money. I replaced the money I took before we were audited. Before I knew it three months had gone by with nothing happening with the development deal. I couldn't pay Nick back and he was running up the interest. He wanted his money."

"How did Irene know about Cappello?" I said.

"She knew him from back east," she said. "I told Irene I couldn't afford a secretary anymore. I was usin' the money I paid her to hold off Cappello. She took a job with this Mrs. Schofield as a personal assistant. Irene nosed around and discovered Schofield was dealing in stolen goods. I think this Cappello was fencing the stuff."

"You two sure pick some interestin' playmates. Then what?"

"The two of us were out one night and Cappello shows up. He tells Irene if she doesn't want anything bad to happen to me, he has a plan to square my debt." Bailey got up from the edge of the bed and started to pace the small room again. "I didn't know what to do. Nick wanted fifteen grand by then. Wanted it all right away."

"How did Irene fit in?"

"She found out this big shipment was coming in, worth fifteen grand or more. We worked out a deal with Cappello."

"Figures. Cappello wanted to cut out the middleman on this big shipment."

"Yeah. The plan was for Irene to get the lot number of the item. She'd get there before Schofield. Buy the item and give it to Cappello and I'd be square. Somehow the whole thing fell apart."

"Yeah. I'll explain what went wrong to you another time."

"I tried to tell her I could probably get some money from another investor but she said everything was goin' to plan. It'd be all over Friday night."

"Irene tell you what was in this shipment?"

"Two rare statues from some Chinese dynasty. Nine hundred years old, or somethin'. That's what she said. I never thought that I'd get double-crossed by Irene. I don't know what she did with the merchandise. I called her Friday from the restaurant. No answer. I called Saturday and Sunday. Still nothin'."

"You didn't go to her apartment to check on her?" I asked.

"I went over but she wasn't in. No one had seen her since Friday. I was really gettin' worried. Then you and that Lieutenant show up at the office. Tell me she's been murdered."

"What are your plans? Gonna skip town?"

"I have to. Cappello thinks we double-crossed him. He had Irene killed and now he's gonna kill me. I got no choice."

"You've got another choice. Call the police. Tell Rickman the story you told me and have him put you in protective custody."

"But I'll go to jail!" Bailey moaned as he planted himself on the edge of the bed again and dropped his head into his hands.

"You help the D.A. get Cappello and Schofield? I'm sure they'll cut you a sweet deal."

"I don't know."

"If you run, Cappello will eventually catch up with you. You have a better chance now to come clean. Believe me. Police will give you protection."

Bailey rubbed both hands across the top of his head.

"You're gonna regret it one way or another. If Cappello doesn't catch up with you, you're gonna have to live with what he does from this day forward. You have a chance to put a dangerous criminal behind bars for life," I said as I moved toward the door. "I've seen it before. Believe me. A nice old gentleman who lived and worked on my beat had a chance to do the right thing but he didn't. Think about it."

I closed the door behind me.

Sully was in the backseat when I returned to my car.

Shortt is scared, he said.

"He's been threatened. Knows Cappello means business."

Crazy how people look to the police for help, then refuse to cooperate when they've been victimized. You can't make people do what you want them to do.

Sully was right as usual. My beat—North Beach—two years with the department, I knew many of the residents and merchants by their first names. Shared their joys, births, baptisms, confirmations and at funerals shared their sorrows. Summer came that second year and the mood throughout North Beach changed. The merchants seemed to avoid wanting to share the details of their lives. I wasn't concerned at first.

Gamella's Grocery on Filbert had a break-in. No money taken. Store vandalized. Living in the apartment above the store Mr. Gamella heard the commotion in the middle of the night. Before he could make his way down, the perpetrators had left, leaving behind overturned shelves, broken bottles and ripped-open boxes of grocery items strewn across the floor. Police report indicated the possibility of juvenile vandals. Angelo Gamella proved to be uncooperative. Several more North Beach businesses similarly vandalized over the next month. Their owners also uncooperative in the investigation. I started to hear rumors of a gang of young punks working with someone in a protection racket. As much as we tried to put together an investigation, owners were tight-lipped.

As weeks passed things became clearer. A criminal organization had recruited juveniles to carry out the vandalism. Head of the criminal enterprise would then offer the merchant protection. If caught, the youths could claim it a prank. Unlikely they'd serve time in Juvenile Hall for a first offence. One evening everything changed. Mr. Gamella suffered a beating from one of the punks involved in the racket. I stopped by the market when I heard he'd returned from the hospital.

"You gave the detectives a statement, Mr. G?"

"I tell them what I know. I say—this man try 'n steal, I stop him."

"That's all?"

"It is enough. I don't want trouble."

"What about a description? It was a man not a boy?"

"Older, yes. Big fella'."

"Did you get a good look at 'im?"

"Too dark, I think. My eyes. Eyes not so good no more."

I pressed for more information, but Mr. G wasn't talking. Back at the Hall I stopped by Inspector Rickman's office.

"I spoke with Mr. Gamella this afternoon."

"Get anything out of him?" Rickman said.

"Nothin'."

"I'm gonna talk to him. Maybe you should tag along."

Finding Gamella's closed when we arrived, we climbed the stairs in the rear of the building, knocked on the door of the residence. Carmella Gamella, a woman in her fifties answered our knock.

"Hello, Mrs. G," I said.

"Giacomo, it is good to see you. Come in, por favore—please."

I stepped inside the apartment, Rickman behind me. We found ourselves in the kitchen. It was warm, the fragrance of simmering tomato sauce filled the room.

"This is Mrs. Carmella Gamella, Inspector."

"My pleasure, ma'am."

"This is Inspector Rickman," I said.

"So nice to meet you," she said. "Sit. I have nice cup of coffee for you."

"Thank you," he said.

Inspector Rickman and I took seats at the small kitchen table.

"Angelo!" Carmella called. "Giacomo's here."

Angelo entered the kitchen. He had a bandage on his forehead over his right eye. Left cheek was bruised and swollen. His look was one of apprehension.

"Mr. Gamella, this is Inspector Rickman of the police."

"You call me today?"

"That's right sir," Rickman said.

"I tolla you I don't want no trouble. It was nothing."

"But it wasn't nothing sir. You were attacked in your own store. Your wife found you unconscious."

"Angelo! Listen to the officer," Carmella pleaded. "You must tell them everyting!"

"Some kid. . .he—he try to steal something. Nothin' more. It wasn't much."

"It's not about that, sir," Rickman said. "It's about these thugs roaming the streets committing crimes."

"I know," Angelo said. "But it wasn't much. I hurt myself more from fallin' down."

"But what about the next merchant who's attacked? What if they are seriously hurt?"

"He is right, Angelo," Carmella said.

"I don't want no trouble. It's over. I let it go."

"Angelo," I said. "It won't be over if you let them get away with it. They'll keep comin' back for more."

"I don't know," Angelo said.

The conversation went on like this for nearly an hour. After three cups of coffee, Angelo revealed his reluctance to talk.

"This man. He tell me not to talk to police. If I do, he says he comes back. He says he kill me."

"We'll give you police protection," Rickman said.

"How long can you do this protect?"

"As long as it takes to get a conviction. You'll have round the clock protection. Once we put them in jail. . ."

"Angelo! Let them help you, I beg," Carmella said.

"You know who did this to you, don't you Angelo," I said.

Angelo nodded.

"Tell us who," Rickman said.

"They call him Flip. Bonatelli. He runs around with this older man. He's the boss. Lazarri. Bonatelli, he beat me. Lazarri tells me not to talk."

"Who is this Lazarri?" I asked.

"Dominic," Carmella said. "Dominic Lazarri. He comes from New Jersey. Mrs. Ferri? She rent a room to him . . . maybe six months ago. Real trouble maker."

The following morning, Mr. Gamella came into the office, filed a complaint. We arrested Bonatelli and Lazarri that afternoon without incident.

Chapter 18

onatelli and Lazarri made bail. Gamella's had a police officer assigned to their house. Rickman ordered surveillance on the two suspects. Three weeks passed without an incident. Court date was set. The day before trial, Mr. and Mrs. Gamella closed up the store. Had dinner at a neighborhood restaurant. Officer Kent Brand waited outside. After two hours, he became suspicious. We found him waiting in front of the restaurant.

"They disappeared," Brand said. "A waiter told me, they came in and slipped out the back."

Rickman issued a warrant. Interviewed anyone who may have known the Gamella's whereabouts but came up empty. When I returned to the Hall, after canvassing the neighborhood, Rickman called me into his office.

"We're callin' off the search," he said.

"Callin' it off?"

"Lawyers petitioned the judge to drop the charges," Rickman said. "No witness."

"Has he ruled?"

"Less than an hour ago. Already released."

A week later, Angelo turned himself in. The judge admonished him for ignoring the summons. Angelo explained that he received a phone call the day before the trial, Lazzari threatened to kill him. Worried for the safety of his wife, they fled the state. No charges filed against Mr. Gamella.

I kept a close eye on the grocery over the next several months. Lazarri seemed to have disappeared. We received news that Bonatelli had been shot to death by police in a bank robbery attempt in Los Angeles. Later that month Lazarri held up a liquor store in San Jose. Shot and killed the store owner. Seriously wounded a San Jose officer. The store owner was from Angelo's neighborhood. They were close friends. Angelo Gamella was never the same.

I stopped at the first phone booth I spotted on a corner a few blocks from Shortt's hotel. I called my answering service. Had two messages waiting. Doc wanted to meet me at Red's Coffee Shop on the Embarcadero. He'd be calling in again, so I told my service I'd meet him at eleven. The other was from Claire. She wanted me to call her at work. After hanging up with my service I called Brooklyn's and spoke with Claire.

"There's a market on Clement," she said. "Lee's Produce."

"Yeah. I know the place."

"Can you meet me there in twenty?"

"On my way."

When I arrived at Lee's Market a woman in her mid-fifties approached the door with her bag of groceries as I was about to enter. I opened the door for her, gave her a pleasant smile and entered the establishment. I meandered around the canned goods section of the small store for ten minutes or so when Claire came strolling down the aisle. She signaled to me to meet her at the back of the store. I surveyed the area before moving to the rear of the building.

In the corner, next to the butcher counter, was the walk-in cooler where they kept beverages and packaged food items that needed refrigeration. I opened the heavy steel door and the two of us slipped in unnoticed.

"What have you got, angel?" I asked.

"I was able to do some more snooping. I found some notes in the files that were connected to Schofield. I asked one of the accountants if I needed to keep the notes, you know, see if they knew anything about Schofield's business."

"Nice work, kid. You're becoming quite the detective."

"Anyway, one of the gentlemen, Glenn, works with inventory reports. He told me that usually one of them would call Schofield to let him know that a shipment of antiques from this dealer in Spain was in customs. Schofield would then schedule a time to come in and get a look at the merch, then offer top dollar. Brooklyn's thought the deal was great because Schofield would always make a purchase right away."

"I see. He always paid top dollar?"

"Yes. He'd take some of the merchandise right out of the crate. But this last shipment there was a change."

"How?" I said.

"When Eric, he's one of the managers, called Schofield to let him know that the dealer from Spain's crate had arrived early, he talked to someone who said she was Mrs. Schofield. She told Eric that Mr. Schofield wasn't going to be available but she wanted to send someone to come by the next day and make the purchase for her. She had Eric change the lot number on a pair of statues and put them out on the floor," Claire said as she rubbed her arms to warm herself.

"Lot number 1135," I said, shaking my head.

"Bingo!"

"A little risky don't you think? Someone other than me could've purchased those statues."

"If that happened, they could call the office and ask who bought lot 1135. But the pre-auction is only for a small group of special customers so the chance of that was small. Besides we'd have names and addresses of everyone invited to the pre-auction, so. . ." Claire's voice trailed off as she shrugged and rubbed her arms again.

"You better get back, you look like you're freezing. I'll call you later. Good work."

I opened the door and Claire cautiously exited the cooler. I waited thirty seconds before I left and headed to the Embarcadero to meet Doc.

Doc was seated at a table in the back corner of Red's when I arrived, eating a plate of fried eggs and corned beef hash with a Bloody Mary chaser. I tossed my hat on a chair and plopped down across the table. Butch, the morning barkeep, materialized next to me with a steaming cuppa joe.

"Just coffee for me, Butch," I said, as I gave him a fiver. "That should cover Doc's breakfast."

Butch nodded and put the money in his shirt pocket.

"Best corned beef hash in the city, Jimmy. Some of these establishments around this fine city just don't know how to prepare a decent plate of hash. Too many potatoes!"

"Great Doc, I'll tell Herb Caen to put that in next week's column."

"It needs to be cooked on a griddle to get that nice crispy crust on the outside."

"I get it Doc. Now what do you have for me?"

"I got somethin' for you?" Doc said as he sipped his drink.

"You called and left a message. You have something on Cappello for me?"

"Ah yes, Jimmy. Cappello. He came here from Philly a couple of years ago after the—"

"Yeah, after Manzetti was rubbed out by the Parone Gang, you gave me that," I said hastily.

"I did?" he said, a bit perplexed. "Yes, I did, didn't I? Just a few days ago. You are correct, my friend. I found something out that's very interesting," Doc sat back in his chair, pleased with himself. "Cappello has been seen around town with a new bird on his arm."

"Any idea who she is?"

"That I don't know, but I can tell you this with unquestionable certainty. This lady is a rare beauty and most assuredly married."

"Married, huh?"

"She and Nick have been seen in several establishments trying to be extremely discreet. If you know what I mean. Nick likes to make a big show when he's about town. Always gets the ringside table. But with this beauty, it's always a dark corner."

"That's not Nick's style?"

"Not at all. There's something amiss with this lady, that I can tell ya. But get this, from what I've been told, she could pass for Susan Hayward's doppelganger," Doc enunciated the German with a self-satisfied pride.

"Doppel. . . what?"

"Doppelganger, Jimmy. Dead ringer," Doc said as he went back to his corned beef hash.

"Thanks, Doc. This is very helpful. Call if you get anything else."

"Sure will Jimmy."

I rose and left Doc to his breakfast.

I got to my car and pondered for a moment my next move—when Sully interrupted my thoughts from the back seat.

Everything keeps comin' around to Nick Cappello. Sully said.

"Only one way Cappello knew that Irene worked for Schofield. Cappello's callin' the shots."

Something doesn't fit. Sully said.

"Give."

"You're right. There has to be something different about this shipment."

I think it's time you had a little chat with Mr. Schofield. If you ask me, Cappello was told the exact same story. Those statues were worth ten grand or more. He had no idea they were used to transport gems. Someone's tryin' to play 'im for a sucker.

"I'm going to give Mr. Schofield a visit right now," I replied as I started the car.

I drove down the Peninsula to the home in Atherton Hills, one of the new developments that started popping up the last couple of years. Residents of Atherton were well to do and their living arrangements showed it.

The sky was clear and a warm breeze rustled the leaves of tall oaks that lined the quiet street. I approached the entrance. Large red oak double doors with etched glass ovals in their centers gave the impression of entering a cathedral. I gave the doorbell my thumb. From the inside, I heard chimes. It sounded like Big Ben striking the hour. I only rang once, since the sound was so loud it could've woken Henry the Eighth from the dead. I turned and as I was admiring the view of the hills and trees that faced the front of the home, I heard the latch click and the door slowly swing open. Framed in the doorway was a middle-aged Asian man dressed in white jacket, white shirt, black tie and black slacks. He gave me the once over then spoke.

"How can I help you, sir?" he said in perfect English.

"I'd like to see Mr. Schofield."

"Do you have an appointment with Mr. Schofield?"

"No," I said. "I called a coupla days ago and he was out of town." I could hear what sounded like a man talking on the telephone. I couldn't make out what he was saying but he sounded upset.

"I'm sorry, but you will have to call and make an appointment. Mr. Schofield does not see people without prior arrangements. He is a very busy person."

"I have something he may be interested—"

That was as far as I got when he bowed, said "Good day" and closed the door in my face. If that had been some dame or mug who shut the door on me like that, I'd have leaned on the doorbell like a drunk on a lamppost. But politeness prevailed. I felt a sense of respect as I walked back to my car.

Driving back to town I stopped by the Doggie Diner on Van Ness and Golden Gate for a chili dog and coffee. After my brief lunch, I headed to the office and checked my service. No messages left me sidelined for the rest of the day just sitting on my hands. This lull made me feel extremely uncomfortable—like taking your mother to a strip club. I went down the street to the corner smoke shop, bought an afternoon *Examiner* and read the whole thing, even the Macy's women's shoe ads. Gave Claire a call and she agreed to have dinner with me after she finished work. I spent the next few hours fussing with a crossword.

When I couldn't stand sitting in my office any longer, I hit the Mauna Loa for a cocktail. Several fortifiers finally calmed my jitters. I dropped by my apartment to drag a razor over my face and change clothes. I made a reservation at Fior D'Italia and picked Claire up at her place just after six.

It was an evening to remember. The food was superb, best fried calamari in town. Claire was as charming as could be and the conversation flowed with the ease of a canoe drifting along the Suwannee. When she spoke, I got a warm feeling inside like a bowl of soup on a cold day.

Claire reminisced about her time growing up in the Midwest, attending art school at the Minneapolis College of Art. Came to San Francisco about three years ago to study art and was lucky enough to land a well-paying position at Brooklyn's. We were at dinner for nearly two hours, though it seemed a lot less than that. The waiter was pouring another cup of coffee for me when Claire looked up, her eyes focused behind me. I paused for a second then felt the tap on my shoulder. I turned and there, in all his surly glory, stood Lieutenant Rickman.

Chapter 19

"Hello, Lieutenant," I said as I rose from the table. "Claire, this is Lieutenant Rickman of the San Francisco P.D."

"Nice to meet you," Claire said.

"Claire Regis," I said to Rickman.

"It's a pleasure, Miss Regis," Rickman said. He bowed and removed his hat. "Can I see you for a moment? It was nice meeting you, Miss Regis."

"A pleasure, Lieutenant," Claire said while flashing me a curious look.

Rickman turned and walked toward the lobby. I dropped my napkin on the table and gave Claire a shrug.

"Must be important," Claire said as I turned and followed Rickman to the lobby.

"You got a tail on me?" I said as I joined him near the cigarette machine.

"I called your service, they said you would be here. I went to see Shortt today. He wasn't in his office. Then I find you talked to Dumont and he told you Shortt was planning on leaving town. You delivered a suitcase to his hotel. The hotel said he's checked out. Where did he go?"

"That I don't know."

"But you met with him. What is he up to?" Rickman demanded.

"The only thing I can tell you is that he and his girlfriend Irene were involved in a scheme to get money to pay off a loan shark."

"What loan shark?"

"Nick Cappello. Cappello was putting the squeeze on Shortt and Shortt offered to make a deal with him to get his hands on a valuable piece of artwork."

"So that's it. You were hired to get the artwork and deliver it to Shortt?" he asked.

"I'm not sure who I was to deliver it to, but it didn't go off as planned."

"You have the artwork?"

"I do not," I said.

"What do you mean you don't have it?"

Sully stood next to the cigarette machine, pushed his hat back on his head.

Easy, he said. *Don't push.*

"I'm not gonna push," I said.

"Push?" Rickman said. "Push what?"

"Look! I don't have it. It's not in my possession. Follow?"

Rickman was visibly upset.

"You'd better stop jerkin me around, Wolf. If you're concealing evidence in a murder investigation!" he snarled, squeezing the words out between his teeth.

Now you've done it.

"Relax," I said to Sully.

"Don't tell me to *relax!*" Rickman barked.

"I didn't mean. . . Listen Lieutenant. The artwork is not evidence. I purchased it for a client at a legit auction house. Irene Talbot was representing someone I never met."

"Listen you—"

"You're gonna snap your cap in about a minute if you don't calm down. I'll get the item to the rightful owner and then we can all sit down together and sort this thing out. You keep crowding me and I'll never get to unravel this mess. Now you run along, my coffee is getting cold. I have some other business to finish."

Throw him a bone. That'll keep him busy for a while.

I turned and started back to my table. "Good idea," I said.

"Huh?" Rickman said.

I turned back to Rickman.

"Shortt has a sister in Monterey—*if* you're interested," I said. "She may know where Shortt is."

Rickman forcefully positioned his hat firmly on his head and scowled at me.

"How long were you goin' to hold back that information?"

I looked back and gave him a little wave.

"So that's Rickman," Claire said, as I sat back down at the table.

"That's him."

"He seems nice. I thought he might've been one of Brooklyn's customers when he walked over to the table."

"Nice? I guess it depends on what you mean by nice. His disposition is on the sour side and that's when he's in a good mood—wait! He's a Brooklyn customer? Doesn't sound like the Rickman I know."

"I thought I recognized him. I guess he just reminded me of someone who seemed nice," Claire said with a chuckle.

We finished our coffee and I took Claire home. It felt good to hold her in my arms. It'd been a long time and I could tell right away that she was the type of woman who could melt a block of ice from a hundred paces with just a look. Her lips were soft and once you've kissed them, you'll be coming back for more like a hungry guard dog at a meat packing plant.

We said our goodbyes and made plans to see each other again. I planted Claire deep into my mind and it would take some serious excavation to remove her. I started my car and pulled away from the curb, right in front of a Muni Bus, its angry horn brought me back to the present. I looked into the rearview and could see the driver giving me a friendly kind of wave with his middle finger.

That was close, Sully said from the back seat.

"Wasn't paying attention."

If you want to be seeing Claire again you better pay attention. There's still a missing component to this caper. Whatever it is. . . it's dangerous.

It was nearly midnight when I finally dropped into bed. Sully was right, there was a big piece missing. I wondered if maybe I'd overlooked something that would clear up the image.

I was exhausted and tomorrow was another day and another chance to get a crack at Schofield. I set the alarm for eight, pulled the bedcovers up to my neck and went to sleep.

Chapter 20

The alarm clock woke me out of my peaceful slumber as gently as a high school bell announces the start of class. I bolted upright, started swinging in the direction of the noise, knocking the clock off the nightstand onto the floor, where it rolled under the bed. It clanged away until it started to die a slow inevitable death.

Long hot shower finally brought me back into the world of the living and conjured up a hearty appetite. Dressed. I removed the gems from the coffee can. Transferred them into two socks. I knocked on Mrs. Vee's door before I left to get myself some breakfast. I'd put one of the socks containing the jewels in a small cardboard box.

"Wondered if you'd do me a small favor," I said when she opened the door. "Would you mind if I left this with you?"

"I don't see why not," she said.

"I might need to have someone call for it later."

"I'll keep it right here in the closet."

"Thanks so much."

Five minutes later, I was at Joe's on Broadway ordering pancakes, eggs, sausage and a pot of coffee. For some reason, I had a good feeling about the day. It may have been a hunch that I was on the verge of cracking the case or the lingering effects of last night's dinner date with Claire still with me. Either way, I had a feeling, things were about to turn for the better.

After breakfast, I went to the office and checked with my service. Ed Bordey had left a message. He had some information for me. Before heading to O'Scanlon's Gym, I picked up the phone and called Schofield. On the fourth ring, I heard the line engage.

"Schofield residence. Can I help you?" the precise voice on the other end of the line said.

"Yes. I'd like to speak with Mr. Schofield, please."

"Whom shall I say is calling?"

"James Wolf. I called on Mr. Schofield the other day."

"Yes sir. Please hold the line."

I waited about thirty seconds before I heard the sound of someone picking up the receiver.

"This is Mr. Schofield," he said sharply. He had a slight accent. Couldn't quite place it—though the name implied a Teutonic background.

"Mr. Schofield, I was wondering if I could schedule an appointment with you today."

"What's this regarding?"

"Irene Talbot. You see—"

"I barely know the woman," he interrupted. "She was my wife's assistant and is no longer working for her. You'll have to speak with her if you want any references," he said irritably. "I'm a very busy man."

The line went dead before I could respond. I dialed back and was told by the butler that he was instructed to tell me that Mrs. Schofield was not available at this time and I should call back to schedule an appointment with her. I told the butler to have Mrs. Schofield call my service at her earliest convenience.

It was 10:17 a.m. when I entered O'Scanlon's Gym. Ed was in the corner ring with a young Hispanic boxer. Kid was lean and muscular and, from my perspective, quick with his hands like the flap of a hummingbird's wing. Ed was working on a left jab hook combination as I approached the ring. I stood and watched the workout until Ed told his protégé to take a breather.

"Your kid looks good!" I called to Ed.

"Jamie, you got me message," he said in his distinctive accent.

"What have you got for me, my friend?"

Ed stepped under the rope and jumped down to the floor. He grabbed a towel from a folding chair beside the ring and wiped the sweat from his face.

"Dis boy gives me good workout. Keep me in shape ya know."

"I'd hate to get into a tussle with him, you can bet on that. His hands are a blur."

"It is de very truth you are speaking. You want to know about Bruiser Durkin?"

"Yeah! Did you find something?"

"He fights tomorrow night in San Jose on de State Campus. Two-hundred-dollar purse for Heavyweights. I tink you will find his buddy there also. He is his sometimes manager."

"Thanks Ed. I owe ya."

I checked with my service after meeting with Ed. They let me know that Zeke had called. He was released from the hospital and recuperating at home. I drove to Noe Valley where Zeke lived with his wife, Lorna, and their young daughter Kelly. Zeke looked like he had gone over Niagara Falls in an oak wine barrel. Happy, at least, he could stand on his own two feet. Lorna put on a pot of coffee while Zeke and I chatted in the living room.

"How are you feelin' bud?"

"Sore, mostly. Doctor has me strapped up for a fractured rib. Makes it hard to breathe," he said, gingerly rubbing his chest.

"Need anything?" I asked.

"No. We've got everything here," he said. "Steve's got everything under control at the garage. My part-time mechanic Pauley is helpin' out. Happy to get the extra hours."

"Glad to hear it. I wanna ask if you can think of anything else you may remember about that night. Somethin' that one of the guys said, or did?"

"Well, I do remember the little guy did most of the talking. The big guy just repeated what the little guy said. He sounded like a big dumb ox," Zeke noted.

"That actually makes sense. Anything else stand out?"

"I'd just parked the car when the big guy grabs me, yanks me out and pins me against the fender. His arm around my neck chokin' me so I couldn't talk. Little guy searched the car and then asked me where the package was. The big guy lets me loose but when I tried to tell 'im they had the wrong guy. I got slugged on the back of my neck. Big goon started to work me over again. Hit me in the ribs. Think he used brass knuckles. I got hit in the head. Then everything went black."

"Did either of the thugs call each other by name?

"Nah. Whole thing lasted a minute. I remember that the big guy had a tattoo on his wrist."

"Tattoo?"

"Yeah. Knife or dagger. Black with red handle."

We talked for a bit more, had some coffee. Zeke couldn't come up with anything else that was useful. Before leaving Zeke's place, I called Doc but he wasn't home. I left Zeke's and started a tour of Doc's favorite watering holes. After an hour of touring the dives around town I found him at Tommy's Joynt on Van Ness at the jukebox singing *Faraway Places* along with Bing Crosby. He was entertaining a couple of bleach-blonde dipso duchesses who were trying to polish off Tommy's entire supply of Johnny Walker. When I approached Doc, he stopped singing and held up his glass to salute my presence.

"Jimmy!" he yelled. "Come join me in a little rendition of faraway places."

"Maybe another time Doc, I need to talk to you for a minute."

"I want you to meet a couple of new friends of mine," he bellowed.

Doc swung his arm around one of the women and said, "This is Alma and over here, Hazel."

"Ladies," I said, as I tipped my hat. "Listen Doc I need to talk—"

"This is my good friend, James Wolf," Doc proclaimed.

"Nice knowing ya," the woman introduced as Alma said.

The one called Hazel just nodded and let out a belch. Classy.

"Yeah, it's been nice. Listen Doc—"

"Jimmy and I go way back. We've had some good times, haven't we Jimmy?"

"Great times. Doc, listen to me, will ya? I need to talk to ya!"

"If you ladies will excuse us. James and I have some business to discuss," Doc announced, as he put a forefinger to the side of his nose.

"Sure! Take all the time you need. We're not goin' anywheres, right Hazel?" Alma said as she elbowed Hazel in the ribs.

"What!" Hazel squawked.

"We're not goin' anywheres for a while I said."

"Yeah," Hazel replied, as I took Doc by the arm and led him away.

We made our way to the other end of the bar and slid into a booth. Denny the bartender swung by and dropped coasters on the table.

"How's things, Denny?" I asked.

"Not bad. What'll ya have?"

"Can I get a ham on rye and a beer? And fix Doc again."

He nodded, turned and headed to the kitchen.

"That Alma is a real animal, Jimmy."

"You better call a vet. Make sure she's had her shots."

"Yes, that would be prudent on my part. So, what can I do for you?"

"I need you to do some snooping around. I found out that this Bruno is scheduled for a prelim bout tomorrow at the San Jose State campus. What I need you to do is try and get a line on this Schofield character. I feel he's connected in all this, but I'm not having any luck. I can't even get him to meet with me. You got friends at the paper, right?"

"That I do. You want me to get some background on this Schofield?"

"Anything you can dig up on him," I said. I reached into my pocket and pulled out some cash. I selected two ten spots and set them on the table. "That's for you. If you have to grease any wheels, let me know and I'll cover it."

Denny returned to the table with our drinks and my sandwich.

"I'm heading to San Jose after I've eaten. Anything you come up with, leave a message with my service. I'll be checking in regular."

"You goin' alone?" Doc asked.

"I'm ready for trouble. They won't get the jump on me this time."

"Hey Doc!" Alma called. "How 'bout another song?"

"Not to worry Jimmy, I'm on the case. Right after I finish my drink."

Doc returned to entertaining the ladies as I finished my lunch. I checked in with Claire to let her know I'd be in San Jose for the evening and she should call my service if need be.

It was 5:10 p.m. when I arrived at the gym on campus. Workers were still setting up for the fights. My inquiries led me to the athletic training facility where the boxers were working out. I asked around but no one had seen Bruno that day.

A short stocky trainer, balder than a cue ball, instructed a young pimple-faced boxer through a sparring session.

"Yer droppin' yer left, droppin' yer left. Get it up. Up I said!"

"Your boy looks good," I said, my standard boxing ring ice-breaker.

"Looks ain't everything," he said. "KEEP… YER…LEFT…UP, DAMMIT!" he yelled.

"You know where I can find Bruiser Durkin?"

"Never listens," the trainer said shaking his head.

"Bruiser Durkin," I said.

"Whatchya wanna know?"

"Is he around?"

"Probably find him at the Union Hotel on the corner of San Carlos and Market Street."

"Manny too?"

"His big-time manager?" he said, glancing over his shoulder at me. "Yeah, that jamoke is probably there. Keep that left up kid or yer gonna' git your head handed to ya!"

I headed over to the hotel. Asked at the front desk for Bruno's room and the clerk informed me that both Bruno and his manager were not in. I grabbed the late edition of the Mercury and made my way to the hotel bar just off to the left of the hotel lobby. Took a seat at one of the tables that gave me a clear view of the reception desk across the lobby. I ordered myself a bourbon and soda. Perused the newspaper while keeping a close eye on the reception desk. I was on my second cocktail, nearly through reading the paper when I saw a short stocky man approach the reception desk. He fit Manny Strupp's description. The clerk gave him his room key and they spoke for a moment. Manny nodded to the clerk then turned to the right and headed for the front exit. I put down the paper and started to rise from my chair when Manny returned and started for the hotel bar. As Manny entered the threshold, the room suddenly became dark. Like someone turned off all the lights in the joint. As I took my eyes off Manny, I realized that I was in an enormous shadow. I turned to look over my shoulder and five steps behind my chair stood Bruno Durkin, all six feet six inches tall and four feet wide of him. His hands, large enough to be used for snow shovels, hung loosely at his side. As I rose, Bruno was a foot behind me as Manny reached the table. Bruno placed his right paw on my shoulder. The sheer weight caused me to collapse back into my seat.

"Relax, pilgrim," Manny said in a distinct Midwest accent as he flopped down into the chair across from me. "Wanted to see me about somethin'?"

A pair of beady dead eyes was Manny's dominant feature. The kind of guy you wouldn't trust as far as you could throw the Queen Mary. The kind of guy that would pick your pocket while you were dropping spare change into a Salvation Army Christmas kettle. One cheap crook.

"Yeah. I wanted to get a little information from you. If you don't mind?"

I gave him a toothy smile. He sat back all comfortable like, picking at his fingernails.

"Depends on what kind of information yer lookin' fer."

"I'd like to get a hold of Nick 'The Hat'."

"What makes you think I can get you connected with Nick?"

"Word on the street says you sorta work for Nick. From time to time, anyway."

"Could be."

I tried to lean forward, but Bruno's bear paw held me back.

"Is there somewhere we can talk privately?" I said. "The parking lot is right out that door," I said pointing with a thumb in the direction Bruno had gotten the drop on me.

"Sure. Let him up Bruiser," Manny said as he rose from the chair.

"O-ka-kay, Mmmm-Manny," Bruno stuttered, his vocal tone was that of a man who had taken too many blows to the head.

I led the way to the parking lot. We crossed to the opposite side of the lot. Found a cozy spot to talk between my car and the hotel station wagon. Slid my right hand under my jacket for a cigarette, but before I could pull my arm out Bruno had clamped down on it with one of his big hands. My arm felt like it was stuck in a vice. Bruno was screwing it down tighter and tighter.

"I'm just getting a smoke, buddy! Ease off!" I grunted as I tried to pry Bruno's hand off my arm with my right hand. It was like trying to open a steel bear trap.

"Ya-ya-ya try fa-fa-funny stuff and I bu-bu-break your arm," Bruno said.

"Take it easy, Bruiser," Manny said, clearly enjoying my discomfort.

Bruno extracted my arm from under my jacket. In my hand was a slightly crushed pack of smokes. Bruno finally loosened his grip and I snatched my arm away from him. I flexed my fingers several times trying to get the feeling back into my hand.

Irritated, I said. "Mind if I light up?"

"Go ahead. Just don't make any sudden moves. Bruno gets excited easily."

"Yeah, I ga-ga-ga-get excited," Bruno said with a weird chuckle he followed with a stupid-looking grin.

"Whadaya wanna see Nick for? I need more information, ya know. Nick is a private kind of guy."

"I think I got something that Nick wants," I said as I took a drag.

"What is it?"

"I'd rather talk to Nick."

"Listen bub. You're dealing with me right now," Manny snapped. "You got somethin' goin' for ya, you tell me what it is. I'll decide if it's worth talkin' to Nick! Follow?"

Manny had gotten a little too big for his belt loops lately. Getting him to cooperate was going to be about as easy as dancing Swan Lake in snowshoes. I was going to have to take some chances.

"I'm gonna level with you guys. I'm James Wolf."

Bruno's mouth dropped. A shocked look covered his giant face. His lips started to move up and down, but no sound came out of his mouth. Wheels were turning, but the hamsters were dead.

"You can't be," Manny exclaimed. "I never seen ya—"

"Listen, I didn't get a line on you two clowns out of the blue. Nick hired you to pick up a package from *me!*" I said, jamming my thumb against my chest. "There was a mix-up and you two idiots beat up my mechanic."

"What mechanic?"

"The mechanic that was driving my car. You saw my car pull up to my address and thought the guy driving. . . was *me!*"

"Listen, bud. I don't know what yer talking about," Manny snapped.

Manny must've donated his brain to science before he was done with it. He was having a lot of trouble trying to put two and two together. I had my opportunity to execute the coup de grace.

"You drove your Aunt's car to my apartment," I said.

"What Aunt?"

"Christ almighty are you really that dumb?"

There was a village somewhere short of an idiot.

"Aunt Agnes. A witness got a partial license number and I tracked down the car to your Aunt's place."

"Jesus!" Manny exclaimed.

"Aunt Agnes know you're usin' her car to commit crimes?" I said.

"Ha-ha-how heeee know 'bout this Mmmm-Manny?"

"Shut up Bruiser," Manny said.

"I see things Bruiser. You two thought you were double-crossed when you didn't find the package at my place. You went to see Irene and she had no idea what was goin' on. I can imagine things got a little out of hand."

"It was ahh-ah-accident. She tried to ssssss-scream and I needed to stop her," Bruno pleaded.

"Shut up!" Manny snarled.

"It didn't take much to stop the little lady with bear paws like yours," I said.

Bruno kind of rocked from side to side and stared down at his shoes, like a five-year-old who'd just got caught pinching a cookie.

"Now I'm mixed up in this mess and I wanna get out of it," I said.

"Knew that Irene was trouble! Stupid broad."

"So, here's the deal. I've got what Nick wants and I will give it to him personally. You set it up or tell me how to get in touch so I can set up a meet and no more bullshit!" I took a card from my pocket. Shoved it in Manny's jacket pocket. "You can reach me at this number."

"I'll talk to Nick right away," Manny replied.

"Good. Tell 'im I'll meet him any evening. His favorite spot. Julie's Supper Club."

"I'll tell 'im," Manny said.

"Oh, and by the way, this is for sapping me when you searched my place," I said, as I slammed my fist in Manny's jaw sending him to the asphalt like a sack of cement.

Manny sat up rubbing his jaw. "I never sapped you, shamus!" Manny cried.

"I figured, but you don't think I would smack Bruiser here for sapping me."

"Ahhh. Bu-bu-but I never sss-sapped you neither. Na-na-never in your apartment."

"You two didn't ransack my joint?"

"Na-na-no. I ne-ne-never sapped no-no-nobody. Never!"

"Really?" I asked.

Manny nodded.

"Well, I guess you owe me one, Manny," I said as I got into my car.

I started the car. Turned to Bruno.

"Good luck tomorrow, Bruiser. Remember, keep that left up."

"Yeeeeah!" he said, bringing his cocked left arm up protecting his face. "I…I…I'll reee-ree-member."

I waved. Pulled out of the parking space and drove out into the street. Pointing the car north, I headed out of San Jose.

That was interesting, Sully commented from the back seat.

"You remember that guy. . . That snitch, what was his name. . . Wendell something?"

Wendell Rankin.

"Yeah, Wendell Rankin. He had his brains scrambled like Bruno. He was so dumb he thought the English Channel was a radio station. There's one thing about people whose brains are that scrambled. They're too dumb to lie."

Looks like another piece just got added to the puzzle. If it wasn't those two jokers, who cracked you on the head?

"I guess I still owe someone a fat lip."

It was late when I returned to the city. I stopped by John's Grill for a bite to eat. After a trio of gin and tonics, pork chops, and a salad I called my service, hoping Doc could come up with something on Schofield. No messages.

Chapter 21

Had breakfast at Tony's in the morning and headed over to my office immediately after. Read the morning papers then scratched out what I'd learned over the last few days to try to get a clearer picture of the case. Schofield was still an important key, but the lock this key fit was nowhere in sight. I was in my office for nearly an hour when the phone rang.

"Wolf speaking."

"It's Manny, shamus."

"Hello Manny," I said, unable to hide a tinge of excitement. "Got somethin' for me?"

"I talked to Nick. He's very anxious to talk with ya."

"I feel the same. What's the skinny?"

"He'll be at Julie's. Tonight, nine o'clock. He'll meetcha there."

"I'll be there," I said and the phone went dead.

A few minutes later, I got a call from my service. Doc wanted to meet me at the Boondocks on the Embarcadero at noon. Things were moving fast, like a dime-a-dance girl on a busy Friday night. I pressed the receiver down to get a dial tone and called Claire. The line rang twice.

"Brooklyn's, can I help you?" said the low plodding voice of Lester Pitts.

"Lester! It's James Wolf. Can I speak to Claire please?"

"Certainly. By the way, police were here. They had several questions regarding the purchase you made. I recounted the scenario as I remembered it."

"Is that right?" I said.

"Yes. They were very interested in getting an accurate description of the items. They took a carbon of the delivery receipt that contained all the details."

"I see. Did they ask for anything else?"

Lester paused for a moment, making an hmmmmm sound then said: "No. Can't say that they did. Once they had the delivery invoice, they seemed happy. They didn't inquire as to the value or the purchase price."

"Who were the two officers?" I asked.

"A Lieutenant Rickman and a Sergeant. . ."

"McNabb?"

"Yes, that's the name. Hold the line. I'll get Miss Regis for you."

Less than a minute went by before Claire was on the line.

"Hello James," she said.

"Hey, sugar. Listen, you got something nice to wear tonight?"

"I'm sure I do. Why?"

"I'm making reservations for Julie's Supper Club."

"Julie's!" She exclaimed. "What's the occasion?"

"Gotta meetin' about the statues. I'm getting close to solving this crazy case."

"We had a little get-together for the owner's birthday there last month. I know just what I want to wear. I hope you like to dance?"

"I can hold my own. Pick you up at seven."

"I'll be ready," Claire purred.

I stepped into the Boondocks. Odor of low tide greeted me immediately. The Boondocks is a little shack that stands on stilts over the bay next to Pier 28. It doesn't matter if the charts indicate low or high tide. Place has been around long enough that the low tide stench has permeated the pilings that hold up the place. Your typical dive. Sleazy little joint where no one will bother you if you pass out in the corner or conduct an illegal transaction in one of the booths. It's owned by Max Keller, an old bootlegger. He's the kind of guy that'd give you the time of day if you're willing to pay for the information. Max knows how to turn a profit. Whiskey is cut more times than a chin at a barber school. Drinks are nice and cheap so no one puts up a stink.

Doc waved to me from a table in the back along the windows that overlooked the bay. I pushed my way through a group of sailors crowded around two beefy longshoremen arm-wrestling at the bar. A cheer erupted as I approached Doc's table.

"What have you got for me, Doc?" I asked as I slid into a chair.

"Plenty. It was indeed a rewarding excursion. I have some very valuable information."

"Don't worry Doc. If it's what yer claiming, you know I'll take care of you," I said.

"So I checked with the county clerk. Schofield purchased his home just four years ago. According to tax records, he's behind on his taxes. The property is subject to a tax lien. He has an import-export license, but I couldn't find out much about the actual business."

"What else?"

"I *was* able to find out through county records that Schofield moved here from Cleveland. Purchased some property in Walnut Creek. I had my friend at the Examiner contact a guy he knows at the Plain Dealer. Schofield was born in Akron in 1922 and went to high school there, then moved to Cleveland. He worked for Steiner and Sons, a fabric manufacturer, as a salesman. Couldn't get any information as to where he served during the war, which I thought was unusual," Doc noted and then finished the drink he had in front of him. I signaled to Max for two more. "We were stymied indeed."

"Trail went cold?"

"It looked that way, but then I decided to take a chance and call his former employer. It seems that Schofield was in an auto accident in 1940," Doc said, giving Max a nod as we got our drinks. "Schofield left that company the following year, moved west. They think it was California, but didn't know where. The injury damaged his right leg enough to where he had to use a cane. They told me that they believed Schofield has no living relatives still in Cleveland."

"Lotta empty space to fill in there."

"Ronny Davis, that's my friend at the Examiner, said he would put out some calls. Maybe he could come up with more information on Schofield. I told him to call me here if he has any information."

"Hey Doc!" Max called from the bar. "Phone call for you."

"Must be Ronny."

Doc left to take the call. I sat back in my seat and lit a smoke. The fog that had hung around the bay for most of the morning was now in the east bay, hugging the top of the Oakland hills. It was pretty in a depressing way. Doc quickly returned to the table.

"That does it, Jimmy. Schofield's a phony."

"What?!"

"Adrian Schofield sold the property, moved to Scottsdale. Doctors recommended a dry climate. Died a year later. Complications from pneumonia, apparently."

"So who's the guy I talked to on the phone?"

I sat back and took a long drag on my cig.

"Whoever the joker is, he must've known this Schofield. Nicked his identity. He gets a clean slate. It's a perfect setup, Jimmy."

"Thanks, Doc," I said. I fished a couple of twenties out of my pocket. "That's all I can throw you right now—"

"Don't concern yourself," Doc said, as he threw open his arms. "I hit a long shot yesterday at Bay Meadows. I'm flush."

"See ya, Doc."

After my meeting with Doc, I called my service.

"Wolf investigations?"

"It's James, honey. Any messages?"

"A Mrs. Barski called. "

"Barski?"

"Yes. She said it was extremely important that you contact her immediately."

"Did she say what it was about?"

"It has something to do with an Irene Talbot. She's at the Broadway Hotel on Van Ness."

"Thanks, doll."

I called the Broadway. Asked for Mrs. Barski.

The line rang twice. A woman, in a tone of extreme distress answered and said, "Mr. Wolf?!"

"Yes, I got your—"

"I'm so glad you called, I'm just about at my wit's end."

"Take it easy, Mrs. Barski and just tell me what's going on."

"It's about my brother, Bailey Shortt."

"You're his sister?"

"Yes. Helen Shortt, Barski now. I talked to my brother a couple of days ago and I tried to get in touch with him yesterday at his hotel and he's checked out."

"I heard."

"I drove up from Monterey to see him. I know he's in trouble. Do you know where he is, I'm very worried," she said almost in tears.

"I don't know where he is, but I can try to find out. How did you happen to call me?"

"When the hotel told me the man in 337 had checked out I got very worried and called Thomas Dumont at the realty office. He gave me your number. I just knew there'd be trouble once he got involved with that Irene girl. She's no good, Mr. Wolf."

"Listen. I'm in a phone booth right now. Let me come to your hotel and you can tell me all about it."

She let out a sigh and said, "Thank you, thank you. I'm in room 410."

"I'll be there in thirty minutes."

"Thank you so much, Mr. Wolf, I'm just frantic over this, I—"

"Try to relax. I'll be by as soon as I can."

I got into my car and started for my place. As I turned up Second Street, I looked in the rearview mirror and noticed Sully sitting smugly in the back seat.

"So, what do you think? This Adrian Schofield turns out to be a phony," I said.

Could be Nick tried pullin' a fast one on ole Adrian. He gets Irene to con you into doin' the dirty work.

"She and Bailey gave themselves an alibi in case anything went wrong. I'd be left looking like a real fat head, trying to explain who Elizabeth Westrom is."

I swung by my apartment and picked up the box containing the figurines then headed over to the Southern Pacific Terminal building where I checked the box into baggage claim. I slipped the claim check into my billfold.

What's next? Sully said.

"Now that I know all the players, it's time to turn up the heat. But first I need to have a talk with Mrs. Barski."

I drove over to the Broadway Hotel.

I tapped my knuckle on the door of room 410. Female voice on the other side said, "Yes?"

"James Wolf, Mrs. Barski."

The door lock clicked and Helen Barski, an attractive woman around 30 years of age opened the door.

"Please come in," she said. "Thank you so much for seeing me."

"You're very welcome."

"Please have a seat."

"Thank you."

At the far end of the room was a writing desk with two straight-back chairs. I took a seat in one of them, tossing my hat on the desk. Helen paced the floor worriedly wringing her hands.

"I can't tell you how upset I am right now," she began. "Bailey has never done anything like this before."

"Can you give me some background, if you don't mind?" I asked as I took a small notebook from my jacket pocket.

"My brother was made manager of the real estate office a couple of years ago. Somewhere along the line, he met this Irene girl and he hires her as a secretary, receptionist, someone to keep track of phone calls and appointments."

"Do you know where he met her?"

"I don't know, only that it was a casual meeting, at some party I think."

"I see."

"Before long she's filling his head with all these ideas about housing developments. Bailey was doing just fine with individuals wanting to sell or buy a house. He let that fall by the wayside to get into these big deals he said he was working on. His sales started to drop."

"Do you know what kind of deals he was working on?"

"No. At one point Bailey wanted to borrow money to put down on an option I believe he called it. We didn't have that kind of money, Mr. Wolf, but Bailey was desperate. I will tell you this. That Irene girl is no good. When Bailey was explaining what they were doing, it sounded. . . I don't know. I could tell he was being evasive. I warned him not to trust her," she said as she sat in the chair across from me. "Then I read about the murder. Bailey told me not to worry, but how could I do that?"

"Did your brother tell you anything about Irene, other than how they met?"

"Not that I can recall. I think he said she came from Seattle. Her and another girl—Rosemary was her name."

"Anything else you can remember?"

"No, I'm sorry. Bailey promised everything would work out. Told me he could be reached at the hotel. He hung up before I could ask him why he checked into a hotel. Something wasn't right. I could feel it. Then I tried to reach him. They told he'd checked out."

"Listen. Try not to worry," I said. "I'll see what I can do."

"Oh! I do remember one other thing. Bailey met this Rosemary once. She worked at the Cadillac Club," she said as she opened her purse. "He would go there often. I have some money with me—"

"That won't be necessary Mrs. Barski, I'm already working on this case. I'll be in touch."

I got change for a dollar from the desk clerk jumped into the phone booth in the hotel lobby and called my service. Doc had left a message. He was at the Boondocks. I dialed the number.

"Boondocks!" the baritone voice said on the other end of the line.

"Max. It's Wolf. Doc still there?"

"Yeah, I'll get him. Hey Doc, phone for you. Wolf!" Max yelled.

A moment later I heard Doc's voice on the line.

"Hello, Jimmy. I forgot to tell you. I ran into a bookie friend of mine at the track. I got a line on Cappello's redhead."

"Spill it."

"Miriam LaSalla's her name. Rico Manzetti's ex. She used to be blonde but even with her red hair my bookie friend recognized her. She doesn't go by Miriam anymore. There's talk that Miriam fingered Manzetti. I guess he slapped her around once too many."

"Well, well. So, Nick is runnin' around with Manzetti's ex."

"What's goin' on with Cappello?" Doc asked.

"I got word to him. Meeting him at Julie's tonight."

"Be careful, Jimmy," Doc said gravely.

"I will Doc. Listen. I need you to check on a Rosemary. She worked at the Cadillac. I don't have a last name but see what you can dig up."

"Fine establishment. They don't water down their drinks. Check with you later."

Sully poked his face into the booth.

You look like you've come up with a plan.

"If the Schofields knew I needed money, that's why they hired me. That's my angle. Money!" I dialed the Schofield's number.

"Schofield residence," said the precise voice of the Schofield butler.

"This is Mr. Wolf. I'd like to speak with Mr. Schofield please."

"Mr. Schofield is not in the residence at this time. Would you like to leave a message?"

"Is Mrs. Schofield in?"

"She is, but she is not taking calls."

"Tell her that Mr. Wolf called. I'm in possession of some merchandise of hers. Very expensive merchandise," I said.

"You have merchandise of hers. Yes. Anything else?" the butler replied.

"Very expensive merchandise."

"Yes sir. Very expensive. And the number."

"Henderson 4, 3267."

"I will give her the message, sir."

I dropped into Tommy's Joynt for a bite to eat. Called my service to reach me there if I had any calls. I ordered myself a roast turkey sandwich and a beer. Some twenty minutes later, Rubin, the busboy came to my table.

"You gotta call, Mr. Wolf. From your service."

"Thanks, Rubin."

I finished the last of my beer and went to the phone.

"Yeah, doll."

"Doc called. You can reach him at the lab."

"Thanks. Any call from a Mrs. Schofield?"

"No. Sorry."

I dialed Doc's number.

"What have you got for me, Doc?" I said when he answered.

"Rosemary still works at the Cadillac. Her last name is Temple. I was able to get her phone number and address. She lives in an apartment. 1105 Fell. Broadmoor 4-3879."

"Good work, Doc."

"Anytime, my friend."

I parked a block away from the apartment building. Air was damp and cool as the fog started rolling in. Traffic was light. Two girls were roller skating along the sidewalk on the other side of the street. I walked up the steps. Found Rosemary Temple's apartment number on the bank of mailboxes in the lobby. She was on the third floor, number 311. I entered and climbed the stairs to the third floor. Her apartment was directly across from the stairs landing. I could hear the faint sound of a radio playing as I rapped on the door. The faint sound of footsteps crossing a hardwood floor grew louder as I waited.

"You're early!" A female voice said as the door swung open. "Oh!" she exclaimed when she saw me.

She leaned against the door and gave a smile so warm it would've melted the iceberg that sank the Titanic.

Chapter 22

H ellooo!" she said.

Her voice suddenly had a smokey quality to it. I'd listen to her recite from the Yellow Pages any day of the week.

"My name's Wolf, Miss Temple," I said, removing my hat. "I'm a private detective. Can I have a word with you?"

She stepped back and opened the door wide. "Come in. I hope you have more than one word for me," she said coyly.

I stepped into the small apartment. It was neat but still looked lived in. She motioned me into the living room area. There was a gold and black striped couch in the middle of the room. End tables held lamps on either side, a glass coffee table in front. An armchair faced the couch in the corner of the room.

"Have a seat. Tell me. What goes in front of the Wolf?"

"James," I said as I crossed the room and sat in the armchair.

"James. I like that. You're tall. I like that too."

She closed the door and moved to the radio that had a home on the table against the wall. She switched it off. I watched her closely. She was tall and slim. When she walked, she swayed. The sway was rhythmic. It reminded me of a cobra, hypnotized by an Indian snake charmer. She had on a silk robe with nothing much underneath. The window was open and the breeze made the robe cling to her body as she crossed the room. She delicately placed herself on the couch.

She patted the cushion beside her and said, "I want you right here James, where I can get a good look at you."

"You nearsighted or somethin'?"

"Something like that. And it's Rose," she patted the cushion again. "Come sit by me."

I got up from the chair without thinking and moved to the couch. She was the kind of woman that if she wanted you to give her a hand, you'd offer your whole arm right up to the shoulder without a question. I sat down. She reached over and patted my knee.

"Now isn't that much better?" she said, flashing that ice-melting smile.

Her hair was a light brown, almost approaching red. It just kind of flowed randomly all over and across her forehead. If you looked hard you could find her eyes. I gave up at her lips.

"I understand you were friends with Irene Talbot."

She leaned forward and opened a silver box on the coffee table. Nominated a cigarette. Slid the box toward me with her perfectly manicured hand and sparked the matching lighter and lit her smoke.

"You come here to see me and you're asking me about another woman?" she said as she blew out smoke, leaned back into the corner of the couch.

Her robe slipped open a bit revealing the thinly laced undergarment that exposed every delicious curve of her body. I reached into the cigarette box. Removed a smoke. The box was solid silver as was the lighter. Furniture and accessories in the apartment were all expensive. I wouldn't be surprised if I ended up contributing to the collection before this little encounter was concluded.

"You know Rose—I like to take care of business before moving on to other things."

"You're cute. You have a certain charm. I like that."

"Yeah, I tend to get like that from time to time. Have you heard from Irene recently?" I said turning the conversation back to the subject at hand.

I noticed her eyes were green as they gave me a meticulous going-over. She drew on her cigarette and blew smoke out of the side of her generous mouth.

"Irene, Irene. What is all this interest in Irene?" her tone betrayed a tinge of frustration.

"It's kind of important. Have you seen her or talked with her in a while?"

"Haven't talked to her in a couple of months," she said as she smoothed her robe with her free hand.

"You knew her when you were living in Seattle, isn't that correct?"

"That's true. We were pretty good friends."

"How did you two come to decide to move to San Francisco?"

"We worked at the Diamond Club together, a real dump. One night Irene got herself into some trouble with the law."

"What kind of trouble?" I said finally getting somewhere.

"This yahoo from Nebraska or Iowa, somewhere in the Midwest comes into the club on a Friday night acting like a big wheel. Flashing a wad of lettuce that would choke a hippo. He's on Irene like flies on a horse. Gets himself good and liquored up, then gets all handsy. She gives him the brush-off and the next thing you know he's telling the manager that Irene lifted his wallet."

"Did she?"

Rose shrugged and said, "I don't know. She said she didn't—but the rube called the cops and Irene had to spend the night in the joint."

"What happened next?"

"They found the wallet stuck in the cushions."

"The money?"

"All there."

"Any charges filed?"

"No. The whole thing was dropped," she said leaning forward and taping ash into the crystal ashtray on the table. Revealing once again her delectable curves. "The rube was all apologetic. Wanted to make things right, he said. Gave her a hundred to smooth things over. Guess he was worried Irene would sue."

"Was she fired?"

"Nah. The club kept her on. She generated a lot of business, if you know what I'm sayin'. But after that, she was determined to leave town," Rose said as she took a drag on her cigarette. "I was looking to find something else too. One day we decided that the two of us should venture out together."

"Two of you decided to move to San Francisco?"

"Yeah. We got an apartment together for a while. I got a job at the Cadillac. Irene got a job house cleaning for a while. Then she got a job as a receptionist for an insurance company. They liked the way she gave the place a little class. She could do that without even trying."

"How long did she work for the insurance company?"

"Six months or more. This one night she comes into the Cadillac. I was giving this guy the once-over when he gets the eye for her. Bailey was his name. They started seeing each other after that."

"You two had a falling out because of this Bailey guy?"

"Nah, that wasn't it. I didn't care about him."

"What happened then?"

"Irene had some big ideas that I wasn't interested in," she said leaning forward tapping ashes into the ashtray. "She was always looking for the big score. I'm okay with gentlemen wanting to give me gifts, but she was looking for a deal that would put her on easy street. Wanted to get her own place."

"I see. When was the last time you saw her?"

"Like I said, coupla months ago. I'd run into her downtown. She tells me that her and Bailey were about to strike it rich."

"And you haven't heard from her since?"

She shook her head and said, "What's this all about anyway? I've told you too much already. Why do you wanna know so much about Irene? She in some kind of trouble?"

I took a drag, braced myself.

"Irene was murdered."

"*What!*" Rose cried. "Murdered?"

"I'm afraid so."

"I told her that something bad was gonna happen if she wasn't careful, gettin' involved with no good gorillas," she shook her head in disgust. "Always taking chances. Was it Bailey?" she probed. Her voice contained a suggestion of ire as she looked me straight in the eye.

"No it wasn't. Sorry I had to be the one to tell."

"Irene could never seem to get an even break," Rose admitted solemnly.

"One last question. She'd stopped working for Bailey and got a job with an art dealer. Did she ever mention that to you?"

"No. She only told me about Bailey. An art dealer?" she said.

"Yeah. She worked as a personal secretary."

"That sounds like her. She could do almost anything, really smart girl. Too smart for her own good sometimes."

"Is that so?"

"I don't like to talk out of school, but when I spoke to her, she told me that she had finally convinced Bailey to show some moxie. Irene figured that they could put together a land speculation deal she called it. Using the company's money to buy options. She was all excited about how they were getting investors to put up cash to get in on it. She said it was easy money. Sounded fishy to me and I told her to be careful."

"Did she say who these investors were?" Rose shook her head. "She never said who else was involved with this land deal?"

"No. Can't help ya there."

"Well you've been a great help," I said as I stood up. "Believe me, the person who did this won't get away with it."

"Poor girl," she said, shaking her head.

Rosemary got up from the couch and strolled to the door. She turned to me as she twisted the doorknob and said, "Now that you know where I live, don't be a stranger."

Her tone was enticing and had a silky quality that made you want to forget all your future plans. I walked right into the web she'd just spun in the short time she had to escort me to the door.

"I work nights but have a lot of free time during the day," she said as she leaned with her back against the door letting that silk robe slip open a few more inches.

I swallowed and replied with what sounded like, "I'll remember that." Or something close to that—I don't really remember clearly. She was good, very good. I was thrown off my game all right. I took a breath, set my hat on my head and moved to the door. She held out her hand.

"It was nice meeting you," she said with that captivating smile.

Her hand was in mine as I turned the knob and eased the door open, still holding on to me. It was soft and warm and I didn't mind letting it linger there.

"Thanks again," I said as I let her hand slip out of mine.

Grasping my left wrist, she maneuvered my hand under her robe against the silky camisole. Then positioned it on her right hip as her left arm slid over my shoulder. Her hand rested on the back of my neck. Tilting her head back, she pulled me down until her soft warm lips firmly pressed against mine. Electricity surged through my body as I became aroused. Her hand, still attached to my wrist, moved slowly up until her soft supple breast filled my hand. Our lips separated—my ears burned—my face flushed with excitement as I slipped both of my arms around her slim midriff.

"I was under the impression that you were expecting company when I arrived."

"One of the girls from work. She's planning on coming by to pick me up."

"Well, I should—" her hand covered my mouth as she turned to the clock on the nearby wall.

"She won't be here for at least an hour. We have plenty of time."

Her lips were on mine again as I lifted her off the floor. With my right hand, I locked the door as our lips separated. With my left arm around her waistline, I positioned my right arm under her knees and scooped her up, kissed her hard and moved to the bedroom, kicking the door shut with my foot. As I moved toward the bed, Rose removed my hat and flung it across the room where it landed on top of a walnut bureau, upsetting a collection of perfume and cologne bottles.

I dropped her on the bed and the bounce caused her robe to come undone exposing the flimsy camisole that barely clung to her agile body. Her long shapely legs, smooth and creamy white, were an image any artist would've desired to sculpt in Italian Marble for the world to appreciate for ages to come—save for the ridiculous fuzzy-pink slippers that encased her feet. Light blue pastel silk panties completed the undergarment ensemble. Rose popped up into a sitting position and began to claw at my tie as I unbuttoned my shirt as best I could, considering the circumstances.

Very little romance was exchanged during the encounter, mostly a lot of thrashing around like an Olympic Greco-Roman Wrestling competition, each combatant trying to get the upper hand. I ultimately decided to concede the match and let the chips fall where they may. Once the grappling had subsided, Rosemary took command and orchestrated the rest of the performance, taking my hand and positioning it in strategic locations on her well-sculpted body. Her skill? Superlative. If I were to award Rose's sexual acumen in an academic sense, she would've earned a doctorate.

I scarcely had time to catch my breath when Rose started scurrying around the apartment to get ready for work before her girlfriend arrived. I splashed water on my face in the small kitchen. Toweled off. Combed my hair and finished dressing. We said our goodbyes with me, promising to call her again.

Chapter 23

When I got to my car, I lit a smoke and took that long first drag. She was something all right, the kind of woman that would give you a run for your money if you didn't mind claw marks. I sat there and enjoyed my cig, mind rerunning the last forty-five minutes, appraising what I did, what I should've done and most of all, what I shouldn't have done. I finished my cigarette and tossed it on the pavement, took a deep breath and I was back on the beam, a little warmer under the collar but focused back on the case. Confident I had everything set up I went straight to my place. Fixed myself a drink and flopped on the couch to relax until I needed to pick Claire up for dinner. I had just finished taking a sip of my drink, holding the cool glass against my forehead, when I suddenly noticed Sully seated at my desk.

"What do you want?"

Nothing, nothing at all.

"I'm sure glad you weren't around a couple of hours ago."

How's that?

"Never mind, you don't need to know."

Sully just sat there and eyeballed me for several minutes. The dead sure can stare.

"Listen, I've got this under control. I'm going to give Cappello what he's been looking for and that should get him off Shortt's back for a little while. Then I'll go to work on Schofield."

Ya think Cappello knows those statues contain jewels?

I got to my feet and paced the floor.

"The way I figure it, Cappello and Deidra were workin' together behind her hubby's back. She tells Nick of a big shipment comin' in. Maybe she tells 'im jewels are hidden in a coupla statues. Maybe she tells 'im the statues are worth a small fortune. Maybe Nick is puttin' the squeeze on her. Maybe Deidra wants Nick involved cuz she wants 'im to remove the hubby from the picture. Permanently."

They're all possibilities, Sully said.

"Or maybe Nick's tired of bein' the second fiddle," I said.

The door buzzer squawked in rapid-fire succession.

"Hold on!" I yelled to make the buzzing stop.

I set my drink on the lamp table and opened the apartment door to find Rickman and Sergeant McNabb gracing my doorstep. Without a hello or good afternoon, the two men pushed their way into the room.

"Come in gentleman," I said sarcastically to the now empty doorframe.

I stuck my head out and looked up and down the hall.

"Just let us know when you're through with the comedy routine," Rickman said sternly. "We heard you talkin'. You got company?"

"Radio."

I closed the door and turned to my guests. I could tell Rickman was not in a pleasant mood. With McNabb by his side, he wouldn't tolerate any needling from me.

"You always talk to the radio?"

"Sometimes," I said. "Why don't you boys have a seat? Can I get you anything? Cup of coffee?"

"We need some information," Rickman said as he took a seat in the armchair next to the couch. McNabb moved to the small desk at the corner, pulled a notebook from his coat pocket and readied himself to take notes.

"I'll give you all I can," I said as I took a seat on the couch.

"Where is Bailey Shortt?"

"I honestly don't know. I have no idea where he went after checking out of the Victorian."

"Where is the item you purchased from the auction house?"

"I told you before, Mike. I don't have it in my possession. It's in a safe place. I don't see what this has to do with the case. No one involved has ever seen the thing. What do you want from me?" I pleaded.

"I want some answers to what *the hell* is going on here!"

I sat back, rested my head on the back of the couch and took a deep breath. I couldn't keep dodging Rickman any longer so it was time to give him something he could chew on.

"The way I figure it, Irene and Bailey came up with a scheme that they thought was fool proof. Irene had discovered some information working for Schofield. It seems he was smuggling valuable artwork disguised as curios into the country. Bailey was heavily into Nick Cappello for a loan. They worked out a deal that they would intercept a valuable shipment, give the item to Cappello and square Bailey's debt."

"That doesn't explain Talbot's murder," Rickman said.

"That was just one of those things that you can't plan for. My car broke down. By the time I was able to get back on the road and get to the meeting place, my contact was gone. My guess is that they got all in a panic and assumed they were double-crossed."

A light bulb popped on in the darkness of McNabb's tiny brain. "That makes sense, Lieutenant."

Rickman flashed McNabb a look.

"You think Cappello killed Talbot?" Rickman said.

"I know who killed Talbot," I answered confidently as McNabb looked up from his notebook.

"What the *hell*!" McNabb exclaimed.

I re-claimed my drink from the lamp table and took a hard swallow.

"If you've been holding back evidence—"

"Relax Mike," I interjected. "Cappello sent two of his boys to accept the merchandise. When I didn't show up, they decided to take matters into their own hands. The way I figure it, they went to see Irene. Told her I didn't show. She tells 'im I double-crossed her. Gives 'em my address. They stake out my place. When Zeke showed up in *my* car, they think it's me and worked him over. Then they go back to Irene's. Things quickly got out of hand, so to speak."

"You know who these two mugs are?" McNabb asked.

"One's a big gorilla named Bruno. Prizefighter. The other is Manny Strupp. He runs numbers for Cappello and other assorted errands Cappello needs done. Not too bright, but from what I understand does what he's told."

"How you know all this?" Rickman asked.

"Got a line on Manny. Did some snooping around and found out that he manages Bruno's boxing career when he's not running numbers. Bruno's fighting in the undercard at the San Jose State Arena tonight. Can't miss him. He's a big dumb ox who doesn't know his own strength. I met up with them yesterday."

"You found out about this yesterday?!" Rickman bellowed.

"Yeah. Bruno actually admitted he *accidentally* killed Irene. They figured she was orchestrating the double-cross. She protested her innocence. Bruno tried to keep her quiet. One thing led to another."

"And just when were you going to let me in on this little nugget?!"

"If I let you clowns barge in throwing your weight around it'd take me months to straighten out the mess."

"Ahh, you're *nuts*!" Rickman yelled.

"Consider this your Christmas present. Go pick up those two tonight. Bruno fights under the name Bruiser Durkin. The morning papers will have you all over the front page telling the world how you solved the Talbot murder. When I read the part where you clowns got an anonymous tip that led you to the killer, I'll know you were talking about me."

McNabb snickered in disgust as he jotted down the information as best he could. I was talking pretty fast and he had to ask a few questions to clarify the story. Rickman pressed again on the location of the artwork I purchased.

"I wanna see the item you were hired to pick up."

"I told you before, I don't have it. You can search if you want. Turn the dump upside down if you have a mind to, just as long as you brought along a search warrant," I said with a warm smile.

Rickman got up, jammed his hat on his head and headed for the door. Turning to me he said. "You're playin' with fire here, Jimmy!"

"Slow down, pal," I said, getting up. "I just gave you Irene Talbot's killer. That's what got you involved with this case."

Rickman turned red. He knew I was right. "You work your side of the street. I'll work mine," I said.

"Goddamit!" Rickman said as he flung the door open.

As he pounded down the hall McNabb rose from his seat. Stuffed his notebook in his pocket.

"This Drukin, fella," McNabb said.

"Durkin. Bruno Durkin," I said.

"Yeah, Durkin. He admitted killin' Talbot?"

McNabb was embarrassed by Rickman's outburst. He just didn't know how to respond.

"Yeah. I figure they accused her of the double-cross. She got upset. Started yellin'. Bruno told me he just wanted to keep her quiet."

"Well, thanks," McNabb said.

He moved to the door. Gave a wave. Gently closed the door behind him.

You sure know how to send that guy over the edge.

"Yeah, I know. I shouldn't do it because it's just too easy."

I flopped back on the couch and took a much-needed nap.

I was up and out of the shower by six. After a shave, I dressed in a starched white shirt, tied a snappy black bow tie and buttoned up my black double-breasted suit. After another look in the mirror to make sure all was in order, I got into my car and drove to Claire's apartment. It was just shy of seven when I rang the buzzer. I was not ready for what greeted me when the door swung open.

Chapter 24

y car keys fell out of my hand and for a moment I couldn't remember my name when I saw Claire, framed in the doorway of her apartment dressed in an emerald green, scoop-neck tight-fitting dress that left nothing to the imagination. I picked up my keys and stumbled into the apartment.

"What do you think?" she said as she spun around.

Even a blind man could see that she was beautiful. I wondered for a moment if I should ask at what age she had her appendix removed, but thought better of it.

"You look. . . amazing is the word that comes to mind," I croaked, clearing my throat.

"I went shopping right after you told me we were going to Julie's. I just couldn't wear the same dress I wore last time I was there. It just wouldn't be right."

"If you say so," I said, recovering my composure.

We arrived at the supper club for our seven-thirty reservation. We had a cocktail and our dinner ordered by seven-fifty. The band played a rumba and we danced. I had a sudden thought that if I was lucky to live a long life, I'd remember this frameable date.

"You're a pretty good dancer," Claire said as we returned to our table.

"Thanks. It's been a while, but it's kind of like riding a bicycle."

The waiter appeared beside the table with a large metal platter that held our dinners. He expertly deployed a little stand for the tray and set down the platter. He placed our selections on the table and wished us a pleasant meal, taking the stand and platter away. Maybe it was the drinks, the lovely babe—but I privately raised a glass to his skill.

"This is so much fun," Claire exclaimed. "I'm so glad you asked me."

"Sure. It's a two-fold proposition."

"How's that?"

"First, it's business. I'll be meeting Cappello in about a half hour or so and secondly, I got a date with you. I was hoping that you'd be induced to go out with me, you know. . . because it's detective work."

"Since we're being honest. I would've accepted your date invitation even if you were taking me to a hot dog stand."

"That's good to know. For future reference."

As we continued to eat our dinner, I told Claire plans for solving the case.

"Once I give Cappello what he wants, I'll work on Mrs. Schofield."

"I remember seeing her that time we had the party here," Claire said. "She was at a table in that dark corner over there with some man."

She indicated the area with a nod.

"Not her husband?"

Claire shook her head.

"How did Irene fit in?" she said.

"She used me to get the merchandise so she had an alibi. Her boyfriend owed Cappello money. Statues were to square the debt."

Claire stopped eating and sat motionless for a moment. Blood drained from her face.

"You okay?" I asked. "Is something wrong with your food?"

"No. I just got really scared, James. These people are dangerous."

"Relax sweetheart," I said. "I know how to handle these kinds of people. You'd only have to worry if I *didn't* know this about them."

I checked my watch. It was ten after nine. Nick 'The Hat' Cappello strutted into the supper club with a blonde buzz saw on his arm dressed in a silver evening gown. The dress held on to her body so tightly you'd have thought it was painted on. Nick greeted the maître-d' with what looked like a fifty-dollar bill and followed him to a corner table in the back of the club. Two of Nick's artillerymen close behind. Nick signaled them to sit at the bar on the other side of the room. The taller of the two nodded and they made their way to the bar, brusquely removing a couple of male patrons from stools that were better suited for them to keep an eye on Nick's table. His two goons sat there motionless, sticking out like a couple of horseflies on a wedding cake. I took a business card from my pocket, flagged down a waiter and told him to deliver the card to Nick's table. The waiter returned with the card. On the back was written: *Men's Room – 5 min.*

Above a small alcove next to the bar, a sign indicated the Men's Room. I opened Claire's purse, stuffed my revolver in it.

"I'll be back in a few minutes," I said.

"Be careful," Clair said.

I made my way to the Men's washroom. As I approached, the larger of the two gunsels, all shoulders and no hips, stuck out a big paw and stopped me in my tracks. He moved the lapel of his jacket enough for me to get a gander at the handle of his .45 automatic. I opened my jacket so he could see I wasn't carrying artillery, but that wasn't good enough. When I tried to move towards the door, that big paw prevented my advance. The other gunsel moved around me and proceeded to pat me down. I've cased these guys before. Same blue pinstripe tailored suits cut to hide the fact they've got a rod parked under the armpit. Same hard eyes, that permanent sneer affixed to their faces. Hundreds of them around but with a little experience, you can learn how to handle them. Just do as they say and maybe you won't lose an eye, or wake up in an alley with a couple of fractured ribs. I let the mug with the slicked-back black hair molest me until he was satisfied. I didn't have a nail file or penknife on me to cause any problems. Once he was through, the other one pushed the door open allowing me to enter. I stepped in and positioned myself in the center of the room, my backside against a sink. A minute or two passed when the door creaked open and Nick stepped in, turned and faced me. After giving me the once over he moved to the sink next to me and regarded himself in the mirror.

"It sure doesn't look like you have anything to give me, shamus," his raspy voice echoed off the walls of the ceramic tiled cavern.

"It's a little too bulky to carry around," I said.

"So just what is it you're looking for?"

"I'm not looking for anything. I've got what you want and I just want to get rid of it. This whole thing was a misunderstanding. I want no part of it."

Nick kept looking into the mirror. He adjusted his tie and the collar of his starched white shirt.

I cleared my throat and said, "No one tried to double-cross you. Not Bailey, not me. I have an envelope," I said, as I slipped my hand under my jacket and slowly pulled it out.

Nick never moved from his position but watched carefully my actions in the mirror.

"In it is a ticket. The package is in baggage claim at the Terminal."

I held the envelope out. Nick just continued to stare into the mirror.

"Put it on the sink," he said.

I set the envelope on the edge of the sink. Nick looked down at it and said, "You can go now."

I stepped past him and out of the door. As I glanced back, I saw the smaller gunsel open the washroom door and Nick stepped out saying something to him before heading back to his table.

"Is everything okay?" Claire asked when I sat down at the table.

"It's fine. Let's finish our coffee and I'll take you home."

"We can go now if you don't mind. Just knowing that guy is here makes me nervous."

I retrieved my gun and slammed down the rest of my coffee.

After dropping Claire off, I swung over to the Victorian to see if I could get a line on Bailey. The desk clerk gave me a smile as I approached.

"May I help you sir?" he said politely.

"I need some information," I replied as I showed him my Private Detective credentials. "Were you on duty when a Mr. Parker checked out yesterday?"

I slipped a five-dollar bill across the desk.

"Mr. Parker?" he said, as he found a home for the five-spot in his jacket pocket.

He flipped the registration book back a page and ran a thin finger down the left side of the ledger.

"Yeah, I remember Mr. Parker. He checked out just a few minutes after I came on duty. I asked him if anything was wrong because he was paying for the night and wouldn't be staying here."

"Did Mr. Parker say where he was going?"

"No. He just said he was checking out and paid. I saw that he got a cab out front. That's all I know."

"What time was this?"

"I come on at five o'clock, so it was a few minutes after that."

I went out to the cabstand outside the hotel and checked with the two cabbies parked there. The first driver in line was across town at 5:00 p.m. yesterday. The second cabby was in his mid-thirties and on the heavy side with bushy eyebrows. He was half-asleep when I tapped on his windshield.

"You need a cab mister?" he said with a yawn.

"I need some information."

"If you want information there's a newsstand down on the corner. If you need a ride somewhere, that's what I'm here for."

"Did you pick up a fair in front of this hotel sometime after five o'clock yesterday?" I asked. "A man, five-eight, five-nine, slim build, dark hair with a brown leather suitcase?"

"I pick up lots of fairs," the cabby said sleepily.

A five-dollar bill cleared the sleep out of his eyes.

"I do seem to remember a man with a leather suitcase though. I think it was around five-fifteen."

I held another five through the window of the cab.

"Yeah, I remember now. He got in. Said he wanted to go to the Hotel Central," he said as he snatched the bills from my fingers. "Nervous sorta guy. Jumpy like. I mentioned that it was a warm night. He tells me to just drive."

"Anything else you can remember?"

"Nah. Did think it was kinda strange. Him leavin' the Victorian for a dump like the Central."

"What happened when you got there?"

"He pays. Gave me a pretty good tip. Went into the hotel."

Ten minutes later, I parked across the street from the Hotel Central. One look at the joint and you got the feeling that this place was about as cozy as an abandoned coal mine. The hotel desk clerk was speaking with an older gentleman when I walked into the lobby. He gave me the once over, then continued his conversation. Across from the reception desk was an old worn dark brown corduroy couch. It could've been green or blue at one time but the years of grease and grime darkened the color to the shade of dirty motor oil. On one wall hung a framed photo of a man who looked remarkably like Calvin Coolidge, which gave me a clue as to when the last time this dump was painted. The old gentleman moved away. I positioned myself in front of the clerk.

"How can I help ya, mister?" he said.

"Man checked in yesterday, between five and five-thirty, Tall—slim build—dark hair. Carried a brown leather suitcase," I said, placing my hand on the counter, lifting it just enough to reveal a fiver.

"You a friend?" he said.

"He knows me. Can you ring his room?"

"We don't have phones in the room," he said.

"Gotta number?"

"Three-twelve. To the right at the top of the stairs."

I walked up the three flights and down the dark narrow hall that smelled like the entrance to a bayside sewer. Only one small wattage light bulb illuminated a section of hallway at the far end of the hall. I found the room. Light bled into the hall from the bottom of the door. Music played on the radio from inside the room. I tapped on the door. It creaked, opened about an inch. I pushed the door open another few inches.

"Shortt! It's Wolf," I said.

No response. I pushed the door halfway open and could see the window on the other side of the room was open and a damp breeze fluttered the flimsy curtain. To the left of the door was the bathroom, its light was the only light on as I moved into the room.

I was only a few steps into the room when I saw a pair of legs in tan trousers on the white-tiled bathroom floor soaking up a pool of bright red blood. I took two quick steps toward the bathroom—then felt a tap on the back of my head. A pitch-black elevator shaft appeared at my feet and I rocked forward and dove in.

Chapter 25

I heard the radio announcer as he reported the news on the half-hour as I opened my eyes. I'd been unconscious for nearly ten minutes according to my watch. I started to raise myself from my prone position when I noticed I had a gun, fitted with a silencer, in my right hand. It wasn't mine. I sat up and opened my jacket. My holster was empty. I got to my feet and checked the body. It was Bailey and he had three neat holes in a tight grouping from his chest to upper abdomen. I must have stood there for five minutes just looking down at him. His body was twisted in an odd angle like it couldn't make up its mind on which way he wanted to die. He was on his back, bent to the right at the waist, head facing left, mouth open like he was trying to tell someone some bad news.

I stepped over the body and splashed cold water on my face, then soaked a washcloth under the tap and placed it on the melon that was growing on the back of my head.

This is getting to be a regular thing with you.

Sully, sitting on the edge of the bed. Hat pushed back on his head, hunched over with his elbows on his knees.

"I thought I'd squared things with Cappello but I guess he felt he needed to get even with Bailey."

Cappello is the kind of sick animal that kills for the fun of it. He had already made up his mind. It wouldn't matter what you did to square things.

"He cleverly left me holding the bag for this murder."

How do you mean?

"He's got my gun for Chrissake," I said, as I opened my jacket. "They've got my—" was the sound that erupted from my mouth. "Hold on just a minute. Shortt was dead when I got here. What the hell?"

I'll give you even odds the gun in your hand killed Shortt.

"Christ!"

It's not this murder it's the next murder you've got to worry about, Jimmy.

Sully was right. This made about as much sense as a trombonist in a string quartet. I only had a couple of choices and neither were very good. I was down so deep in this case—I was nearly halfway to China. I put the pistol left behind in my jacket pocket and wiped any prints off the doorknob. I checked the hallway and then slipped out of the room, down the back stairs, out of the hotel.

I parked the car at a garage on O'Farrell and walked to the Warfield Hotel on the corner of Taylor and Turk. After checking into a room, I went to a liquor store on Eddy and picked up two much-needed buddies: a pint of bourbon and a bottle of club soda. Back in my room, I fixed a stiff one, lit a cigarette and flopped on the bed to figure my next move. It was easy to stay focused when you lay on a mattress stuffed with concrete cinder blocks.

It was after midnight when I finished my last drink and found a reasonably comfortable position to get some sleep. The sounds of distant police sirens kept me awake for hours before sleep finally was able to take hold and I drifted into oblivion.

Noise from the street woke me just after eight o'clock. After a shave, I dressed and hit the pavement. I grabbed the morning *Call* from a newsstand, folded it and shoved it under my arm. Several blocks down from the stand was a little diner. I situated myself at the end of the counter, giving me a clear view of the street traffic outside. I ordered eggs, bacon and coffee and opened up the paper. Page 3 had the story of Shortt's killing. One of the other tenants called the desk around 1:00 a.m. complaining about music coming from room 312. The desk clerk let himself in when no one answered his knocks. He found Shortt's body and called the police. The clerk gave the investigative officers an accurate description of me. After a pot and a half of coffee and something on my stomach, I was feeling half-human again. I needed to lay low but at the same time get enough information to clear myself. I gave Claire a call.

"This is Claire, can I help you?" she said pleasantly.

"Can you talk?"

"No, I'm sorry but Mr. Pitts is with someone right now. Could you call back in about ten minutes?"

"Got it," I said and hung up.

I had another cup of coffee and waited the longest ten minutes ever. The cops were talking to Claire. Rickman had put two and two together and got five. Just like him. The squeeze was on and I began to feel like a fat lady stuffed into a size two corset. I went to the phone and called Brooklyn's again.

"This is Claire," she said in an anxious tone.

"It's me."

"That Lieutenant Rickman was just here asking about you."

"Thought so," I said. "What did he want to know?"

"If I knew where you were. He said you were involved in something and needed to talk to you right away."

"Did you see the paper this morning?" I asked.

"No, I don't like to read the paper first thing."

"Bailey Shortt was killed last night. Shot three times in the chest."

"Good Lord."

"Cappello . . . or one of his goons did it."

"Oh no, James. Can't you call Rickman?"

"I can't. I need to get the goods on Cappello and Schofield. Bring the package all nicely wrapped and tied up with string to Rickman or I'll be sittin' in a cell for who knows how long as the cops poke around looking for clues. I've got to handle this myself."

"Just be careful."

"I'll keep you posted. If you need to get a hold of me, call Howard-3-5144. That's Doc's number. He'll know how to reach me."

"I will," she said nervously.

"Don't worry. I just need a little time to sort this all out."

It was unusually hot. One of those San Francisco days that makes an appearance every few years. The air refuses to move and the cloudless sky allows the sun to bake everyone and everything into a bleary malaise. Not even the birds had the energy to chirp. I went back to the hotel room and paced the floor for several hours easily working up a sweat. I was in a spot.

You wanna stop pacing? It's starting to get on my nerves.

"I'm boxed in Sully."

You're gonna need to get some help.

"The only person I can trust right now is Doc."

He's a bit of a loose cannon, but—

"Yeah. Any port in a storm. I gotta pull him in deeper. I need Doc to be my legs. He could move around town freely without churning up any suspicion.

I went to the phone booth in the hotel lobby and started making calls to the likely joints where I might find him. After a half-dozen calls, I hit pay dirt. Doc was holding court at the Jackdaw on Connecticut.

I hailed a cab.

"Why do you think they took your gun, Jimmy?" Doc said.

"I don't know," I said gravely. "They couldn't use it to kill Bailey. He was already dead. We suspect Nick will set me up with another murder."

"Who's we?"

I glanced up. Doc had a puzzled look on his face.

"We! You and me. Right? I mean what else would he want my gun for?"

"I don't see how you get yourself into so much trouble. It seems you just walk right up to trouble and introduce yourself," Doc said, shaking his head.

"Walk up to it?" I cracked. "I just have to stand still for five minutes and it's all over me. I need to lay low."

"Do the police think you did it?" Doc inquired.

"Rickman was with Claire when I called Brooklyn's. They got a good description of me from the desk clerk. He wants to talk to me."

"You're welcome to bunk at my place."

"No, I'll be fine at the hotel. Just in case Rickman finally figures I'd come to you for help. You may end up with a tail and I don't want you to get into trouble for harboring a fugitive."

"Very nice of you, Giaco," Doc said with more than a tinge of sarcasm. "Who do you suspect did it?"

It felt good to be addressed by my birth name. Fortifying.

"I figure one of Cappello's men."

"But why, Giaco? You gave Cappello what he wanted. Doesn't seem like a Cappello move. Too bold. He knows the cops will find out this Bailey fellow owed him money."

"I don't know why he might have done it," I said resignedly. "Maybe he wants to make a point. I don't know."

"So! What do you want me to do?"

"Nose around your newspaper buddies, see what the cops are up to. Maybe one of your bookie buddies can get a line on Nick."

"Certainly, my friend. Where can I reach you—your service?"

"No, I'm sure the cops will be on that in no time. I'll be at the Warfield. Room 210. Mr. Kirkland."

I called my service from the Jackdaw. I had a message from Mrs. Schofield. I called the Schofield's number. It rang several times before the butler picked up.

"Schofield residence."

"This is Mr. Wolf. I received a message to call Mrs. Schofield."

"Just a moment please."

It was only a minute, but it seemed more like ten that passed before I heard the phone receiver pick up again.

"Mrs. Schofield will be with you shortly, please remain on the line."

Two minutes passed before I could hear the sound of high-heeled shoes echoing across a hardwood floor.

"This is Mrs. Schofield. What do you want to speak to me about?"

Her voice was as smooth as syrup dripping over a stack of hot flapjacks. If she had a radio show, she could read from the phone book and mesmerize any red-blooded man with ears.

I took a moment to clear my head.

"I have the statues you're looking for," I said.

"I'm not sure what you mean."

"Let's cut the games. Your boys grabbed the wrong guy the other night. I'm James Wolf. I've got what you want and I'm willing to make a deal."

"I see," she said, hardly fazed by my bluntness.

"There's a joint on Chestnut. Santino's. Across from the movie theater. Meet me there in forty-five minutes." For a moment I thought the line had gone dead. I still had an ace in the hole. "My next call will be to your husband! Your choice."

"Forty-five minutes," she said.

I hung up the phone. There was something odd about this affair, like a stripper wearing long johns—but I was going to get to the bottom of it, one way or another. I got in my car. In the rearview, I saw Sully in the back seat.

You gotta plan, he said.

"Remember the Chen Po affair?"

Sully gave me that patented smile, said. *Gonna play the 'I'm desperate for money Jimmy Wolf?'*

"Just like the Chen Po affair."

Chapter 26

It came to be known as the Chen Po affair. I had just been promoted to Inspector. Sully and I were called into Captain Haller's office, head of narcotics.

"You wanted to see us, Cap?" Sully said as we entered.

"Close the door. Take a seat," he said.

I could tell by his demeanor something was up and it was serious.

"Narcotics has been workin' a case for over six months. High grade 'H'. Nearly pure heroin, floodin' the Bay Area."

"We've heard," Sully said.

"Then you know we haven't a clue how it's comin' in. Narcotics been rousting every junkie—pusher—dealer from here to San Jose. The East Bay, Marin County. So far, we've got nothin'."

"How can we help?" Sully said.

"I want the pair of you to investigate," Haller said. "Drop whatever you're workin' on. You've got one mission. Find out how the stuff is gettin' in. Hopefully, *that* will lead us to who is movin' so much junk."

Over the next three weeks, Sully and I worked every angle we could think of. Contacted every snitch we ever worked with. Nothing. Another week dragged on with nothing to show. We were off Sunday. It was a warm afternoon. I sipped on a cold beer while listening to the radio. Seals were trailing 3 to 2, bottom of the sixth. They had a man on third with one out when my phone announced a caller. I turned down the radio and answered.

"Hello."

"It's Sully. I just gotta call from Greg Pinder at the morgue."

"What's up?"

"Man died of an overdose. Greg found somethin' interesting. Meet me at the coroner's office."

"On my way," I said.

Twelve minutes later I entered the lab at the coroner's office. I found Sully bent over the desk in the far corner of the lab. A single body, covered by a white sheet, lay on one of the porcelain tables located in the center of the room.

"This better be good, Greg," I said. "You pulled me away from a great ballgame."

"Don't know if it's good or not. It's interestin' for sure. Victim is Tan Ling. Resident of Hong Kong. Died of a heroin overdose. Did a test on what he still had on his person. Ninety-nine percent pure."

"Christ!" I said.

"Guessin' Mr. Ling must've thought it was cut," he said.

"Take a look at this, Jimmy," Sully said.

I moved to the desk. Sully pointed to some documents on the desk.

"Those were found on the body," Greg said.

"Ling was a sailor," Sully said. "Oiler on the Chen Po."

"That *is* interesting," I said. "How did he come into havin' pure heroin?"

"My thoughts, exactly."

"I may be way off base," I said. "But. . . if I was to wager a bet. I'd say someone on the Chen Po was transporting 'H'."

"Yeah," Sully said. "It'd be a simple plan to have a boat meet the Chen Po at sea. Transfer the drugs before she enters port."

"Finding that boat is like findin' a needle in a haystack," I said.

Sully picked up the phone.

"Who you callin'?

"Harbor Master," Sully said. "Hello?" Sully said. "This is Inspector Sullivan. Can you look up when the freighter Chen Po docked? Yeah, I'll hold," Sully said as he turned to me. "At least this will give a time when Mr. Ling—yeah, I'm here. Thanks."

Sully dropped the receiver back into its cradle. "Last night. Five-thirty."

"We need to talk to Danny Hung."

Danny Hung, Private Investigator, lived in the third-floor apartment on the corner of Clay and Taylor.

"Jimmy Wolf!" Danny said. answering his door. "And is that Inspector Sullivan?"

"How are you, Danny," I said.

"Fine. Good to see old friends," he said, flashing a wide smile. "Come in. I have tea."

We entered his small but neat apartment.

"Sit, gentlemen," he said then disappearing into the kitchen.

Sully and I sat on a couch upholstered in embroidered red and gold silk. Danny returned from the kitchen with a pot of tea and cups on a tray. After setting the tray on the table in front of us he expertly poured tea.

"To my friends," he said as he held up a cup.

We sipped tea. Danny sat in a stuffed chair across from us.

"How can I be of service?"

"A sailor, name's Tan Ling. Sailed from Hong Kong on the Chen Po. They docked Friday evening. Ling died of a drug overdose sometime Saturday night," Sully said. "Heroin was pure. We think it was part of a shipment the Chen Po smuggled in."

"I hear many stories," Danny said. "Fear it is Chinese mob. Try to—how you say. Corner market."

"We're guessin' they're using a fishing boat to meet the ship out at sea," I said. "Maybe you could do some checkin' around."

"For you! Can do," Danny said.

Sully and I poked around all Monday. Talk on the streets, the same story. Dealers of Mexican 'H' losing business. Another supplier was offering better deals to the pushers. Tuesday morning, we got a call from Danny. We met him at his office located over the Ming Li Asian Market on Grant.

"Heroin come from Chung Yee—Han Zhu Mob," Danny said. "They work together. Very hush-hush. Maybe Lin Cai, Dragon Lady involve. She give money for fisherman to buy boat."

"Do you know which boat?" I said.

"Not sure. Maybe Captain's Pride. Maybe Fisherman's Fortune."

"Can I use your phone?" I said.

Danny nodded.

"I'm callin' narcotics. They need to search those two boats."

"How can we find this Dragon Lady?" Sully said.

"Maybe I know someone. You be careful. Han Zhu very dangerous."

By the time we returned to the Hall, Narcotics searched the Captain's Pride and Fisherman's Fortune. They hit paydirt. Traces of heroin were found on the Fortune. Feds ceased the boat. Chung Yee mob was out of business in the Bay Area. Following morning Sully and I met with Haller. We had a plan.

"It's takin' a big risk," Haller said.

"I think it's worth it, Cap," I said. "With the Fortune out of commission, they'll be lookin' for another vessel. I know how to handle a boat."

"Wolf will let word get around that he's strapped for cash," Sully said. "Owes a loan-shark a hefty sum. Could lose his boat—or worse. We have feelers out right now. Just need to make a connection with the mob."

"They'll wanna hire my boat. If they believe I'm desperate enough," I said.

"What about a boat?" Haller said.

"I can get the use of one. Pop has a buddy in Monterey."

"I'll get the Chief to cover the cost of the boat," Haller said. "With one caveat."

"What's that, Cap," I said.

"Anything goes sour, you get outta there. Follow?"

After twenty-two hours of sailing up the coast, I pulled into San Francisco late in the afternoon. I booked myself a room at a flea-bag on Mission. At the crack of dawn, I was at the wharf. Fueled up the boat on credit and sailed up the coast. I did some fishing on some days. On others, I'd let the boat drift in the current as I caught up on a couple of books I'd been interested in reading. For the next two weeks it went like this. One morning, as I moored at the fueling station, I was met by the station manager.

"I'm gonna need some cash, bud," he said. "You owe nearly three hundred. Can't give you any more credit."

"I've got thirty bucks on me," I said. "No gas—I don't go out—I don't sell fish."

"Gimme the thirty. I'll give ya forty gallons. I gotta business to run."

I gave him the thirty bucks and tied my boat up at the slip. I cooled my heels for the next forty-eight hours in my cramped room on Mission waiting for something to happen. I met up with Sully across from the church in Washington Square.

"Haven't heard a word from anyone," I said.

"Patience. Give it a couple more days. The Chen Po just sailed for Yokohama a few days ago."

"Heard anything from Danny?"

"Hasn't been able to make a connection between Lin Cai and Chinese drug dealers."

"Been stuck at the hotel for nearly a month now. Room's gettin' on my nerves."

"I can tell. There's one good thing about that," Sully said.

"Good thing?"

"Yeah. You're lookin' more desperate by the day."

When I stopped at the fueling station the following morning, the dock attendant refused to sell me gas. I offered some cash but was told my account was closed. I needed to pay the full amount owed before they'd sell me any more fuel.

"I've barely enough gas to get back to my berth!" I said.

"Can't help ya, pal. Unless . . ."

"Unless what?"

"I know someone who needs a boat. Needs to make— let's call it a late-night-pick-up. No questions asked."

I processed the information for a moment.

"As long as the pay's good," I said. "No questions."

"Nine o'clock. Skip-Jacks," he said. "Don't be late."

I ventured into Skip-Jacks on the wharf at 8:40 p.m. I ordered a beer. Took a seat at a table and smoked a cigarette. I'd nursed the beer for twenty minutes when an Asian man approached my table.

"You have boat?" he said.

I looked up. He was short and stocky. Dressed in a black suit, black shirt buttoned up to the collar.

"I do. Sixty-five-footer. You wanna hire?"

"Maybe yes," he said as he sat down across from me. "Li Peng. American call me Lenny."

"Lenny huh!"

"Correct."

"What's the deal? I need to make some money," I said.

"You very impatient man."

"When you get desperate, you become impatient."

"How I find you?"

"I'm at the Fremont. Room 206. You can—"

Peng got up, turned and headed for the door.

Days piled upon days. Not a word from Peng. I checked in with Sully. There was nothing in the files on a man named Li Peng. I'd just returned from dinner at the Snack Shack two blocks from the hotel when I entered my room and I found Lenny Peng relaxing in the only chair, smoking a foul-smelling cigarette.

"Lenny!" I said. "I was beginning to wonder if I'd be hearin' from you."

He crushed his smoke in the dirty ashtray on the bed stand. Rose from his seat. Reached into his jacket pocket and produced an envelope.

"For you," he said, dropping the envelope on the bed. "Pay your debts. Make your boat ready."

"Yeah, sure," I said. "What's the deal?"

He walked past me. Opened the door. Turned and said, "In due time."

I called Sully from the lobby pay phone.

"Peng just left my hotel room. Gave me an envelope full of cash. Enough to pay off my fuel bill and what I admitted to owing a loan shark."

"I'll come by and pick up the cash after I call Haller."

It felt like we finally got over the hump. I readied the boat and waited for the call. Three days bled into four. A full week and not a word from Peng. I lay in my room listening to the radio when there was a knock at the door. I opened the door to find Peng.

"Get coat. We sail tonight."

"What?! I don't have a crew!"

"No need. We meet crew at docks," he said. "No time to waste."

I grabbed my coat. There was no time to call Sully. I followed Peng down to the lobby. A car waited for us in front of the hotel. He headed directly to the wharf. Three Asian sailors were on the pier when we arrived. Peng spoke to them in Chinese. We boarded the boat.

"Where we headed?" I said.

Peng handed me a slip of paper with a compass heading. Due west.

We sailed on the compass heading for an hour and a half.

"How much longer," I said to Peng when he entered the pilot house.

Checking his watch he said, "Maybe two hour."

"Stayin' on this course? We'll be in the middle of nowhere!"

I waited for a reply. Peng lit one of his foul cigarettes. Left the bridge without a word. I sailed west on the heading for another two hours. Off in the distance, I noticed running lights on a ship heading east southeast. Peng came up to the bridge.

"You slow down now," he said.

"We meetin' this freighter?"

Peng left the bridge without a word. Twenty-five minutes later we came alongside the Chen Po. Peng gave commands in Chinese to the deckhands. Two medium-sized bails, wrapped in burlap, were lower to the deck of my boat. Peng waved to a deckhand on the Chen Po. Returned to the bridge.

"We head back," he said, giving me a slip of paper with a compass heading east.

"What's in the bundles?" I said.

"Not for you to know," Peng said. "You will be well paid for your service."

Three and a half hours of sailing east I could make out the coast line. We were heading toward Marin. Peng returned to the bridge.

"Stay on heading," he said.

Less than a mile off the coast Peng ordered me to turn north. Muir Beach was just off my starboard beam. Peng pointed a large flashlight toward the shore, began turning it on and off in a specific pattern. A light from shore responded to the signal. Peng ordered me closer to the shore.

"I can't get much closer," I said. "We'll run aground."

"Stop engine," he said.

I could see a small motorboat approaching. Peng went down to the deck. I turned on the radio. Harbor Police had cleared a frequency to be left open twenty-four hours a day. I could only transmit. They would not respond to my message for my security.

"Merchandise arrived. Transferring to motorboat—Muir Beach area. Muir Beach area."

I switched off the radio. Peng returned to the bridge.

"Return to port," he said.

"When do I get my money? I didn't know you'd be smugglin' drugs."

"I take you to get money when we dock," he said. "Not for you to worry. Good boat. We have more work for you."

We docked. Peng was all over me like a cheap Montgomery Ward suit. One of the crewmen had his car parked at the docks. Peng ushered me into the rear seat, climbed in after me. We traveled across town. The irony wasn't lost on me as we entered China Basin. We stopped at a warehouse on 3rd Street. Two quick blasts from the car horn and the large door began to lift. We pulled into the building. Peng got out.

"Come with me," he said.

I followed him to the back of the warehouse. We climbed a flight of metal stairs. Followed him to a single door. We entered. Two Asian men, dressed in navy-blue pinstripe suits moved to me. One indicated I raise my arms.

"I don't carry a gun," I said.

He lifted my arms and patted me down. Turned to the other pinstripe suit and nodded. He moved to the door in the corner. Opened it. In the doorway stood a slim woman. Dressed in silk. She stepped into the office. Lin Cai, I assumed. The Dragon Lady. She spoke Chinese to Peng. He answered. She nodded. Peng moved to a metal cupboard. He unlocked it and retrieved an envelope.

"Peng tells me all went well," she said.

"Piece of cake," I said.

"Cake?" she said.

"Easy," I said. "No problems."

She nodded to Peng. He brought the envelope to me.

"It's better if you don't use," Peng said.

"What? Drugs?" I said.

"Got other captain in trouble."

"Not me, pal. Never touch the stuff. Is there anything else?" I said.

"You not count," Cai said.

"That would be rude," I said as I slipped the envelope in my pocket.

Dragon Lady smiled. Nodded to Peng.

"I take you back to dock," Peng said.

I followed him down the stairs. When we reached the car, he signaled the man at the entrance to open the door. He pulled on a chain. The great door slowly rose. It was half way up. The bottom of the door eight feet off the floor, when we were all blinded with an intense light.

"POLICE!" a voice shouted through a bullhorn. "YER SURROUNDED! "PUT YOUR HANDS OVER YOUR HEAD!"

A dozen officers rushed into the building guns drawn. I put my hands on my head. Two of Peng's men ran for the rear. There was a crashing sound. Six officers poured through the rear door of the warehouse. An officer in uniform pushed me against the fender of the car. Cuffed my hands behind my back.

"Take 'im outside!" I heard a voice command.

I was hauled out of the building where I was met by Sully and Captain Haller. Sully took out his key and unlocked the cuffs. I slid into Haller's vehicle. Sully next to me.

"Where'd you guys come from?" I said.

"On a hunch, I checked with a contact in Hong Kong," Sully said. "The Chen Po had sailed last week. Expected her to dock tonight. We had your hotel on 24-hour surveillance. When Peng showed up, we knew the deal was on. It was just a matter of time before you'd be on your way back."

"You followed me here?" I said.

"That's about the size of it," Sully said. "When you radioed the drop off at Muir Beach. We mobilized. Had an entire division on alert."

"Good work, Wolf," Haller said.

That was the Chen Po incident. We broke up a large drug ring. Arrested some key figures in the Asian drug organization, including the officers of the Chen Po and the S.S. Tian Sing.

Chapter 27

It took me a little over fifteen minutes to make the drive to Santino's. A dark local watering hole. Kind of place people go who don't want to be seen. I parked myself at the bar and ordered a drink. Angling myself in the stool to keep my eye on the entrance, I waited. Time passed and I ordered another drink. I'd gotten halfway through my second highball when she walked into the place. I slipped from my perch. She moved toward me with the grace of a soft kiss on the lips. Rita Hayworth, I thought. Doc was right. She looked like Rita Hayworth. Deidra Schofield was Miriam LaSalla. Rico Manzetti's ex-parakeet he flaunted around Kansas City. She stopped about a foot away from me. Her eyes locked on my face, exploring every feature as if she were planning to paint my portrait.

"Can I get you a drink?" I asked.

"No thank you. I'd like to get this over with," she replied in a voice so low it could strike oil.

"Let's get a booth," I motioned to her to follow me. "This should be private enough," I said.

I let her slide into a back corner booth next to the jukebox. I fished coins out of my pocket and selected several tunes to cover our conversation. She spoke first.

"So what kind of a deal do you want to make Mr. Wolf?" her voice sweet and smooth like chocolate frosting.

"Irene hired me to purchase a couple of items from Brooklyn's and deliver them to a couple of. . . how should

I say? Questionable characters. I believe those items were intended for you."

"You do—do you?" she said as she slipped off her white cotton gloves and placed them on the table with an air of indifference.

"I do. The fact of the matter is, the items were not delivered and I still have them and they're in a safe place. I'd like to get them off my hands. I'd like to deal with you, but I can always make a deal with Cappello if you prefer. I guess it all depends on who's willin' to pay."

It was like flinging wet spaghetti against a wall to see what would stick. I had no other choice. "You tell your husband that I know about the smuggling and if he wants to keep his little enterprise going, he needs to deal with me."

"Blackmail, Mr. Wolf? It hardly becomes you."

"Blackmail is such a strong word. It's more like. . . insurance. A small premium to pay for the security of knowing that all this will be kept. . . how should I put it? Under wraps."

"I see," she said as the words practically dripped from her lips.

"Let's set up a meet, we can make the exchange. No funny business."

"Like you said before, let's not play games. How much do you want Mr. Wolf?"

"Ten grand, in cash," I said.

She paused. Looked down at her hands.

"Or—I could find another interested buyer."

"Ten thousand," she said flatly.

"And I'm outta your hair for good."

"That would be agreeable," she replied.

"How soon can you get the money?"

"The money's not a problem," she said evenly.

Her cool manner gave me a chill. She was as dangerous as getting in bed with a rattlesnake.

"Good. I'll call you with a time and a place to meet tomorrow evening. Both you and your husband."

"I don't see why we have to involve my husband with—"

"Both you and your husband, or no deal. Follow?"

She looked at me and her eyes went cold. I had this dangerous animal cornered. I could see in her steely eyes that she'd have no trouble ripping my throat out just as easily as ordering a scotch and soda. I could feel a bead of sweat begin to work its way out from under my armpit down to my ribs.

"As you wish, Mr. Wolf. We will be there."

"Tomorrow night at ten. I'll call and give you the address at nine-thirty," I said. "You bring the money and I'll bring the merchandise."

She didn't say a word after that. She just gave me a loathsome stare. Then she picked up her gloves and slid out of the booth, making a beeline to the exit.

Sully was leaning against the fender when I returned to my car.

That one is more dangerous than Cappello, Sully said.

"She made me sweat."

Five'll getcha ten, Cappello's been blackmailin' her.

"It's a sure thing," I said as I got into the car. "You commin'?"

Sully smiled. Faded away.

"Yeah! What was I thinkin'."

I headed back to the hotel.

Chapter 28

I picked up several newspapers and a fifth of bourbon before returning to the hotel. Started leaning on the booze again to keep me going. I scanned the papers. Accounts of the Bailey murder were mostly the same. All had somewhat of a description of a man wanted for questioning as a material witness, who had been seen going into the hotel before Bailey's body was discovered. None of the papers had any indication that the police were looking for a former SFPD cop and private dick by the name of James Wolf. I had a suspicion that Rickman was keeping that information under wraps until he met with me. After I finished poring over the early editions, I felt hungry. I walked a couple of blocks down the street from the hotel to a small delicatessen. Picked up a corned beef sandwich and slaw and headed back to the hotel.

I cooled my heels for much of the afternoon. It was around 2:11 p.m. when the desk clerk slipped a note under my door. Doc had called and requested Mr. Kirkland to meet him at the Old Ship Saloon on Pacific and Battery. I found Doc seated in a back booth. I took a seat across from him.

"What have you got for me?"

"It's not very good news, Giaco," he replied gravely.

"Spill it."

"The police want you for questioning in the Shortt killing, according to my Chronicle contact. That information will be coming out in the late edition from what I understand."

"Now everyone and their sister will be out looking for me," I moaned.

"Whacha gonna do now?"

"Looks like I'm running out of time fast. I've got to get a handle on this mess before Rickman and his flatfoot brigade are down around my neck. I'm meetin' Mrs. Schofield tomorrow night."

Doc said sternly, "You're really takin' chances, my friend."

"Believe me! I've seen her up close. I wouldn't be alone with her in a room again without a whip and a chair," I said. "There's a mystery man lurkin' somewhere. I can feel it."

"Be very careful. I've come to enjoy our little excursions," Doc replied coyly.

"If this doesn't work send my mail to San Quentin. Hopefully, I'll only get twenty."

I left Doc at the Old Ship and called Claire from a phone booth across the street. She'd just returned from lunch.

"There was something about the supper club last night that's been on my mind," she said. "The trouble is—I can't put my finger on what it is."

"You may have recognized Cappello from a time you were there before," I said.

"No, I'm sure I never saw him before. Maybe it was because Mrs. Schofield was at that table when we had the birthday party. She was with some man and it wasn't her husband I can tell you that for sure. Anyway, be careful."

"I've made an appointment with Schofield for tomorrow night. I'd like to meet at your apartment if that'll work for you. Will you be able to stay with someone tomorrow evening?"

"Sure, that won't be a problem. I could be there to help if you want."

"No," I said. "Just in case there's trouble. I've met Mrs. Schofield to set up the meet. She's dangerous with a capital D."

"Oh my!" Claire exclaimed.

"Don't worry. I'll be fine."

"The icebox is stocked, so you are welcome to help yourself to food and drink," Claire said wearily.

"Thanks. You've been an angel."

I hung up the phone then dropped another coin in the slot to call for a cab.

"City cab," The female voice said flatly.

"Can I get a cab to—"

The booth door squeaked open and a beefy hand pressed down the receiver. A booming baritone voice intoned:

"You won't be needing that cab friend."

Chapter 29

"Well, if it isn't Sergeant McNabb. How are ya Sarge?" I said as he unceremoniously yanked me out of the booth. "Hang on Mac, that's my nickel."

McNabb stuck his finger in the slot.

"Funny guy," McNabb said.

"You're always good for a laugh."

"Shut up. Rickman wants to talk to you." He shoved me toward the police vehicle. "Put your hands on the roof," McNabb said. "I'm gonna pat you down."

"Not carryin' today, Sarge."

Satisfied with his search, McNabb stuffed me in the backseat then wedged his big frame in next to me. Behind the wheel was Inspector Silks. A boyish-looking 30-year-old officer. I'd seen him around the precinct from time to time, he was a straight-up kind of cop, firm but fair.

"You're Silks," I said. "Heard good things about you. I'm James Wolf."

He looked at me through the rearview mirror but made no overt reaction to my introductions.

"So, what's Rickman want to see me about now?" I said to McNabb who just looked out of the window at the pedestrians walking along the street.

"Yeah, I guess he needs some help. Did you guys pick up Manny and Bruno?"

We drove along in silence.

"It's always good talking with you, McNabb. Stimulatin', you know what I mean?"

"Just shut the hell up, Wolf!" McNabb snapped.

"Sure thing, my friend. If you're not in the mood for a chin-wag, I can understand that. I am in no way opposed to just enjoying this lovely ride on a beautiful afternoon with two of San Francisco's finest—"

"Are you gonna shut up, or do I have to make ya?"

Through the rearview, I could see Silks choke back a snicker. We continued the trip in silence for another ten minutes. I contemplated my future. This could go very wrong, despite my cheery bonhomie. We pulled into Police Headquarters.

McNabb escorted me through the building and deposited me into an interrogation room. It was a small space with four wooden straight-back chairs, two on either side of a wood table. Walls covered with sound-absorbing panels. A two-way mirror was located just a couple of feet left of the interrogation room door. This was a clear sign that Rickman meant business. I was not going to talk with him in his office. This was official. I dropped my hat on the table, took a seat facing the mirror and waited. Typical police formula when they have suspects in custody. Let them stew for a spell before any questioning. Let them worry about what will come next. On this side of the fence, I discovered there was some validity to the procedure. I lit a cigarette to calm me down and get my mind off what was to come next. I was halfway through my smoke when Rickman entered. He dropped a file on the table, leaned over, put his two hands on the table, then looked me straight in the eye. I took a drag on my cigarette, crushed it out in the ashtray in the middle of the table. Rickman opened the folder and started leafing through papers. I made myself busy inspecting the calluses on my hands. My inspection revealed a need for a manicure.

Rickman finally broke the silence.

"Where were you last night?" he said in a matter-of-fact manner. His head down perusing papers in a folder.

"Date with a lady."

"I didn't ask what you did, I asked where you were."

"Do I need to get my lawyer? Am I being charged with anything?"

"Look! You know you'll get better than a fair shake with me. I'm going to need some answers."

"I was on a date with a lady at Julie's!" I snapped.

"You met with Nick Cappello?"

"He was there."

"I believe you had an opportunity to have a conversation with him?"

"Christ! We shared a sandbox."

"I had a man keeping an eye on Cappello."

"Figures. So, what did that get you?"

"Did you visit Shortt last night?"

"I think you know I did. You've already spoken with Claire. I wanted to tell Bailey that I'd squared things with Nick."

"Squared things?"

"Did you pick up Manny and his pal?" I said.

"I'm askin' the questions."

"Okay, let's back up. Bailey was worried that Nick was out to get him because Nick thought he'd double-crossed him. Nick frequents Julie's several times a week. I wanted to explain the mix-up."

"Then what happened?"

"Well . . ."

"Come on Wolf. I need to know."

"I told Nick where he could get the merchandise."

"You did *what*!?"

"The item I was hired to purchase was supposed to be delivered to Nick. Indirectly, but it was ultimately supposed to get to Nick. I stored the box containing the items at the Terminal baggage claim. I gave Nick the claim check."

"What the *hell*!"

"I'm guessing he's picked it up by now." Rickman was on the verge of blowing a gasket. I've seen that look before. "Bailey had changed hotels, but I was able to track him down at the Central. I went there to let him know that Nick got the merchandise and he was off the hook. Shortt was dead when I got to his hotel room. I think one of Nick's boys had a tail on Bailey—theory is that Nick gave his boys the word that he wanted Shortt to disappear—permanently. They understood the message. The way I figure it, they must've gotten there just before I did because I got sapped on the head when I entered his room. When I regained consciousness, my gun was gone."

"So, now your gun is missing, is that it?"

I rose from my chair and positioned myself in front of the two-way mirror. I could see Sully standing directly behind me.

"Yeah, I need to do something about that. You have an extra piece floating around?"

Be careful...Sully said. "You know, one of those heaters you use to plant on a suspect—"

Rickman was on me in an instant, both hands grabbing my lapels as he slammed me against the wall.

What did I tell ya? Sully cracked.

"You really screwed things up this time Jimmy boy," Rickman snorted through clenched teeth.

You went too far! Sully groaned. *You still haven't learned when to ease off.*

"Yeah, I know," I said.

"You know what?" Rickman said.

"I screwed the pooch on this one. I figured Nick would let Shortt slide since he got the package."

Rickman was about to dice me like a meat cutter at a slaughterhouse when the door opened and McNabb entered. Rickman let go of my jacket and proceeded to straighten my tie and smooth out my lapels. McNabb whispered something into Rickman's ear.

Hey listen. You're on Rickman's side, remember?

"Yeah," I said aloud.

"What now?" said Rickman.

"Look. We're on the same side here," I pleaded.

"I'm ready to book you for interfering with an investigation," Rickman growled. "I could have you locked up for the rest of the century!"

"Come on. Gimme a break here. I'm workin' a different case. I can wrap this thing up. I just need a little more time. There's still one more piece to the puzzle."

"Book him, McNabb.

"What charge, boss?"

"Withholding evidence, for the time being. I can come up with a few others later."

"I apologized for crying out loud, Mike! When have I ever done that?"

"Take him away," Rickman commanded.

"You got another murder on your hands," I pleaded, as McNabb took me by the arm. "You're gonna look pretty stupid when the real King Pin of this operation gets away because you've got me locked in a cell."

Take it easy, Sully whispered.

"How can I take it easy when he's not listening to me?" I howled.

McNabb said, "I think he's losing his marbles, Lieutenant," as he raised his hand next to his head and made a circular motion with his index finger.

"I'm telling you there's more to this than just those statues. I got proof."

Don't say another word, Sully advised. *Let him chew on that.*

Rickman sat back in the chair. I could see him run scenarios in his mind. I was way ahead of him on the facts of this investigation and he had two murders on his plate right now.

"Believe me," I said. "Cappello only got a fraction of the delivery."

"Damn it, Wolf!" Rickman said as he slammed the folder flap shut. "What the *hell's* goin on here?"

"Can't tell ya right now. But I can tell ya this. Cappello was only the muscle in this caper. I'm about to blow this case sky high."

Tell him you need twenty-four hours.

"You give me 'til tomorrow and I can deliver you the leader of an international smuggling ring. The solution to two murders, not to mention you'll put Cappello behind bars for the rest of his life." Rickman twitched and picked at the folder on the table. "What've you got to lose? Bruno Durkin admitted to me that he accidentally killed Irene Talbot. I figure that Nick killed Bailey to keep *his* mouth shut."

"He's right, Lieutenant. There's nothin' to lose," McNabb chimed in.

"I have a plan. Just need a little more time," I said. Rickman drummed his fingers on the table for several moments. "I'll have the whole case laid out like a menu at the Top of the Mark."

"Wolf's not goin' anywhere, Lieutenant," McNabb said.

Rickman scooped up the file on the table.

"You've got until tomorrow," Rickman said reluctantly, as he got up from the table. Opened the door and signaled to McNabb with a nod. "Turn him loose!" he barked storming out of the interrogation room.

I waited until dark before I approached Claire's apartment, found the key, let myself in. Turned on the light switch and surveyed the living room. Built-in shelf containing books, mantel clock and knick-knacks directly to the right of the entrance. Hallway on the left led to the bedroom. A closet situated directly across from the entrance. In the center of the living area, Claire had two matching flower print loveseats facing each other with a coffee table between. One of the loveseats faced the apartment's bay window. The other faced the wall that separated the kitchen from the living room. Along the wall was a small desk and chair. On top of the desk was a telephone. An archway to the immediate right of the desk led to a small kitchen.

I took the smaller sack of jewels from my coat pocket and stashed it behind some books on the bookshelf. I hung my topcoat in the closet and checked the automatic I took from Shortt's hotel room. Removed the silencer. Three live rounds were in the clip. I looked up. Sully was leaning against the entrance door.

You better find a place to stash that where you can get at it fast.

"Yeah, you're right."

I went to the loveseat with its back to the bay window and slipped the gun between the cushion and the armrest on the right side. Seated there I could observe the entire living room and part of the kitchen.

"There. I'll sit here and have 'em sit across from me. Now all that's left to do is wait."

That's the hard part, Sully noted, then vanished.

I fixed myself a drink and made a sandwich. I read several of the magazines Claire had in the apartment, chain-smoked a half dozen cigarettes and drank a couple of bourbon and sodas to kill the next few hours. Finally, 9:30 rolled around and I picked up the phone and dialed Mrs. Schofield. After giving her the address, I cleaned up my dirty dishes, made one last check of the apartment and sat back down to wait the final thirty minutes. One way or another, this case would be solved tonight. I closed my eyes for a minute to clear my head when Claire's phone began making an impression. I got up and lifted the receiver.

"GIACO!" Doc's voice yelled before I had a chance to say hello.

"What is it, Doc?"

"My bookie just told me Nick Cappello's body was found in his parked car."

"Christ! Where?"

"Golden Gate Park. Chain of Lakes Drive. Shot to death. I checked with my Chronicle contact just ten minutes ago. Point blank range from what he heard. Both Nick and his chauffeur. Guy walkin' his dog found him coupla hours ago. They think it happened sometime late last night."

"Manny and Bruno must be on the run now. Who the *hell* shot Cappello—Schofield?"

"Doesn't seem plausible," Doc said. "This Adrian Schofield doesn't have the guts from what I've been able to dig up. May slap a woman around once in a while, but murder?"

"Deidra! Nick probably contacted her once he got the package. Yeah, she could slither up to Nick real cozy-like and pump a few ounces of lead into his liver. She's just cold-blooded enough. Well, she's on her way here right now so she knows I have the jewels."

"Do you have any last requests, Giaco? Where would you like your ashes scattered? If I were you, I'd get the police over there right now."

"Thanks for the advice, Doc. I'll handle it my way."

"Good luck, Jimmy," Doc said, then hung up.

I took a deep breath and surveyed the room. "I'm way out on a limb on this one," I said to Sully, as I placed the phone back on its cradle. "Deidra all along."

Gotta figure she could never trust Nick once he found out she was livin' here. He'd bleed her dry.

"She strung him along. Waitin' for that right moment. Whatta sap."

You're on your own on this one, pal. No backup, so be careful how you play it. Only one out away from a complete game.

I noticed that my hand was shaking terribly. I glanced at the clock. 9:36 p.m. I sat back on the couch, no time to write my last will and testament let alone get a witness.

Chapter 30

Deidra sat on the edge of the print couch, twitching and wringing her hands, looking nervous. Red hair pulled back and stuffed under a floppy felt hat, she still had that distinctive look of elegance. Her light brown eyes darted around Claire's apartment.

Adrian Schofield dressed impeccably in a cream-colored linen suit. Light blue starched shirt, yellow bow tie. He arranged himself in the stuffed armchair next to the couch, his knees together, feet flat on the floor to minimize any wrinkling in his trousers. He was a half-inch shorter than Deidra and much older. He carried a few extra pounds around his middle but looked quite fit. He rested his hands on the gold parrot-head handle of a black cane. Adrian had the look of a man who was always impatient. He wanted this thing over with and soon.

"May I offer you a drink?" I said. "Scotch—bourbon?"

"Scotch and soda, if you don't mind," Adrian said.

"Deidra?"

"Nothing for me," she said.

I went into Claire's tiny kitchen. Mixed a scotch for Adrian and a bourbon for myself. I returned to the living room, handed Adrian his drink and sat at the end of the loveseat. As I sipped my drink, Adrian set his glass on the small round table next to the chair.

"Are we going to get down to business or are we just going to sit here and waste my time? I am not a man to be trifled with."

"I have something you want and I'm willing to sell."

"I have the money," Adrian said. "Let's see the merchandise. If it is worth what you say. We have a deal."

"There are some details I'd like to go over first," I said.

"Get on with it," Adrian sneered.

"Let's review, shall we? Late last Friday morning, I had a visitor to my office. She called herself Elizabeth Westrom. I was to purchase on her behalf a certain pair of statues from a particular lot delivered to Brooklyn's Auctioneers. After I secured the purchase, I was to deliver said purchase to an address in Burlingame." A puzzled look crossed Adrian's face. "To my misfortune, as well as yours, my car broke down. I had to borrow my mechanic friend's car. By the time I arrived, considerably late—I discovered the place locked up. I can only assume that the person or persons, expecting the delivery, panicked believing they'd been double-crossed."

"This is all very interesting, but I've never heard of . . . what was her—"

"Elizabeth Westrom," I interjected.

"Never heard of her," Adrian said.

"Elizabeth Westrom was an alias. Her name was Irene Talbot."

Adrian shot a look at Deidra. He was starting to put two and two together and didn't like how the math was adding up. "Thinking that Irene had changed plans, she was visited by someone in an attempt to get her to reveal where she had the items delivered. They put the questioning to her a little too hard and well . . ."

Adrian slammed the point of his cane on the floor.

"This woman, sir, worked for us but resigned," Adrian's eyes followed me as I rose and leisurely paced the floor.

He said, "I hardly knew the woman. I thought I made that clear."

"I understand," I said. "I can assume that Irene told this individual where I lived. She did have my address in her diary. After leaving Irene's apartment, this person proceeded to my address and staked out my place. I planned on meeting my mechanic at my apartment so we could exchange cars. But when my car arrived, it was assumed that the driver was me and the people waiting gave my mechanic a good working over, not realizing they had the wrong man."

"So, you had this item with you at the time?" Adrian asked.

"I did. They were statues of two Chinese Water Carriers."

"This is preposterous! What does this have to do with me? This is the first I've heard of Chinese Water Carriers," he said turning to Deidra.

I shot her a look. I could tell he was worried.

"Your beef is with *whom*?" Adrian spat out the words. His petulance seemed phony.

"I had no idea at the time. The following mornin' I started to investigate what was going on with these two statues. It was a complex problem, but this is the way it figures." I sat on the loveseat across from Deidra and Adrian. "Before taking a job with you, Irene worked for a man named Bailey Shortt. Irene wasn't on the up and up from the get-go and had talked Bailey into putting together this real estate con. Bailey used company funds to finance the con. When the deal didn't go as planned, they started hocking Irene's rings and watches to cover the payroll of his office manager so no one would be the wiser. Irene then left and took the job with you," I said, looking directly at Deidra.

"Is there any way we could move this along?" Adrian grumbled. "Who is this Bailey anyway? Never heard of him either!"

"Bailey was in a serious jam. The roof was about to fall in on him when the head office scheduled an audit. Irene tells him he can borrow money from a loan shark, Nick 'The Hat' Cappello, to cover up his embezzlement." I took a sip of my drink to get a chance to take a good look at Deidra over my glass. She was sweating like a hooker in a confessional. "How Irene knew about Nick Cappello, I haven't figured yet, but I have my suspicions," I said looking directly at Deidra. "Bailey's able to put the money back and balance the company books but then Nick wants his money."

"I fail to see the connection here, Mr. Wolf. What does this Cappello have to do with *anything!?*" Adrian was practically shouting now—you could hear the growing panic in his voice.

"Here's the way it shakes out. Irene discovered your smuggling operation and told Bailey."

Deidra bolted up from the couch, hotter than a two-dollar pistol. Her face was glowing red like a hot coal.

"You bastard!" she spat out viciously.

"Sit down lady!" I said with authority.

"You'll pay for this, mister. I don't much like your manner," she said, still hot under the collar and in a panic.

I said, "That's okay, I don't much like it either, but it's all I've got."

"You, sonofabitch! This wasn't part of the deal!" Deidra said.

"I think I've heard about enough," Adrian uttered as he stood and reached for his hat. "You invite me here under some pretense. I won't stand for it."

"Well then, *sit down!*" I said as I continued my story. "Nick wanted the money Bailey borrowed and offered him an out. He knew Irene worked for you and you were smuggling stolen artwork into the country."

Adrian slowly lowered himself back on the couch at the same time Deidra rose from her seat.

"How is that possible?" Adrian said.

Deidra walked around the back of the couch and stood behind Adrian. She put her hand on his shoulder. He reached over and patted her hand in a calming manner.

"What is he talking about, dear?" Adrian said.

"I'm talkin' about a shipment of jewels hidden in the statues," I said. "The jewels that would square Bailey Shortt with Cappello."

"Jewels?" Adrian said.

"Yeah! Jewels. Now *Shortt's* dead."

"Dead?" Adrian said.

"Caught up with him as he was about to leave town. He figured Cappello was close on his tail because he didn't get his money and was afraid to hang around. I told him that he should contact the police, but . . ."

"Cappello killed him?" Adrian asked.

"Stands to reason. You didn't kill him, did you?"

"I wouldn't know this Bailey fellow if he walked into this room."

"I met with Cappello the other night. I explained the mix-up and told Nick where to pick up the merchandise. He has it by now. I understand that the police want to question him for the murder of Irene." Deidra's face went whiter than the Rockies on Christmas Day.

"I don't understand." Adrian's voice trembled.

"Nick has the statues but I have the jewels."

Adrian looked at me as if I had three arms.

"Christ almighty!" I said. "You're a bigger sap than I am!"

Adrian looked as sick as if he had eaten a plate of bad oysters.

I walked to the bookcase to the left of the couch, reached behind a set of Funk & Wagnall's and produced the jewel sack.

"I don't care if you're a smuggler, or how Irene found out, or any of that. All I'm interested in is a payoff," I said, as I slipped the tie off and dumped a load of gems onto the coffee table.

Adrian made what sounded like a cough and mumbled something I couldn't make out. My eyes followed the gems as they rolled across the mahogany tabletop.

"What the . . ." a shocked Adrian said.

"I figure these little baubles must be worth nearly a million," I said looking up. "What do you think?"

Adrian swallowed hard. "Deidra—"

"Shut your mouth, Adrian! *You!*" she said to me. "Put your hands over your head!"

In her hand, a shiny silver-plated .25 caliber Beretta—a tiny but deadly instrument—pointed directly at my chest. Adrian raised himself from the couch and gave me a broad smile of satisfaction. I just stood there with a stupid look on my face.

"I guess I should've patted you down before we started this little soiree," I said, raising my hands.

"I'll get the jewels, dear," Adrian said.

"Sit down and shut up! You're a fool," Deidra spit through clenched teeth.

"What's going on, Deidra?"

"I said *shut up!*"

Dejected, Adrian sat back on the couch. This is what happens, I thought when you're out of practice. I tried to figure all the possibilities, but this had more angles than a geometry quiz. Deidra turned to me.

"Your gun," she said. "Put it on the table."

I opened my jacket wide and said, "I don't like carrying iron all the time. Ruins the cut of my jacket. Makes this bulge right here—"

"Shut up funny man. Put the stones back in the sack."

I picked up the sack and started to drop the gems into it.

"There's another one of these, you know."

"Get it!" she barked.

"It's not here. I can have it brought over. I just have to make a phone call."

"Do it. And don't try any tricks. I know how to use this."

I pointed to the small desk along the wall that held the phone. Deidra waved the gun in the direction of the desk.

"So you and Nick go way back. Whose idea was it, Miriam, for you to pull off this scheme—you or Nick's? Or was Nick blackmailing you?"

Her face started to redden again. Adrian's mouth moved but no sound came out.

She said, "You think you're pretty smart, Wolf."

"I do have my moments," I said as I walked to the phone. "I'm guessing it was blackmail. Nick either threatened to tell Adrian here—or whatever his real name is—that you were Rico Manzetti's ex. Or he'd let Vic Manzetti know you were here living in San Francisco as Mrs. Schofield. I'm thinking it's the latter."

"Shut up and make that phone call," she said.

I started to dial a phone number.

"Did Nick know about the jewels?"

She just stood there. I could see rage in her eyes.

"There's one thing that doesn't figure. Why did Nick kill Bailey?" I asked. "I gave him what he wanted."

"Who knows why Nick does anything?" Deidra laughed.

"Doc! It's Wolf," I said into the phone. "Listen. Make the call. The box is with my landlady. Bring it to 1722 Steiner, apartment 'A'. Got it?"

I hung up the phone.

"Deidra! What the hell . . ." Adrian moaned. "I thought that we—"

"I SAID SHUT UP!" Deidra yelled. "You know who this is Wolf? Johann Hofmann. Nazi clerk. A lousy Corporal. He was in charge of storing the valuables taken from Jews that were sent to concentration camps because he worked in a jewelry store before the war."

"Deidra, what are you doing?" pleaded Adrian.

At that moment, I detected a clear German accent. I'd noticed it before—but honestly, it seemed almost like a speech impediment. I can be a little slow on the uptake. Now it all made perfect sense—Schofield was a brown shirt bockwurst—with the emphasis on worst. I moved back over to my seat. Deidra kept a wary eye on me the whole time as she nonchalantly pointed her gun at Adrian.

"He tells me he wants to make an honest woman out of me," she said "How's that for a laugh."

"And that didn't fit into your plans?" I prodded.

"He wanted to go into a legit business. White picket fence—the whole nine yards," she said as she moved close to Adrian's ear. "I'm *sick* of you!" she barked. "I'm done. I'm gettin' out. This shipment is worth close to a million, at least. I'll get five hundred, maybe six hundred thousand for the lot. If not more."

"That would set you up for life. You said we earlier. Who are you planning on sharing this with?"

Adrian gave Deidra a pleading look as she moved closer to me.

"You think you're cute, Wolf."

"I know I am. It gets me into trouble sometimes. So, what happens next? I mean when the rest of the gems get here. You gonna shoot us?"

"That won't be necessary. As soon as the package arrives, I'll be on my way and you two can commiserate together."

Adrian slumped over and put his head in his hands.

"Can I fix you another, Deidra?" I said, holding up my glass.

"Just shut up."

"But I like to talk. For example, why didn't you just intercept the information about the jewel shipment and go and get the thing yourself?"

"For the same reason that Irene told you. I would've been recognized."

Adrian moaned something unintelligible.

"So, who were you planning to share this haul with? It certainly wasn't Cappello. Who was it?"

"None of your damn business," she said, waving the pistol in my face. "You enjoy needling don't you, Wolf?"

"One of my favorite pastimes, outside of poker and billiards," I said. "Why don't you put that thing away? You waving it around like that gives me the heebie-jeebies."

I heard a faint sound in the hallway of the apartment, followed by a light tapping on the door. Deidra moved to the door, her hand holding the pistol moved behind her back as she turned the knob. The door slowly swung open. Adrian turned to the door and a *"Whaaa?!"* escaped his lips as a tall man in a tan trench coat stepped into the room.

"Took you long enough," I said.

Chapter 31

Rickman took off his hat as he entered the apartment. He looked to me first, then to Adrian, then Deidra. She stiffened. A shocked look crossed her face. Her pistol still trained on me.

"Everything okay here?" he said.

"Fine, now that you're here," I said, relieved.

"I'll take that, sweetheart," Rickman said to Deidra.

She relaxed. Moved to him. Handed her gun butt first. "The other half of the jewels are on their way," she said.

"I've got 'em right here," Rickman said, patting his hand on his trench coat pocket.

This case just blew up like a silk skirt in a tornado. That sap on my head that night in my apartment. It all became clear.

"I should've figured your landlady," Rickman said, as he removed the tied sack from his overcoat pocket.

"You've been playing me for a sucker all along. My god! How stupid am I?" I said, rubbing the top of my head. "This lump on my head? I'm guessin' I owe ya one, pal."

"Who the hell is this?!" whined Adrian.

"Lieutenant Michael D. Rickman, of the San Francisco Police Department," I said as I started to rise from the couch.

"Just sit down and relax," Rickman said. "I'm sorry about the rough treatment. Did you get his gun?"

"Didn't have one on him," Deidra said.

As a kid, I had a puzzle. It was a carnival scene with colorful balloons. A little boy and girl were standing next to an ice cream cart. The ice cream vendor was handing the little girl a cone. The face of the vendor was a single puzzle piece, a star shape. I remember losing that piece, so when I put the puzzle together, it all looked great, except for the blank space where the man's face should be. This is what this case had become. I could see a clear picture but the key character was missing. It all made sense now. Rickman was that missing piece.

"Just how do you think you're going to get away with this, Mike?" I said as I leaned a bit forward. I pushed my right hand between the couch cushion. My fingers touched the handle of the .38. "You can't start shooting. Too many neighbors," I said.

"There won't be any shooting, Jimmy," Rickman said. "Don't worry."

"It was a good performance, Mike. I didn't even realize you were aware of everything from the starting gate."

"I knew what was going on with you. Broke and you needed money. A little assignment like this, I was sure you'd go for. You tend to overlook a few things for the right price. You're not as honest as you try to make people believe. Besides, we worked together. You do tend to follow directions to the letter. That stupid jalopy of yours. Couldn't figure that into the equation. I couldn't come right out and ask you to give me the jewels. I had no idea you even knew they were hidden in the statues."

I shook my head, "What made you do it?"

Rickman moved closer to Deidra, slipped his arm around her waist.

"On my salary, I couldn't provide the kind of life that Deidra was accustomed to."

It always seems to come down to a woman. For a woman he threw his career into the sewer.

"She's Miriam, my friend. Miriam LaSalla, Rico—"

"I know all that," Rickman interrupted. "She's Deidra now and that's the way it's gonna stay."

"Have to admit. Things are working out for ya. Cappello kills Bailey, so he's out of your hair. Deidra kills Cappello—"

"Cappello didn't kill Bailey," Rickman said.

"He didn't?"

"No! That's all on you, pal. Bailey took your advice after you met with 'im. Got in touch with me and was about to spill his guts. He figured that Irene had double-crossed him and when she was murdered, Cappello'd be after him next. He was going to blow the whistle, come down to the Hall and give himself up, right then and there. We would've had to pick up Adrian here," he said tossing a thumb in Schofield's direction. "Which would have only gummed up the works even worse. Had to do somethin' drastic. Told Bailey to stay at his hotel until I got there. I told 'im to sit tight but he wouldn't have it. Wanted police protection. If he'd only decided to make a run for it. I was about to leave when I hear this tappin' at the door. You again," Rickman said, shaking his head in frustration. "Made me have to leave the gun behind."

"I find out what hotel Bailey had moved to and then I get sapped again. That's two concussions I owe you," I said. "You kill Cappello?"

"I picked up his tail at the terminal. Thought it was my lucky night. Imagine my surprise when I smashed the damn things only to fine gravel," Rickman said. "Cursed you a blue streak." Rickman pulled a couple of pairs of bracelets from his coat pocket. "You two gentlemen will be going for a short ride to the warehouse district. Found a spot where we can keep you safe and sound for the next twenty-four hours until we're safely out of the country. When they open the place up in the mornin', you'll need a shave but not much the worse for wear."

"It won't work, Mike," I remarked as I opened my jacket a bit. "Can I get a smoke?"

Rickman nodded and said, "I think it will. You're already wanted for questioning in the Shortt killing. I made sure of that," Rickman removed my .38 from his trench coat. "Ballistics will find that it was your gun that killed Cappello," he said, letting out a contemptuous laugh. "By the time the department sorts through this mess, you'll be lucky if they don't pin my disappearance on you."

I lit a cigarette and blew out a stream of blue-gray smoke.

"You're a real sonofabitch, Rickman," I said.

"I wish I could be there when you start telling the story of how this woman paid you to buy a statue at Brooklyn's. Then ends up dead. Then her boyfriend is killed. Then your gun is used in the Cappello murder. I'm really sorry you're the one who's getting the short end of the stick on this one pal," Rickman said with a snicker.

"I bet you're sorry," I snapped back. "You're okay with letting me fry for this."

"It won't go that far. The department will figure what really happened before too long."

"That's so reassuring. What made you go so wrong?" I said. "I really want to know."

"There comes a time, Jimmy. That you have to look out for number one," Rickman said as he tapped his chest with his thumb. "Fifteen years on the force, putting my life on the line every day, for what? Mahoney, making sure I wouldn't get a Captain's promotion because I went to bat for you. I should've been promoted to Commander by now. But what have I got to show for it? Not much. A couple hundred in the bank and no future." He turned. Look at Deidra. "Then I met Deidra."

I could see that he'd fallen for her hard. What a chump.

He said, "Dealing with the sewer rats that dirty up this town . . . well that's over now. Nothin's gettin' in my way."

I shook my head. Looked straight at Rickman. The two of us locked eyes.

"Yeah, I guess that's the way you were when you were walkin' a beat. Build up that arrest record. Get that next promotion. Youngest to ever make Inspector. You didn't care if there wasn't sufficient evidence. Plant some. The perp was already a two-time loser," I said. "Didn't matter if he didn't do this crime. He was surely guilty of some others."

"Damn judges. We lock 'em up. They turn 'em loose. Tired of the merry-go-round."

I shook my head. There wasn't much left to say, he knew it and I knew it. I could sense the pressure he was feeling. Something simple had gone terribly wrong. He killed two men in cold blood. He was up to his neck with no way out. There was an eerie stillness in the room. No one moved. I shifted my eyes toward Adrian. His head was in his hands again. Deidra, standing to Rickman's left side, didn't take her eyes off of him. I could only imagine that Rickman was replaying the events of this last week over in his mind. He was wound up tighter than a five-and-dime watch. Spring ready to snap. The clock on the bookshelf ticked out a slow rhythm. The moment seemed to last an excruciating long time when suddenly the silence was shattered by the shrill ring of the telephone.

Deidra shrieked and fell into Rickman. Adrian shot up and I slid the .38 out from between the sofa cushion. The next moment ran in my mind in slow motion. I swung my arm up and pointed the revolver at Rickman. He had a puzzled look on his face as if he'd never seen a gun before. He was frozen—unable to move. I squeezed off a round hitting him in the lower right side of his chest. The impact threw him back and to his right. He crashed to the bookcase. I squeezed off another. Second shot hit him in the stomach, pitching him toward Deidra, knocking her against the wall and into the desk. Phone crashed to the floor. Rickman took two steps back when his knees gave out and he fell on his back in the hallway. Adrian just stood there motionless in a state of shock.

"MIKE!" screamed Deidra as she scrambled to Rickman's side.

Rickman moaned in agony as I bolted from the couch darting across the room. Deidra's .25 lay just a few inches from him. I picked it up. Slipped it into my jacket pocket. I reached inside Rickman's coat. Pulled back his suit jacket. Took his revolver out of its holster. I retrieved my gun from the left side jacket pocket. With all the artillery collected I moved to the phone. I could hear a voice coming through the earpiece yelling "HELLO, HELLO—SOMEBODY?!" I picked the receiver off the floor.

"Yeah," I said.

"Jimmy. It's Claire. You alright?!"

"I'm fine," I said as calmly as I could. "Listen. Call the police and have them get an ambulance to your place right away. There's been a shooting."

"Oh my god! Yes. I'll call right away. I wanted to tell you. I remembered who the guy was I saw at Julie's with Mrs. Schofield. It was Rickman."

"Yeah, I know," I said.

I hung up the phone and checked on Rickman. He was bleeding badly. It appeared that the bullet smashed a rib. He was barely conscious.

Nearly hysterical Deidra kept repeating. "You killed him! You killed him!"

"Shut up and get a towel from the bathroom!"

Deidra, on her knees, straightened herself up. She stared at her hands. They were covered with blood.

As I knelt down at Rickman's side the apartment door opened then closed. I heard Adrian's footsteps rush down the hall.

"Get a towel, DAMNIT! NOW!" I yelled.

Deidra rose to her feet sobbing.

"Mike. Can you hear me, pal? Stay with me. Can you do that?"

A hysterically crying Deidra returned with a towel and just stood over me wringing the towel in her hands. I grabbed the towel from her and pressed it against the wound to help stem the bleeding. It didn't look good, but it was all I could do.

Rickman opened his eyes a bit.

"Ya pulled a fast one on me, Jimmy," Rickman said.

"Don't try to talk," I said. "Had no choice, Mike. Ya put me in a jam."

Someone was pounding on the apartment door. Off in the distance, the sound of sirens grew louder.

Chapter 32

McNabb arrived on the scene just a minute before the ambulance. A crowd of tenants had gathered in the hall. Ambulance attendants pushed their way through the crush of humanity clogging the hall.

"Please, *everyone!*" McNabb announced. "Clear the hall, please! Go back to your rooms."

The attendants loaded Rickman onto a stretcher. McNabb and I followed them to the meat wagon.

Rickman was conscious for most of the ten-minute ride.

"Wasn't like I could come out and ask ya if you had the jewels," Rickman said.

I turned my head. McNabb was taking notes.

"Take it easy," I said.

"Couldn't put a tail on ya. You'd spot that in a minute."

"Save your strength, Mike," I said.

"It's all over for me," he said and smiled. "That stupid jalopy of yours."

Rickman slipped into unconsciousness as we arrived at General Hospital.

Doctors rushed Rickman into surgery. McNabb and I sat in the hospital waiting room.

"I'd gotten a feelin' somethin' wasn't right. Rickman didn't seem too concerned over Durkin and Strupp," McNabb said. "I didn't want those two still on the streets. So, I had the San Jose Police pick 'em up."

"Rickman must've figured that with those two on the loose, it would leave the department stretched thin to run down all the leads. By the time they figured what was what, he and Deidra would be safely in South America."

When Durkin and Strupp ratted out Nick and most of the caper, that really must've got McNabb's ears burning. He may be big and dumb, but McNabb was a good cop and he knew something didn't sit right.

I hung around the hospital waiting room for two hours before I went down to the cafeteria for a sandwich and coffee. As I stepped into the elevator, a smiling Sully met me.

"Who would've figured Rickman was behind the whole affair?" I said.

Ya never know. But when you keep your wits about you, you're prepared for almost anything.

"The only question I have after all this is said and done is, how the *hell* did Rickman know I'd have Doc call *him* to pick up the gems?"

Dumb luck, Sully said.

When I returned to the waiting room McNabb told me that Rickman died on the operating table. We went to Police Headquarters where I proceeded to reconstruct the whole case in an official statement.

Johann Hofmann, alias Adrian Schofield, lived in Pittsburgh for three years before he moved back to Germany when Hitler came to power. He started pocketing precious stones and artwork as soon as he was in charge of the confiscated valuables. In '45, he slipped out of Germany into Switzerland. In '46, he contacted an old friend, Rodrigo Perez. Thief by trade living in Spain. Perez had an import/export business and shipped merchandise to Brooklyn's. Hofmann moved his merchandise from Switzerland to Spain then made his way to the U.S. He assumed the identity of a dead man, Adrian Schofield. He passed himself off as an antique dealer and began to smuggle stolen jewels and artwork into the U.S.

The way it worked. Both parties possessed an inventory ledger of confiscated valuables. The two worked out a coding system. Perez sends a telegram to Schofield, letting him know what the lot numbers of low-priced curios have the hidden items. For a sawbuck, Adrian would give the lot numbers to the guy who handles receiving at Brooklyn's. He would call when those lot numbers arrived. Schofield would then offer top dollar for the shipment before it was up for auction. Only problem was fencing the stolen gold and jewels. Schofield was selling the stuff for pennies on the dollar. He meets Deidra, aka Miriam LaSalla. When she discovered he was fencing stolen property on the cheap she made a few calls and meets Nick Cappello.

Nick discovers that Deidra is Miriam LaSalla and Vic Manzetti is looking for her for fingering his brother Rico. Nick, having Deidra over a barrel demands a bigger cut. This causes serious tension between Adrian and Deidra. That tension overflowed when they were out at a restaurant one night. A public argument ensued. A drunk Adrian slapped Deidra across the face. Rickman stepped in. There was immediate chemistry. They started seeing each other behind Adrian's back. The way it figured, Rickman and Deidra saw their chance to start over with a clean slate. Rickman had fallen for her hard and there wasn't anything that he wouldn't do for her. She knew it and played it to the hilt. I figure what Deidra didn't count on was falling in love with the guy. Rickman was the only man who treated her with love and respect.

Strupp's statement filled in a lot of the blanks. For a time, Irene was the girlfriend of one of Cappello's gunsels. She convinced Nick to loan Shortt the money he needed. When she had to leave Shortt's employ, Nick got her the job as Deidra's assistant. He now had someone on the inside of the Schofield operation. Feeling the heat from Nick's demands, Deidra wanted out—for good. She and Rickman hatched a plan. Deidra started intercepting telegrams from Perez looking for a big score that would free her from Cappello's grasp. She makes a deal with the shipping clerk at Brooklyn's that she'd get the calls when shipments came in. She gets Cappello involved. Tells him she's double-crossing, Adrian. She'll need Nick to take the delivery for her and promises him a big payoff. Cappello goes for it. Has no idea he's being set up. Rickman planned on killing him all along. When the telegram arrives indicating a large shipment of loose gems they put the plan in operation.

It was Rickman's idea to have Irene hire me as the bag man. Adding another buffer. If Irene agreed to set me up as the fall guy Deidra promised to get Shortt off the hook with Cappello. It was all a neat plan until my car broke down. When Manny Strupp called Nick, he thought he'd been double-crossed and the proverbial shit hit the fan. In the end, Deidra loved Mike. When McNabb told her he didn't make it out of surgery, she became inconsolable and had to be put under sedation.

When the story hit the morning papers all hell broke loose at City Hall. The mayor wanted a full investigation into the police department. D.A.'s office was under siege by the press. Me, I had my name plastered all over the front page as the private dick who recovered a million dollars in Nazi-stolen gems and precious artwork.

As for Schofield, once the shooting stopped, he bolted out of the building like a horny sailor getting shore leave. The police caught up with him at the San Luis Obispo Greyhound Terminal two days later. On his way to Mexico with a suitcase stuffed with several rare paintings. The police department notified Interpol and took Adrian's partner into custody and the rest of the stolen items were recovered. Experts concluded that the gems I found could have been sold on the open market for at least three-quarters of a million dollars, depending on where they would've found buyers.

It all worked out well for me. I received a check for twenty-five thousand dollars for the recovery of those gems. Zeke sold me his car and promised he'd keep it in excellent running order. All the notoriety from the case got me clients. I was able to vacate the old dump on Turk Street. Move into the Hunter-Dulin Building on Sutter. D.A. Mahoney ran for State Assemblyman and resigned from his post as District Attorney. With him out of my hair, I have a better relationship with the D.A.'s office. Just finished an investigation for them on Tuesday of last week.

Claire runs the office and keeps me on top of things. Sully approves of the relationship. Claire and I went to the pictures Saturday night to see "The Loves of Carmen" with Glenn Ford and Rita Hayworth. The second she appeared on the screen I was astonished at the resemblance of the two women. I have to admit. When it came to looks, Rickman had impeccable taste.

The other day I was sitting alone in my office. I looked up at Sully smiling.

"Hey stranger," I said.

Looks like you're sittin' pretty these days. New office? Seems like you landed on your feet.

I laughed. My feet were in fact up on my desk, shoeless. "Yeah, how 'bout that."

He chuckled.

"Hey Sully, I gotta question for ya."

Shoot.

"I appreciate your help, being able to bounce ideas off you and all. But tell me this: If you're real, you must be all-knowing, right? How come you didn't just tell me Rickman did it? Why'd I have to go through all that?"

Sully smiled again and didn't say anything.

Just waved and vanished.

END

We hope that you enjoyed this title and look forward to many more to come. Please, leave us a review! Reviews matter to all of our authors.

Take a look at some of our other award-winning series at https://threeravenspublishing.com/series-universes/

Visit us at https://www.threeravenspublishing.com and sign up for our newsletter for the latest and greatest news on upcoming titles and events.

Other series and titles you might enjoy.

JOINT TASK FORCE 13
HOLDING THE LINE
BETWEEN HEAVEN AND HELL
AMAZON

B.E.N.T.
BIOLOGIC   ENHANCED   NASCENT   TALENT

STARFLIGHT

IT CAME FROM THE
TRAILER PARK

You can also keep up to date with our latest release announcements on Scifi.radio and get some of the best fandom programing on the planet.

Scifi for your Wifi

And don't forget to check out our other Sponsors and Affiliates

A southern Appalachian jewel for craft beer lovers, Buck Bald Brewing offers something for everyone.

To discover more visit us at buckbaldbrewing.com

Revolution X is a testament to the power of collaboration, blending four unique styles into a cohesive, revolutionary sound. When these four individuals unite, the result is nothing short of musical Revolution!

Would you like to learn how to write and market your own titles? The following affiliates links might be helpful.

Don't forget to check out the latest edition of Car Warriors: Autoduel Chronicle fiction series.

SHEPHERD'S MEN

Comprised of active or retired servicemen and civilian volunteers, Shepherd's Men enthusiastically raises awareness and funds for the SHARE Military Initiative (SHARE) at Shepherd Center in Atlanta, GA.

This nationally renowned program focuses on assessment and treatment for American military veterans who have sustained mild to moderate Traumatic Brain Injury (TBI) and Post-Traumatic Stress Disorder (PTSD) during post-9/11 service.

Find out more at: https://www.shepherdsmen.com/

www.ingramcontent.com/pod-product-compliance
Lightning Source LLC
Chambersburg PA
CBHW020737310726
48969CB00002B/297